I0538365

A SHOT AT HAPPY

A SHOT AT HAPPY

CHRIS GUITON

NEXTGEN
Press, LLC

Copyright © 2014 by Chris Guiton

All rights reserved. No part of this publication may be
reproduced in whole or in part, stored in a retrieval system
or transmitted in any form or by any means, electronic,
mechanical, photocopying, recording, or otherwise, without
prior written permission of the publisher.

Published by NextGen Press, LLC
nextgenpress@gmail.com

eISBN: 978-0-9915426-0-4
ISBN: 978-0-9915426-1-1

ACKNOWLEDGEMENTS

I would like to thank my family and friends for their overwhelming love and support throughout the writing, editing and publishing process. Your encouragement and enthusiasm inspired me to overcome the clouds of doubt that come along with writing, and sharing, my first story.

In particular, I'd like to thank Kristie Ceruti for editing the manuscript, my sister Maureen for her artistic input into the book cover, and my sister Mary Jo who has been with me every step of the way. MJ, your energy and spirit are contagious and this wouldn't have happened without you.

Most of all, I'd like to thank my wife, Kelly, for putting up with my random pursuits, and my three kids, Jack, Drew and Gabriella, for being a constant source of joy and for making me want to be a better person every moment of my life.

PROLOGUE

"I'm so sorry," I blurted out, startled to have touched anything other than a spoon.

"No, by all means, if you're that hungry, please go for it," a woman replied with a straight face, but in a tone that was in no way serious.

"Of course not. It doesn't matter that I was here first, and you had to sneak up on me to beat me to the spoon. It's all yours."

"I'm not even supposed to be here," she said looking over her shoulder. "My bush league little breakfast is over there somewhere. Please, you go."

"I'm not supposed to be here either," I said, eager to one up her. "And I don't have a breakfast waiting for me anywhere in the place."

She burst out laughing. I laughed too, surprised at the rare moment of honesty. I reached again for the spoon, scooped up a pile of eggs and plopped it on her plate. "Here you go. You can't get in trouble if someone else gave it to you, right?

"I guess, but I'm not really that afraid of getting caught, are you?" she asked as she reached for the serving spoon next to the potatoes.

"Obviously not," I replied as I started piling on the ham and bacon.

CHAPTER 1

The early morning pick-up basketball game at the Sports Club is a long-standing tradition. A few guys have come and gone over the years but the core group has remained essentially the same. I am a relative newcomer. I began playing with this group a few years ago and I don't believe I have missed a single game since I started. You might say I plan my life around it.

Don't get me wrong. It is not that I am obsessed with this particular basketball game, I'm just unusually dedicated to doing what I love, and, among other things, I happen to love to play basketball. Pretty simple actually. I grew up loving to play and I have made it a priority as an adult to feel that joy every day of my life. If that makes my lifestyle a bit unorthodox, then so be it.

This morning's pickup game was fulfilling—both competitive and fun. Blade and Tony were on opposite teams, which always made for a good battle. Tony and I had won the first four games and were on the verge of a clean sweep in the final game.

"Help me on the screens," Blade yelled to his teammates in anticipation as he tried to cover me on defense. "They're going to Drew on this play."

He was right. My teammates were going to try to get me the ball and Blade was going to need some help.

I ran off a screen by Robby on the right wing into an open area of the court. As I pivoted around to square up to the hoop, I could see Blade out of the corner of my right eye trying to fight through Robby's screen and lunge toward me. I bent my legs more than usual as I caught the pass from Tony. This was the last game of the morning and we were all exhausted. I needed a little extra lift to be able to get the ball over the rim. I didn't want to leave this one short, not with a tie game and bragging rights for the day on the line.

I released the ball high above my head a split second before Blade's outstretched hand blocked my vision. He was too late. The shot felt good and I knew it was in before it reached the rim.

Swish! Game over.

"Great picks, Robby," I said as I walked over to slap him five.

"Good shootin' today Drew," he replied, his hand meeting mine in the air.

Blade came over and gave me a friendly bear hug.

"Good shootin' Drew," he said, mockingly. "You got me again. You'd think I'd know by now that you like that little fade into the corner. I'll get there one of these days. I'm getting older and you're somehow getting younger, but, mark my words, I will get there."

Tony sauntered over to interrupt our love-fest.

"I hear that same lame excuse after every time you lose," Tony said to Blade. "Don't you worry, Father Time will catch up to Drew at some point too."

Tony was a few years older than Blade, which was partly why he got away with talking as much trash as he did. They were actually pretty good friends despite their on-court banter. They had played in the same basketball circles for many years. They grew up locally and played for rival high schools. Both played in college and continued in every competitive league in the area ever since.

"Thank God we'll never be as old as you though, Tony," replied Blade.

When Blade and Tony embraced, I felt reassured that there were no hard feelings between the two. I worried that their constant verbal sparring would trigger some deep-seeded hatred but it never did. These guys genuinely liked each other and that's what made it fun.

Tony then put his arm around me in a half hug and rubbed my head like I was his kid brother. In a lot of ways, that was the type of relationship we had. I looked up to him in that he was older with a wife, kids and a house—all the things that grown, responsible men were supposed to have. My life definitely appealed to him too though. I was younger, fitter and seemed to live an entirely carefree existence. These were luxuries Tony no longer had.

"Great playing as always, Tony. You always find me right on the money. You make the game easy."

"Of course I do, that's why God made point guards. To spoon feed hungry shooters like you and to bring home victories."

I hung back with Tony as the rest of the players hurried off the court toward the locker room. I was never in much of a rush and Tony was usually willing to spare a few minutes after our games to get the latest scoop on my social life.

"Please, tell me what you were up to last night," begged Tony. "I need to know."

"Nothing exciting at all," I replied nonchalantly. "Why are you always so interested?"

"Are you kidding? Do you know what I did last night?"

"Please tell me." I braced myself for his response.

"I changed about five diapers, got puked on, played horsey,

mowed the lawn, took out the garbage, unplugged a blocked toilet and passed out before 10 pm from exhaustion. That's why I'm interested!"

Tony lived in a beautiful house in the suburbs with his wife, their 12-year-old girl and two boys under the age of four. He married his wife when he was in his early 20s and started a family right away. Even though he truly had it all by anyone's standards, a small part of him regretted bypassing a decade of adult fun only properly experienced by the unattached—years of social activities missed as a result of what he laments to be premature commitment.

"What's wrong with being an all-star family man," I asked, knowing full well that he was envious of the benefits of being single and child-free.

We entered the section of the locker room where most of the basketball guys changed. Not sure why we were such creatures of habit, but we always congregated in the same spot even though the locker room was sprawling and there were plenty of other options. Perhaps it was because this section was closest to one of the lounge areas with ESPN on television 24/7—just one of the many ridiculous perks provided by this gym.

"There's nothing *wrong* with it," Tony explained. "It's just that the most exciting thing about my nights is whether my baby's ass is going chapped or not. Do you even know what Butt Paste is? I dig my finger in that stuff every night and spread it on Billy like he's a cupcake and I'm about to take a bite. That's literally the most fun I have at night now, frosting Billy's backside!"

"How cute," I replied sarcastically, intentionally egging him on.

"Yeah, cute, thanks a lot. I just want to hear that someone, somewhere is out on the town living the good life. I haven't had a story worth sharing with a locker room in years. It's not that I need to live through you or that I get off on hearing your encounters. It just helps me believe that there is a higher purpose out there. If just one person is happy, then I can go on playing my humble role of the pissed-off family guy."

"Tony," I said with sincerity. "You wouldn't change a thing about your life, so what are you griping about?"

I had to call him out.

"That's the sick part about it. I wouldn't. Don't you see how twisted that is? Like families are designed to wrap you up, suffocate you, wring out your will to live, and then leave you hanging there just wanting to do the whole thing all over again . . . forever."

We undressed in front of our lockers and went into the shower area. Another great part about this gym: spacious, individual showers. I had spent enough time in communal showers through my sports career that I appreciated a little privacy. More importantly, I didn't have to deal with witnessing the bizarre grooming rituals of some of the other guys in the gym. No inhibitions whatsoever. Disgusting.

"Well I wish I had something exciting for you today," I continued. "I went to the bookstore to do a little reading, watched the ball game at the bar, and then called it a night."

"That's it?" asked Tony, dumbfounded that I had nothing better.

We showered relatively quickly. Even though I took 100% of my showers at the gym, I still didn't like to spend any more time than I had to standing on the same wet blue mat that hundreds of other men stood on every day. I was not a germaphobe but I could not help but think I could see actual foot fungus walking around the shower floors. I used the soap and shampoo provided in each of the showers. A lot of the guys brought their own products but I never understood why. Seemed like a waste of money to me. The gym provided virtually every health and grooming product you could possibly need and I took advantage of every single one of them. Shaving cream. Razors. Q-tips. Nail clippers. Nail files. Lotion. Tissues. Hair Dryer. Hair spray. Deodorant spray. Floss. Toothpaste. Toothbrushes. Mouthwash. Unbelievable.

Most of the other players finished before us and were half dressed by the time we came out of the shower area. Blade was in the middle of a story about a recent gambling bust that made big news a few days earlier. He was a cop in the city and was always a good source of information. He never gave away anything top secret but we always learned a little more from him than we would by watching the news or reading the newspaper.

Apparently a number of detectives had infiltrated the gambling ring and patiently waited several years before the timing was right to make a move. Big John peppered Blade with questions about every detail. Sometimes nicknames were counterintuitive and needed explanation. Not true with Big John who had been called that as long as I had known him. At about 6'5", at least 275 pounds, and full of personality, he was big in every way. He was a good basketball player even though he was well above his optimal playing weight. You could tell he was very good in his day. He knew the game well and had that rare combination of great strength with soft hands. You couldn't take the ball off of him but he had a nice shooting touch around the hoop.

Big John owned a number of excellent restaurants in downtown and he clearly didn't miss many meals. More than eating, though, he enjoyed meeting and greeting his patrons. He was the type of owner that made his way to every table at some point during meals. It seemed like he knew everybody and everybody knew him. He liked getting the scoop from Blade so that he had a little extra to add to conversations at his restaurants. Big John enjoyed being in the center of the action. He didn't need to be the focal point of the attention. He just liked to be involved in all things social. He loved people and it showed at all times. What I admired most about Big John, was that even though he was very wealthy you would never know by talking to him.

"Drew, when are you coming by Luigi's again?" Big John asked me as he shifted focus away from his game of 20 questions. He knew the little Italian BYOB was my favorite of his places. The food was spectacular—completely authentic Italian cuisine, décor, ambience, and energy. Although I had purely Irish blood, I had a soft spot for Italian food and eating at Luigi's was an experience, not just dinner.

"I know, Big John, it's been too long," I agreed with a smile. Part of the reason I hadn't been back to any of his establishments in months was because he never let me pay. While I certainly appreciated the gesture, and the overly-full stomach, I always felt a little awkward not paying. Nothing made him happier than to be generous to his friends so he was in no way responsible for my guilt. I just didn't feel right taking too many free meals from him.

"Why don't you come by this weekend?" he suggested. "You let me know what night you can come and I'll make sure I reserve a perfect spot for you and whatever lucky devil you pick to join you."

"Thanks John. I miss Luigi's but I'll have to check with those devils to see if this weekend will work."

"Well whatever day works, this weekend or any other time, just let me know. The lobster ravioli is calling you."

"Drew, you'll love it," Robby chimed in as he grabbed his suit jacket and closed his locker. "My wife and I both ordered it last weekend. Best thing I've had there yet!"

"You don't need to convince me," I replied. "I want to move to Italy after every time I go there."

Robby was a partner at one of the big law firms in the city. He worked long hours but always made time in the early morning for basketball. He said he didn't mind working late into the evenings on a regular basis as long as he had his hoops fix. Not all of the firms required business attire, but Robby was a bit old school for his age and felt like he garnered more respect from his colleagues and clients when he looked the part. It clearly worked because he was one of the most successful young attorneys in the city.

"Take care, guys. Good playing today, I'll see you tomorrow," Robby called out.

"I'll walk out with you, Robby," said Jeff, another one of the guys as he grabbed his gym bag and jogged after Robby. "Later, fellas."

We had all types at our morning game. Jeff was a teacher and a Junior Varsity basketball coach at a local private school. Steve went to college with Jeff and was a real estate agent. Steve's brother Tommy was a major player in the tech world. He played with us when he wasn't flying around the world promoting new apps he created for the iPhone. It was a diverse group of professionals who valued those moments of exercise, competition and camaraderie before they started the rest of their meeting-filled days. Like a Catholic who goes to Mass every morning, or a Yoga nut who is on the mat at sunrise, we viewed hoops as our morning ritual. I'm not saying basketball was our God. There were plenty of guys in the group who practiced one religion or another in addition to their basketball devotion. But just like the way prayer or meditation can be an opportunity for some to find peace of mind before jumping into the chaos of information, activity, work, family and all the rest, the game was a source of positive energy which kick-started our day. Morning hoops was our meditation. The jump shot was my Om.

It was 8:30 am and nearly everyone had bolted for the door

trying to make it to work on time. I was at the sink shaving when Tony poked his head in to say goodbye.

"I'll catch you tomorrow, gunner!"

"See you bud," I yelled back. "Tell Nikki and the kids I said hello."

"Will do man. You'll have to come out for another visit soon. Nikki is bent on finding you a nice girl and getting you settled down."

"Great. Another setup?" I asked with raised eyebrows.

"Don't worry, I will be screening all future setups," Tony replied. "I still owe you one for that."

Tony's wife had set me up with a "young" friend of hers who she swore was just gorgeous. I knew better than to trust her—or any woman's opinion of a friend—but she beat me down until I agreed to take her friend out. She was very nice and it was her prerogative if she decided that 32 was the age that her biological clock turned into a ticking time bomb. We had a nice time but she wanted to have a baby by the end of the date. I would have been flattered if it were my baby she wanted to have, but it was really just anyone's baby. I happened to be the poor sucker sitting in front of her at that point in time.

With Tony gone, I was the last one from our game still in the locker room. I took this opportunity to utilize every hygienic product at my disposal since I treated the place like my own personal bathroom. By 9:00 I had finished, put on my khakis and sports coat and grabbed my briefcase. The laundry bag went into the chute and I was on my way.

"Have a great day, Jenny!" I said to the woman working at the front desk.

"You too Drew! See you in a little bit!"

Jenny thought I was going to work, at least that was what I had hoped she thought. It's amazing what a sports coat and dress pants will do for your image.

CHAPTER 2

Before stepping foot on Walnut Street where the pace of pedestrian traffic at 9:00 am was nothing short of breakneck, I paused on the stairs outside of the gym to take a deep breath, smile, and appreciate the moment. The rest of the guys had already scurried to work. Not me. I had nowhere to be, no one to check in with and nothing on my to-do list. I felt free in the truest sense of the word. Considering what I gave up to create this phenomenon, I made sure to soak it in a few times a day just so I never took it for granted.

The city was absolutely bustling at this time of the morning and many of the city's biggest businesses, best hotels and popular bars and restaurants were nestled along a six-block stretch of Walnut that ran through Center City. People were practically racing down the sidewalk trying to get to work on time. The revolving door at Starbucks never stopped spinning. There were people talking on cell phones. There were people texting on cell phones. There were people staring mindlessly at their cell phones, flipping through a myriad of up-to-the second information that streamed out of Facebook, Twitter, Instagram, Pinterest, CNN, the Weather Channel—an ever-evolving list of sites—while somehow navigating their way through the throngs of people.

No one simply walked down the street without urgency or some type of multitasking. The concept of enjoying the journey seemed to have gotten lost. It wasn't generational either. Sure teenagers were significantly more adept than their elders at texting behind their backs while pretending to have a conversation with someone standing in front of them. But this technology and information overload has been adopted by seemingly everyone. In fact, the older generations seem to get even more lost in the technology than the kids because with an advancing age comes a decreasing ability to focus on competing tasks. When my mother texts, she's excruciatingly slow and it takes every ounce of her attention to *press those little buttons*. Amateur.

As I stroll alongside my media-obsessed fellow pedestrians, I feel like an anonymous participant in a surreal movie. Rarely did someone notice me, because rarely did a person notice anyone or anything at all. But I observe them, just like I observe the rest of my surroundings. Buildings. Storefronts. Restaurant menus. Cars. Bikes. Sun. Clouds. Birds. People are missing out on their immediate environment. Digital information has taken over for the classic sights and sounds of city streets. Rather than getting lost in some handheld device, I prefer to get lost in wondering what each person's story is. Where they are going? Who they are talking to on the phone? What Facebook gossip is so important that it needs to be read right then and there in the middle of the street with the bus bearing down on them?

I found it amazing that at any given time there were more than 1,000 people converging on the same block at the same time and all with their own unique stories of how they arrived at that spot. I guess old fashioned people-watching still fascinated me even though everyone around me preferred to people-watch remotely through some type of handheld device.

"How ya doin?" I off-handedly asked a very attractive woman holding a cell phone to her ear. I saw her coming part way down the street and hoped to catch her eye. For some reason, I always enjoyed the chance—the challenge—to exchange a look, or a smile, or even a hello with a woman I did not know. The occasional spark could be exhilarating, even if only for a brief second and even if I never see the woman again. I wasn't much of a voyeur. I got nothing out of just looking at women. It was the mutual acknowledgment and personal engagement that I liked.

In a society where no one recognizes anything around them because their eyes are buried in a mobile device, catching someone's eye has gotten so much harder. Downright rare. This particular woman was on the phone but was at least looking where she was going. If she were in mid-sentence on the phone, I wouldn't have said hello. But since she was clearly in the middle of a listening pause—also a rare event anymore—and since she noticed me noticing her, I mumbled a barely audible greeting. It wasn't a cheesy *how YOU doin?* like you'd get from some overly-aggressive muscle head. It was more of a friendly, I think you're cute but I'm not going to throw myself at you kind of hello.

To me, this is just good harmless fun. It's win-win. I win because if I get any type of positive response, then I've officially engaged in flirting—and who doesn't love flirting. The woman wins because I'm essentially complimenting her by checking her out in a non-offensive way. At least that's what I hope she thinks. Every now and then I get a scowl in return—probably justified, but I usually convince myself that the scowl was more a reflection of her bad attitude than an inappropriate glance from me. Or perhaps she's just disgusted by my looks which is fine too. Attractiveness is completely subjective and I'm OK with that.

Mostly, I either get a look of surprise and confusion, or a return friendly glance. Occasionally I get an actual return flirtatious glance or hello. This is the ideal outcome. For some strange reason, that is gratifying to me. Every once in a while, though, you have that exchange with a woman who is a bit forward and you actually find yourself in a conversation. That's pretty unusual for the walk-by exchange and not always that desirable because you really don't know what you're going to get with a conversation like that.

This particular exchange went as usual. She shot me a smile that spoke of both surprise and mild delight. That's about all you can ask of someone on the phone walking down a busy street at 9:00 on a Wednesday morning. She wore a tight-fitting, but professional black skirt down to her knee with a white button down top. She was a little too sexy and not in enough of a hurry to be a lawyer, but I assumed she was a professional of some sort. She was definitely not married or engaged, based on the lack of rings, not based on the return flirtatious look. Sometimes the married women were the most eager to return an unexpected look. She was definitely in a relationship, though, because a woman who looked like that always had a boyfriend and a few others lined up in case it didn't work out. My guess was she was 27 but I wasn't great at that game. The older I got the worse I got at distinguishing between early and late 20s. Or early and late 30s for that matter. She definitely had classy tastes and she definitely had a good heart. People quick to smile, I found, were people who were genuinely good inside.

These observations were not ones I deliberated over for a long period of time. I usually drew these conclusions in the 20 seconds before, during and after a walk-by of a person. I wouldn't normally give it more thought unless someone really struck me. And I was fully aware that these conclusions were entirely a fiction made up by me based on next-to-nothing. I wish I were more of a Sherlock Holmes but my observations were more imagination than anything else.

After a few more blocks of people-watching and background-creating, I ducked into the Downtown Marriott hotel. The Marriott was one of my favorites because the lobby was expansive and there was always a lot of action in the morning. Thanks to the navy blue sports coat and khaki pants that I wore virtually every day, I blended in nicely. I could easily get lost in the hustle and bustle and the staff would never know if I had a reason to be there or was just passing through. The hotel had a fresh supply of newspapers on the concierge counter to which I helped myself. With the paper under my arm, I headed up the escalator to the banquet floor which held a city-block worth of meeting rooms and banquet halls and no fewer than five events going on at a given time during the week. At the top of the escalator was a handy big screen monitor that scrolled which conferences were being held where. Several other hotels in the city hosted such events, but none were laid out as conveniently for my purposes as the Marriott.

As I headed down the main hallway that linked most of the meeting rooms, I walked by a number of breakfast spreads put out by the hotel for the meeting guests. Large signs designated which spread went with which group. According to the signs, Ballroom A was hosting the Prudential Insurance Company Annual Meeting. The food looked great but I didn't stop because at a single company event there was always some risk that you would run into that one person at the meeting who literally knows everyone there. It's a situation that I can get myself out of but it's not easy and I prefer to avoid it if possible. It also wasn't one of my favorite meetings because I always assumed that insurance folks by nature were not all that interesting. So if I did get stuck in a conversation with someone, it had a high likelihood of being boring.

If I didn't already have my eye on Ballroom C, I may have still stopped simply because of the food options: eggs, bacon, French toast, pancakes and hash browns on the hot side, and bagels, muffins, cereal, yogurt and fresh fruit on the cold side. It was the deluxe hot and cold menu, the top of the line that the Marriott served. During slow times in the economy like this, there weren't too many meetings that ordered this package. It wasn't so rare that I felt compelled to stop though.

Ballroom B was a teacher's conference. Conversation would be more interesting—at least they would be my kind of people. But the menu package was predictably the bottom of the barrel. Bagels and muffins with a fruit salad bowl. It was still good quality because it was the Downtown Marriott, after all. In fact, I preferred this spread when I was on the go because bagels and muffins were portable and easy to load in large quantities. I didn't stop today because I was starving and planned on sitting for a while.

Ballroom C was all that I had hoped it would be. It was a pharmaceutical industry meeting with people from a number of different companies. This was perfect. Very few people knew each other. People only randomly wore their name tags, particularly for breakfast when the day's meetings hadn't yet begun. I was always prepared to make up who I was and who I worked for, but the occasion rarely arose in these industry-wide meetings and where so few were wearing a name tag. Seldom would someone just introduce themselves to a complete stranger at a group breakfast like this. Usually people just stuck with the one or two people they already knew. This was as safe as can be. And the spread was the deluxe menu. I knew the deep pockets in the drug industry wouldn't skimp. They charged an arm and a leg for people to attend these conferences so it wasn't a huge deal to provide some good grub.

I threw my briefcase strap over my shoulder and grabbed a plate. There was no line on one side of the table. I scooped a healthy portion of everything hot. I only had bacon once every few weeks so I didn't feel too guilty piling on all that fat. I needed some extra protein so I had a few more scoops of eggs than I probably should have. I loaded up on the French toast too, because it was simply the best thing they served. Soft with plenty of cinnamon. I added a few strawberries on top and doused it in maple syrup, one of my most powerful vices.

Instead of entering the dining area itself, I saddled up on a bench in the hallway alongside the windows overlooking Washington Square. I pulled out the newspaper and feasted. No one bothered me. I was starving so I savored every morsel. My syrup seeped over into the eggs a bit. That used to really bother me but I had gotten past that in recent years. I preferred to have my French toast or pancakes on a separate plate but the situation didn't lend itself to having a different plate for every type of food. I made do by just eating the French toast faster. I was a notoriously slow eater but I could wolf down anything doused in syrup like I was in an eating contest.

After about 15 minutes, I left my briefcase and newspaper on the bench and went over for another round. This time I grabbed a few bagels and muffins and huge helpings of sliced pineapple, cantaloupe and honeydew. I sat back down and wrapped the bagels and muffins in a few napkins and placed them into my briefcase. I ate the fruit and then put the new plate under my other plate. I took them over to the large round tray outside of the ballroom door designated for dirty dishes. I was finished with the newspaper after I breezed through the front page, the business section and the box scores on the sports page. I tossed the paper out, grabbed my bag and headed for the escalators. This meal had hit the spot and I had provisions for the rest of the day, just in case I decided not to bother finding a place for lunch. When you weren't sure when or where you'd get your next meal, it was always nice to have a little something in reserve.

CHAPTER 3

After leaving the hotel, I took a left onto 23rd Street and began walking south from Walnut. In just a few blocks, the landscape began to change dramatically. The street widened and there was less traffic. The sidewalk seemed to double in size but it may have just appeared that way because there were so few pedestrians. The trees that peppered the sidewalk were significantly older, larger and had more presence than the saplings that lined Walnut. The recent renovations to Walnut, however, were very well done and very well received by the city's inhabitants and visitors alike. It had a fresh new look and feel, but was still distinctly urban.

23rd and Vine marked the start of University City. Crossing Vine felt like entering a different world. Although only a few blocks removed from center city, the noise and activity seemed miles away. The main entrance into campus was another block ahead on the right. There was no gate or guard that tried to keep out random pedestrians. Instead the whole area had a welcoming feel. The next few blocks contained large, old fraternity-style houses. The university wasn't known as a party school, but this row was the center of campus entertainment.

I walked across Founders Green, which was a traditional college quad found just inside the main entrance. The college was nearly two centuries old and a handful of trees on the

Green must have been there from the start because they had so much character—oversized trunks with thick branches curving in unpredictable directions. Behind the Green was Founders Hall, the campus' original building which still housed the administration offices. Walking paths went around both sides of Founders, the left leading to a series of classroom buildings and the right leading to the college library.

I loved walking down this main stretch of campus, in different ways than I did back in my college days. At that time, I used to love strolling through campus seeing the familiar faces of my friends and classmates. Never did I feel so close to so many people as I did in college. I miss those relationships but I don't miss the burden of homework, tests or any number of deadlines that constantly loomed over me in college. I don't have the bonds of friendship I did then but I don't have the stress either. I wasn't a kid anymore, but I was more carefree than any one of these students laying on their blankets or playing Frisbee across the lawn. With the pressures on today's youth to excel, succeed, and find a job, particularly in this impossible market, I guess it isn't that challenging to be less stressed than them. I envied only that they had younger bodies and undoubtedly sharper minds. But I was sure that I was as happy as anyone out here.

Besides a few people who seemed to make a career out of going to undergrad, college by most definitions was, among other things, a stepping stone to get somewhere else in life. To me, this approach to anything is a recipe for unhappiness. Don't get me wrong, I fully believe that college is the best time of most people's lives. I just can't help but imagine how much fun it would be if there were no stress to go with it. I know it's not realistic necessarily at that stage of someone's life, but at some point people need to figure out how to eliminate the stress and focus on the happy. I know that it's practically blasphemy to say that being content is a good thing. It's usually considered a dirty word that means you are not striving hard enough for something, challenging yourself to be the best you could be. To me, you could be content and striving at the same time, but it's hard to find that balance.

I was only momentarily refreshed by the walk through campus. I couldn't wait to take a load off my feet. I had been awake for nearly 15 hours. As I reached for the front doors to the library, one of the few students I knew by name had just opened the door from the inside.

"Hi Drew! How's it going?"

"Hey Sandra!" I replied excitedly. "What's happenin' with you?"

"Off to class. Remind me to tell you about this book idea I have. You might think it's silly but I know you're too nice to laugh at me so you have to be my sounding board, Ok?"

"Of course," I said encouragingly. "Anytime. And I promise not to laugh too hard, except at the funny parts. Deal?"

"You got it," she smiled. "Have a great day!"

"You too. See ya!"

I tried not to get to know too many students. Even though at 28 I wasn't too many years older than the matriculates, I really didn't want to be known as that old guy who is trying too hard to hang on to his college days. It wasn't even close to true and it was about the most embarrassing reputation I could imagine. I was certainly friendly to everyone but I didn't go out of my way to start conversations.

Sandra asked me what I was working on a few months ago when she saw me scribbling into my notebook in the library. When I said I was supposed to be writing something spectacular without any success, she opened up to me about her novel-writing dreams. She was a very sweet girl with very creative ideas. She was pretty, but plain—long, brown, straight hair and pale skin. I made sure to keep her at friendly distance because I certainly wasn't there to find a best friend, and I couldn't afford to get romantically involved with just anyone I met, particularly at the college. I was very selective with whom I fraternized at the school, and Sandra didn't fit the mold.

I passed through the doors and into the lobby toward the turnstiles you have to walk through to enter the main area of the library.

"Hey Maria, how are you today?" I said to the woman sitting at the front desk.

"Drew! Love to see your smiling face in here. You having a good morning?"

"Of course, of course," I responded. "Played a little ball, so I'm a happy man. Busy day here?"

"Good to hear," she said. "No, not busy at all. Even had a chance to do some reading myself, but don't tell anyone."

The gate next to the three sets of turnstiles opened and I walked through.

"Thanks, Maria. Have a great day!"

"You too, Drew."

I thanked God for Maria all the time. She thought I was working on a big project so she never questioned me on why I was at the library or why I liked going there so much. She seemed to genuinely like me and let me in without fail. She didn't have to do that, considering I wasn't a student or on the faculty, but from her perspective, a man dressed in business attire who came into to do some reading, writing and a little internet research didn't present much risk. I was friendly, didn't disrupt anyone or anything, and seemed like I had something important to do. She had no reason not to trust me.

I headed up to the second floor computer room where a few students were using the printers. It was a beautiful room with rows of the latest and greatest computers, but there was rarely anyone working in there. Most students had their own computers for school work and some type of handheld device for mobile access to the internet. I'm sure the school needed to have a state-of-the-art computer facility just to say that it had one. But it had become virtually unnecessary except maybe for the printers which were a lot faster than the average personal printer.

It was great for me though. I nearly had the whole room to myself most of the time and no one ever monitored the place. I stopped in frequently to check email, IM, Google anything I wanted to know, and Skype on occasion with my family.

As I opened my email, I saw that I had a few non-junk messages in my inbox, mostly from my parents and sister wondering how I've been and when I'm coming to visit. It had been a while since I had been home and it drove them crazy that I didn't have a cell phone, or a house phone for that matter. There was no way for them to get in touch with me if they needed to, other than through email, which I only checked every few days. I loved them dearly but it was sometimes difficult to speak with them. Catching up on their lives and what's going on in the world was great. Inevitably the conversation would turn to my life and what I am or am not doing with it. I didn't like to lie to them but I certainly couldn't tell them the truth. I usually just did my best to avoid the topic, give some cryptic answers, and jokingly accuse them of being nosey. That tactic generally held them off for a bit but the conversation would not ultimately go away until I gave them some satisfactory answers, or got off the phone.

I read the email I got from my sister and a few I got from some high school buddies. I couldn't bear to read the one from my parents. I knew it was nothing urgent or life-shattering because the subject line read, "Miss You!" I wasn't in the mood to read about how out of touch I've been and that they are worried about me. They had enough faith in me to know that I was safe and not in any trouble. But they worried that I didn't give much consideration to my future or my career. The joke is that they were not the type of crazy parents who push their kids to excel and brainwash them into having a career-first outlook on life. They truly just wanted me and my sister to be happy. But happy to them includes a steady job and a family, or at least the prospect of a family. They weren't even in a rush to marry me off. They just wanted me to be working remotely in that direction.

What they didn't know was that though I did not subscribe to their idea of happiness, I was just that: happy. I was actually the happiest person I knew. Every minute of my day was spent how I wanted. I was perfectly content, but if my parents, or even my sister, had a clue about my lifestyle, they would be floored, and probably lose a lot of sleep over it. How ironic. I put my happiness as the top priority in creating the life I lead, and the people I cared most about were still worried sick about my happiness. And the only thing that stood in the way of my happiness was their worry.

I walked out of the computer room and downstairs to the back corner of the first floor. There were a few semi-private big comfy chairs back there. The space was usually empty, especially in the morning. I fell into the red one and pulled out the novel in my bag: *Outliers*, my third straight Malcolm Gladwell book. I was hooked on his work because his ideas changed the way I viewed the world. I love books that do that. I love all kinds of books, but ones that can impact your life are my favorites. I only had a few chapters left but my eyes started to get heavy as soon as I finished the first page. I tried to fight it but I kept nodding off.

After the third time I felt my head snap forward, I decided to put down the book and take out my notebook. It was much harder to fall asleep while writing than while reading. I had been scribbling book and screenplay ideas in this particular notebook for months with no direction and really no purpose. I had lots of scattered ideas but putting them down on paper hadn't provided the clarity that I had hoped it would. I figured trying to assemble a story line or an outline would be my next step.

After a few minutes of doodling, I realized that I was no longer in danger of falling asleep but I was definitely too drained to be creative. I needed sleep and I needed it now. I packed up the notebook and pen and zipped my bag. I reluctantly crawled out of my favorite chair, put on my sports coat and walked out of the library.

CHAPTER 4

I did not always stop for lunch but sometimes it was the best meal for packing leftovers. The breakfast spreads were always my favorite meals and where I loaded up the most. Lunch usually offered sandwich options though which were very easily packed and transported and doing this never drew any attention. Many of the typical conference-goers used meal breaks to re-connect with their day jobs instead of socializing with fellow attendees. Anytime between 11:30 and 12:30, conference room doors would spring open and people would flood out, all looking down at their handheld device of choice. They seemed to instinctively move toward the window, either seeking better cell service or some semblance of privacy, a concept that has really changed over the years. No phone booths anymore, that's for sure.

Others emerge from the meetings with a starved look in their eye that only free food can elicit. They are the ones in the meeting that blanked out on the last 15 minutes of the speaker because they couldn't stop thinking about what might be on the lunch menu. They lead the initial rush which results in a long, senseless line. Why people wouldn't stagger start this process is beyond me.

It was not a coincidence when I strolled up to the buffet line along with the final stragglers from one of the morning sessions at a conference in the Doubletree. These folks were usually engrossed in conversation, so I did not worry about some awkward encounter. They were usually more polite and just generally friendlier than those who positioned their seats in the conference hall specifically for quick and multiple exits for food.

"Is that ranch or blue cheese?" asked a short, attractive woman in a standard navy blue business suit.

"Has to be ranch," I replied.

This was the type of small talk that I didn't mind at all, in fact, I excelled in it. It was about food. It didn't involve personal questions like "Who are you, who do you work for or why in the world are you here taking this food?" I also happened to be good at identifying mystery foods at these types of events. It wasn't because I had any special senses, I simply learned the hard way enough times that I became adept at which bowl contained whipped butter versus cream cheese when they looked identical.

"You're right!" responded the woman after she poured a small amount of dressing on her plate, dipped her finger in and gave it a quick lick.

I just smiled and finished making a turkey sandwich with lettuce, tomato and mayo. I was planning on eating it soon so I didn't need to be concerned with how it would keep unrefrigerated. I already had bagels and muffins from breakfast that I would eat later. I took my sandwich over to the side of the wide hallway. I set my plate down for a moment while I unfolded a napkin. I packed the sandwich neatly in the napkin, and then wrapped another one around it for extra protection. I slipped the sandwich in my bag without even giving a glance around to see who noticed. My theory: if you acted like what you were doing was normal and that you weren't hiding anything, then no one would give it a second thought. It didn't hurt that it was becoming more common for people to grab food to take back to their hotel rooms to eat while catching up on emails and phone calls missed during the conference.

After adding a banana and an orange to my bag of goodies, I grabbed a bottle of Gatorade out of the cooler next to the coffee station and headed out. I stepped out into lunch-time pedestrian traffic on Walnut. As much as I loved to people watch, I was way too tired to spend any time checking out the scenery. The Doubletree was just across the street from my breakfast spot so I only had a few blocks to get back to the gym. I didn't see Jenny on my way into the lobby. She usually took her lunch break around this time. Not that it would have been a big deal to see her again, or rather, have her see me entering again. But it just seemed like it would raise fewer questions if she weren't there. Desmond was on duty when I walked through the gate but he was in the middle of answering questions to a young couple who looked like they were considering a membership. I scanned my card without notice and walked into the locker room.

I quickly changed out of my coat and khakis into my cargo shorts and T-shirt. I hadn't put them into the laundry bag in the morning knowing that I would need them as I usually would in the afternoon. I used the bathroom there again, although this time my routine was quicker than in the morning: just toilet, toothbrush and gone.

I did not exactly move fast, but I was not wasting any time either. Although I had gotten a second wind after leaving the library, I knew I needed to get some sleep. I slid out the gym exit without notice again and made my way out of the building and back onto Walnut Street. This time I headed East, away from the college, and virtually sleepwalked the four blocks that led to the city park.

This was easily my favorite place in the city, but I wasn't in the frame of mind to properly enjoy the park. I made a bee-line for my favorite old oak tree in the corner of one of the long fields. This wasn't only a beautiful, shady spot to enjoy a sunny summer day; it was also a quiet oasis in the middle of the hectic city. It was not a coincidence that the two places in which I chose to spend my days were the park and the college. I needed open space and fresh air to survive. It wasn't just that it made me feel like I was home or a kid again—I grew up in the middle of no place after all. It just seemed to be a part of my chemical makeup. I loved the culture and action of the city, but I needed the balance that these spots provided. Plus I needed the opportunity to get some sleep without notice.

As I approached my tree, I was relieved to see that no one had infringed on my territory. In fact, there was no one nearby at all. I didn't mind some activity. Sometimes the classic sounds of kids playing and people talking were soothing to me and provoked a peaceful, enjoyable sleep. It made me feel like I wasn't alone even though I didn't know anyone.

I unzipped my backpack and took out my book, sandwich and Gatorade. I took one of the T-shirts out of the bag and left the rest inside so I could use it as a pillow. I devoured the sandwich, more because I was in a hurry to sleep than because I was hungry. Because of my big breakfast I wasn't in dire need of sustenance. But I knew the sandwich wouldn't last all day and I didn't want it to spoil. I never wasted food. In fact, I liked to think of myself as personally taking up the cause against wastefulness. With so many people hungry in the world, it never seemed right to throw away perfectly edible food, something I know the hotels and the hospitality industry did as a matter of course.

I saved half of my Gatorade in case I got thirsty later which was usually the case after I slept. I tossed my book aside and laid down on my back with my head resting on my backpack. I had used one T-shirt to cover the backpack so it was softer to the touch, like an actual pillow. After a deep breath I looked up at one of my favorite views in the world. The underside of tree leaves against the backdrop of the sky gave me a sense of peace and contentment like nothing else.

I have seen more awe-inspiring sights in my travels but nothing beat the feeling I got lying under a tree, like a kid with not a worry in the world. Everyone talks about being in the moment and the benefits of meditation or prayer which can bring clarity of mind and soul. That's what this position did for me. I don't know if it was the hypnotic effects of the leaves gently rustling in the breeze or just an overwhelming sensation that I was a part of the same natural phenomenon as the ground on which I lay, the tree a few yards above me and the clouds and sky miles and miles away.

There were times when I could stare up for hours, and other times that I would drift off to sleep in a matter of seconds. This time, I drifted off quickly as I thought about how there was nothing else in the world I'd rather be doing. That was the essential premise upon which I tried to live my life. I tried to fill my days and hours with the activities that I most enjoyed and made me feel good. I saw so many people get carried away with their lives that their priorities got buried. It was not intentional and was not because their priorities changed or were out of order. It was simply bad planning and a matter of how quickly and powerfully the momentum of today's society can sweep you away. I was pretty proud of myself. I created a life where that would not and could not happen to me.

I was sitting at a café with a beautiful woman and two little blonde rambunctious boys. I was feeding yogurt to the younger one and begging the older one to take another bite of his grilled cheese. There was about a year between them and they were thick as thieves. In an otherwise quiet and subdued place, these two clowns kept looking at each other, breaking into hysterical laughter.

The older boy would mock his brother, "Da-da-da-da-da!" They both cracked up and I could not stop laughing. Their mother looked at them and me disapprovingly but she could not help but find it funny, too. This routine continued for what seemed like 20 minutes. Although we were concerned that we were annoying the other diners, everyone who walked by remarked how adorable our family was and how we should cherish every moment as it goes by so fast. With each comment, I experienced a pang of pride combined with a strange feeling of dread. As the meal continued, I had an increasingly sinking feeling that I had done something irrevocably wrong. The boys stopped eating and could no longer be contained by the highchair and the dinner table. They climbed down and were on the verge of wreaking havoc on the café.

The woman turned to me, "Drew, we need to get these guys out of here. They're done and we need to get them to bed pretty quickly. I'll clean up the rest of this mess. Why don't you go up and pay."

I couldn't make out the features of this beautiful woman because I could not bring myself to look directly at her. The pit in my stomach started to take over my entire body. I felt mortified and ashamed as it dawned on me why this idyllic moment wasn't bringing the pure joy that it should have.

"I don't have anything," I murmured into my plate. The laughter stopped and I could feel the woman's eyes bear down on me. I could tell she was not surprised, like she was expecting to be disappointed by me. The boys didn't say anything and although they were way too young to comprehend how pathetic their dad looked at that moment, I could feel them longing for a real father to be sitting in my chair.

"And I don't have anywhere to take us," I continued. "I can try to get us into the library . . ." I stopped, knowing that I had no plausible solution to this dilemma. I had no money, no home and no hope for this family.

Instead of telling me what a loser I was and that I was not fit to be anyone's father or husband—which would have been the truth—the woman just began crying, defeated. As I still couldn't look her in the eye, I only knew she was crying because her tears and sadness were absolutely deafening to me. I began to cry deep in my heart, wishing with every fiber of my being that I had not let this happen. How could I have been charged with such a noble responsibility as having a family, only to have selfishly ignored the obligations necessary to take care of it? The hurt of this realization was overwhelming. I wanted to scream and literally rip my own skin off until I became unrecognizable.

"Janie, time to go!" yelled a woman from across the meadow as my head bolted up off of my backpack. Breathing quickly, I wasn't sure if I had yelled in reality or in my dream. I was certainly relieved to find myself under the oak tree, but it took a few minutes for my heart to stop racing. It always did. The emotional effects of this recurring nightmare usually hung with me long after I calmed physically. It only happened once a week or so but it was always haunting.

Luckily once I got my mind on something else, I could usually forget about it. I had one true gift in this world and that was to block out of my mind topics I didn't want to think about. It didn't hurt that my memory as an adult was pitiful. I used to have a great memory. When I was a kid I could tell you the year-by-year stats of practically every major league baseball player after memorizing the backs of their baseball cards. In 5th grade I could rattle off the U.S. presidents in order and tell you the names of the states and capitals in an instant. But my brain maxed out around the age of 20 and practically nothing has stayed in there since.

This pervasive memory malfunction comes in handy when it's time to block things out though. This nightmare was a good example. It was not always the exact same dream but it always centered on the same basic premise. I'm with my loving wife and kids having a great time when it eventually dawns on me that I'm an incredible loser who somehow forgets to get his act together in order to provide for his family. Clearly my subconscious was dealing with issues I didn't deal with in my waking hours. I hated to admit that I still had some latent anxieties even though I designed my whole life around happiness.

I saw a girl, probably the Janie whose mom was calling, running across the meadow to the woman down the footpath pushing a stroller. The sun was low in the sky and I guessed that it must have been a little after 6:00 pm. I felt pretty well rested even though I got just less than six hours of sleep. I took the shirt off of the backpack and put it inside. While still sitting on the ground trying to orient myself, I finished the remainder of my Gatorade. Then I threw my book in my bag, zipped it and slung it over my shoulder as I stood up.

I started walking toward the southeast corner of the park on my way to the gym. I was comforted by the fact that I'd have a basketball in my hands in just a few minutes. Nothing made me feel like everything was right in the world more than being on the basketball court.

CHAPTER 5

It was almost 7:00 when I saw the boys enter the far end of the court. I had been shooting around by myself on court two for a few minutes. They were always early but I liked to spend a few minutes shooting before they came, partially to get my thoughts together for the coaching session and partially because I wanted to be ready in case they challenged me to a shoot-off.

"Hold that follow-through!" yelled Kijana as he ran down the court toward me with his hand in a gooseneck position straight above his head. He heard me say that probably a thousand times so he was clearly mocking me, albeit in a good-natured way.

"Coach KJ!" I responded. "You almost sound like you know what you're talking about."

"He's been watching me!" yelled Hakim, who sprinted past his twin brother to steal the ball I had passed. He took one dribble and pulled up for a shot at the foul line.

"Not in my house!" KJ barked as he swatted Hakim's shot just as it left his hand. I quickly raised my hands to catch the ball before it hit me in the midsection.

"Easy fellas," I said. "Don't hurt the old man before the lesson even starts."

"How are you, coach?" KJ said as he we shook hands and brought it in for a quick shug.

"Good, buddy," I replied. I gave Hakim the same shake and shug before handing the ball over. I told them to take a minute to loosen up and that we would start soon. As I turned back toward half court, I saw Keisha smiling at the scene as she was walking toward us. I took a few steps toward her, returning her smile.

"Are you sure you want to put up with these guys today, Coach? They are in rare form."

"Of course! It's my favorite hour of the week. And these jokers are more fun to be around than anyone else I know."

"Fun for you because they actually listen to you."

I knew she said this just to make me feel better. They were extraordinarily well-mannered, entirely because Keisha was a mother who got through to her children, even ones just entering their teens. She was a great combination of loving and strict. She was an intelligent hard-working mother who seemed always composed and in charge of every situation. I think she remained so focused as a way to compensate for the kids' father not being around. I don't know what the story was but I knew that he was not in the picture at all.

"How are you Keisha?" I asked while giving her a quick handshake. We had known each other long enough now that it would be natural to give her a hug or a peck on the cheek, but for some reason, most likely to not confuse the boys, we always stuck to a handshake. This moment was always a little awkward in my friendships with women. For men who you know well, haven't seen for some time, or with whom you are simply very close, you can just shug. Shake, pull in, and pound on the back. Affectionate and manly all-in-one. There was no such thing for the man to woman interaction. It was either hug and kiss or shake hands, nothing in between.

"Great to see you, Drew."

35

"What's new with the boys? How was their game on the weekend?"

Keisha lit up immediately, but kept her voice low as if she were hiding something.

"The team played well. The boys shot the ball really well, but Hakim was so quick off the dribble that he was able to pass to teammates for layup after layup. Don't tell him I said that, though. You know you're the only person who I brag to about my kids, right?"

"You have the right to brag to everyone. They're awesome kids. Are they ready to get to work?"

"They're all yours."

I jogged in toward the key and snatched the ball as it caromed off the rim. I held it up high as both boys tried to jump to knock it out of my hands.

"Alright fellas," I said, as I tried to calm them down and get them focused. "Let's get started with our usual warm-up: one hand, three spots to the free throw line. Then repeat, adding the second hand."

Hakim took the ball and walked to about five feet in front of the rim. He held it in the palm of his right hand, his left hand hanging loose at his side. He looked down at his feet to make sure they were aligned properly, shoulder width apart with the right foot about a half a foot in front of the left. Then he looked up at the rim while turning his right hand over and lifting it just above his right eye, his wrist cocked back and the ball balancing on the pads of his fingers. He looked down again toward his right foot, then his right elbow which was directly under the ball and then back up toward the rim. With everything in line along his right side and his knees slightly bent, he straightened his legs and extended his right hand upward and flicked his wrist toward the rim. The ball lifted gently, rotating backward as it arced over the rim. Swish.

This was a thing of beauty. For me it was better than looking at a famous painting or listening to any masterful musical piece. A pure shooting stroke followed by the splash into the net was poetry in motion. Such artistry did not happen by accident, but by hard work and incredible discipline. I understand that anyone can put a ball in a hoop from time to time. It's a different thing entirely to have such a refined shooting motion that you can put that ball in the hoop over and over again and from anywhere on the court. It takes more than just practice. It takes the proper form, mental concentration and supreme confidence. Then it takes practice. Lots and lots of practice.

KJ grabbed the ball out of the net and tossed it back to Hakim, who repeated the same routine. After five shots from the first spot, Hakim took one giant step backward and repeated the routine for another five shots. Then he took one more giant step back to the foul line and repeated the routine again. After taking those 15 shots, they switched spots. KJ's routine looked virtually identical to Hakim's, except everything was done with his left hand, his left foot slightly in front of his right, his left elbow underneath the ball. KJ's stroke was just as pure and even more aesthetically pleasing than Hakim's because lefties always looked smoother. I never understood why but lefties always just looked more natural shooting or throwing a ball.

We had been doing this warm-up sequence for several months. It started as a method by which we transformed their previous poor forms into proper shooting technique. Then it evolved into a muscle memory warm-up before doing more sophisticated shooting drills. The concept was simple, really. Break down shooting into its most basic parts. Master those parts before moving on to the next and gradually introduce more complex concepts as they can handle them.

"OK, let's get moving now. Elbow to elbow drill. Twenty-five apiece. Don't get tired!"

For the next 45 minutes, the boys put up 300 shots apiece. As usual, they worked very hard. We took a few breaks where they drank water and took two foul shots. Other than that, they were busting their butts in these drills. When they finished the final one, we huddled under the hoop for a talk. I saw Keisha walk into the opposite corner of the gym a few minutes earlier. Our session was nearly over but I liked to talk to them for a few minutes before letting them go.

"You guys are really progressing. Hakim, your foot preparation is so much better. You are getting your shot off so much quicker now that you are focused on it. KJ, I can count on one hand the number of times you faded right or left during your shots. So much better! You're better balanced and you're taking your time to shift your momentum instead of just letting your speed carry you into your shot before you're ready."

"Thanks Coach," they muttered together trying to catch their breath. They were always less playful and better listeners when exhausted.

"Guys," I continued. "No one else your age is putting in the kind of time on shooting that you guys are. There are other kids working hard, don't get me wrong. They might be putting up more shots than you guys, believe it or not. But I guarantee you they aren't working on the types of shots that will help them be great shooters down the road. They are simply further reinforcing bad habits that they will have to fix later in life. You guys will simply raise your release as you get stronger. You'll have the same stroke at age 20, heck, 60, that you do now."

I wanted to say "when you're playing in the NBA" but I very consciously did not feed those kinds of expectations or pressure. They would be able to shoot at a professional level, I was certain of that. But whether they grew tall enough or strong enough or stuck with it long enough to be great, that remained to be seen.

"So, more importantly, how is school?" I said, shifting topics.

"It's fine," said Hakim, breathing a bit easier now.

"I don't want 'it's fine,'" I replied. "I want some details. Are you guys studying hard? Grades good? Any teachers you like?"

"We were both on high honors again, coach," chimed in KJ. "We can't stand Mr. Bush because he gives us more homework than a 10th grader. It's ridiculous!"

"OK, now that's more like it. And are you guys helping your mom around the house, being an absolute pleasure to be around?"

"I can hear you so you better answer that honestly," said Keisha sternly but with a smile as she made her way over to our huddle.

"Of course, we're always good for mommy," Hakim said mockingly as he lunged over to hug Keisha with his sweaty body. Keisha showed some quickness of her own as she sidestepped him.

"Get out of here you sweaty pigs," she said as KJ cornered her from the other side. "You see what they do to me? Torture, I tell you. Torture!"

I loved seeing the boys interact with their mother like this. I knew they didn't have a man in the house to play with or learn from, more importantly. I think that was why Keisha continued to send them to me once a week. Sure they loved basketball and I was helping them get better. But Keisha loved having a positive male influence for the boys. The boys looked up to me and I looked up them. I found their spirit and enthusiasm inspirational.

"Thank you, Drew," Keisha said as the boys grabbed two Gatorades out of the bag she had handed to them. She took a few bills out of her pocket and moved toward me to give them to me. We had the same interaction every time. She always tried to pay me for the lessons and I always tried to refuse to take it.

"Keisha, please. You know I don't want anything for this. I love working with these clowns."

"I know you do and I know you'll take this because I also know you respect me too much to not take it."

"Why do I even fight with you? You always get your way, don't you?"

She grabbed my hand, turned it over and slapped $50 into my palm. I thanked her and she corralled the boys. I quickly closed my hand around the money so I didn't have to look at it. I hated taking it from her. And I hated that I needed it. I looked up from my hand to shift my attention to something else. Something I could bear. But looking at this family walk off the court gave me another pit in my stomach beyond the one created by the money.

I had this same sinking feeling every time I watched them leave a session. It was so fulfilling to play this role in their lives, but I felt like an imposter, potentially exposed at any point. It wasn't that I didn't know what I was talking about when it came to shooting or that I wasn't truly interested in their off-the-court well being. It was just that I think they would be severely disappointed if they knew how I lived my life. I couldn't blame them.

Would they call me a hypocrite? A liar? I was never dishonest with them but I felt like the facts of my life wouldn't live up to the persona that they witness. It wasn't necessarily anyone's fault, but it made me sick to my stomach nonetheless.

I don't know if it was a rationalization or if I really believed it, but I told myself that role models can hinder personal development—that these boys need to find their own way, develop their own opinions and create their own goals. In the spirit of Emerson, it would be a disservice if they only looked to me as a role model and tried to emulate a life that they think I lead. Rather, they'd be more true to themselves to appreciate me for who I am, and then forge their own paths in life. I hadn't touched on this concept with them yet, but perhaps it is time. If they can grasp that, then perhaps they won't be so terribly disappointed to learn more about my off-the-court life.

CHAPTER 6

When I finished refereeing, I headed to the locker room to take a much needed shower. Most of the players were still cooling down or talking and I snuck out as soon as the buzzer sounded. I didn't exactly love officiating these men's league games, but I was the natural choice. I didn't play in this league because the talent level was too varied—mostly low—for my liking and I preferred playing with the guys in the morning. I got along with pretty much everyone in the gym so the league lobbied to have me ref to cut down on the arguing and general controversies that typically arise in men's leagues. Gym ownership liked the idea since to them I was a trusted regular. The deal we struck: I would ref a few games a week and receive a free gym membership—premium package no less—and the virtual run of the place. Everyone wins. What they didn't know was that this little deal was the key to my existence over the past few years.

I dried off in front of my locker and reached into my clean laundry bag for fresh clothes—a pair of jeans, a T-shirt and flip-flops. My sweaty clothes and my clothes from earlier in the day went into another laundry bag. The gym did laundry twice a day, morning and night. I usually threw in a load each cycle that way I always had something clean to wear. My locker contained two pairs of basketball shorts, one pair of swim trunks, one pair of cargo shorts, one pair of jeans, three pairs of socks, several pairs of underwear, one sports coat, one sweatshirt, one long sleeve T-shirt, four short sleeve T-shirts, one hat, one pair of basketball sneakers, one pair of running shoes and a pair of flops.

That was it. Although it was a lot for a gym locker—even an oversized one like they have at the Sports Club—it wasn't much considering it was the entirety of my worldly possessions. I rotated through those clothes as best as I could. The key to a limited wardrobe was simply not caring what others thought of your appearance. Otherwise, you'd live with the constant threat of embarrassment. Who saw me wearing what and when? I wasn't interested in playing that game so I just put on whatever suited the occasion. Sports coat for hotel meals. Cargo shorts for day trips to the park or library for sleep. Sweatshirt when it was chilly.

I couldn't decide what to do that night but I was leaning toward going to a book store. There were a few in the city and I hadn't been to my favorite in a few days. They were all comparable as far as book selection but I liked the atmosphere of the café in Cocco's better than the others.

I went back in the bathroom again to brush my teeth and was ready to go. I placed my book and notebook in my backpack. Then I threw in a bagel, a muffin and an apple I had left over from this morning. I tossed my laundry bag down the chute on the wall next to the far row of lockers, and headed out with backpack in hand.

"Later, Lafayette," I said to the person standing behind the front desk.

"See you, Drew," he replied. "Hey, when are you going to join us for some afternoon ball? I need some shooters out there to hang with me."

"Soon, buddy, soon," I lied. Lafayette was not a good shooter, or player for that matter. But he loved to play ball and he was always trying to get me to play with his group. He knew I didn't love playing with them, but that didn't stop him from asking every chance he got.

When I arrived at Cocco's, it was just before 9:00 pm and there were a few open seats along the windows in the café area. I always preferred a window seat so I went straight over to the tables before they were taken. As soon as I sat down, I caught a woman a few tables away from me in mid-stare. I smiled and looked away quickly.

I unloaded my backpack piece by piece on the table, intentionally not looking back at her. I did not want to seem as though my goal was to hit on women. I was there to relax, read and do some writing if the mood ever struck me. When I did peek at her a few minutes later, she was buried in what looked like a test preparation book. I noticed then that she was very attractive with dark hair and complexion. I guessed she was Latina but could not tell for sure. Her hair, long with flowing curls, gave her a wild look that I liked. I looked back down and began reading my book.

After about 30 minutes of unusually focused reading—my mind had a tendency to wander easily—my head snapped up in response to an audible sigh I heard. This same woman was leaning back in her chair with an exasperated expression and her hands on top of her head. She looked like she was going to pull her hair out of her head but her smile showed that she wasn't truly upset. She looked over at me and shook her head, making it clear that her studying efforts were driving her crazy. I smiled back at her and said at a volume intended only for her to hear, "You having a tough time?"

I was always embarrassed when I overheard people having a first conversation. This happened a lot at cafés where people often came with the purpose of meeting others. I had no problems with this practice in theory. I just didn't like to hear the awkward dialogue. So whenever I engaged in one of those conversations myself, I made sure that I wasn't being overheard by anyone.

"Does it show?" she replied with a laugh. She shook her head again, this time at the material in front of her. As I looked closer at the book and papers, I could tell that she had been taking a practice test of some sort.

"What are you studying for?"

"MCATs" she said, breaking into a long cat-like stretch like you would after sitting in the same position for a significant period of time. She yawned and murmured a light giggle as her body regained its original position.

"They're killing me," she continued as she rose and took a few steps over to my table and slid into the seat across the table from me.

"Have a seat," I said wryly, as she had already made herself comfortable without my invitation. I smiled at her to let her know that I was in no way bothered by her assertiveness.

"Thanks! I just really need a break and you look like you can handle a little intrusion."

"I guess I can handle it. How long have you been studying?"

"Do you mean in general or just tonight?"

"Both."

"Two and half months and three and a half hours."

"Is it killing you in general or just tonight?"

"Both."

We both laughed, catching each other's eyes a little more intensely now. I sat up straighter in my chair after realizing that I was practically lying down when I was reading. No one likes a slouch.

She ended our mutual gaze by dropping her head into her folded arms on the table. Her hair seemed to flow in all directions. I wasn't always a huge fan of random hair all over my stuff, but for some reason this didn't bother me. Her wild locks sprawled across the table onto my book and slightly onto my hand, which was resting on the table.

"Do you care if I catch a quick nap?" she asked innocently and in a tone muffled by her own arms.

"I'm not saying I'm not offended by you nodding off smack in the middle of our conversation, but if you're tired, you're tired I guess."

"I'm sorry, that is incredibly rude, isn't it?" she said as she picked up her head.

"I'm just kidding."

"I know but it's still rude. I'm sorry."

"Don't be silly. In a few minutes I was going to come over there and just throw my head on your desk and start snoring."

"Oh really?" she asked, laughing.

"Yes, this book is really kicking my ass. I've been reading for 30 straight minutes and I don't know how much more I can take," I said with as much exasperation as I could muster.

"Are you making fun of me or trying to make me feel better?" she said accusatorily.

"I'm not sure."

I paused for a second to gauge whether she appreciated a little teasing.

"So, what are you reading anyway?" she asked.

"It's the new Malcolm Gladwell book."

"Nice. I loved "Blink." How's this one?"

"Thought-provoking," I said after a second's delay.

"Of course it is . . . it's Malcolm Gladwell," she replied.

"So, when is your test?" I asked.

"Not for another month, but I feel like I have so much more to do."

"Do you have more subjects to review or are you just taking practice tests at this point?"

"Mostly just tests."

I hadn't taken the MCATs but I had plenty of friends from college who did. I knew they were difficult and that you never felt completely prepared. Not that different from the LSATs. Very different subjects and skill sets, but a similar overwhelming feeling. It had been nearly 8 years since I had taken them and I still remember the uncertainty I felt regardless of how many hours I prepared. The Bar exam was the same thing, except longer and harder.

"Sounds fun," I said facetiously.

"A blast." She rolled her eyes and looked over at the café counter. "I either need to drink something to wake up or I need to go get some sleep. I need to be up at the crack of dawn tomorrow."

"Sunrise yoga?" I asked.

"Yeah, not quite. I have to be at work at 7:00 for a 12-hour shift. Who has time for yoga?"

"Where's work?"

"St. Luke's," she said referring to the city's largest hospital.

"What do you do at St. Luke's," I probed.

"I'm a nurse in the cardiac care unit, that is until I'm a heart surgeon in just a few short years," she winked at me. She had eight plus years before she would finish med school and her residency. She was at the beginning of a long journey and I admired her determination to go for it knowing how much work it would take.

"Do you think they'll make you shave your head so your hair doesn't fall into any major heart valves? Or will they start making extra large skull caps just for your hair?"

I was successful in making her laugh with this question but I had truly always wondered how someone with that much hair managed to not get it into everything—food, dangerous machinery, hearts, just to name a few items. She tilted her head at me, clearly not pleased with the question.

"Is there an issue with my hair?"

"What? Of course not. It's sexy as hell. I would just worry about it causing serious infections and compromising patient care," I said as I slowly pulled a very long black hair off of my book, gave it an exaggerated look as it dangled from my finger tips, and then dropped it to the floor.

"Real sexy, huh?"

"I love it, but I'm not being operated on by you."

"Not yet," she said threateningly and with enough sass for me to grasp the double entendre.

I definitely liked how this was going. To me, there was nothing more exciting than discovering good chemistry with someone who I found attractive. Mutual flirtation was at the core of my dating philosophy. Everyone likes to flirt. It's fun. It's exciting. It's innocent. It's improvisation at its finest. My theory was to live in those moments as often as possible.

Of course that was easier said than done. There were plenty of conversations that lacked chemistry. But when it worked, it worked beautifully. Even those most jaded by relationships gone badly would admit that the memory of the initial spark was a good one, if not the best one of the whole relationship. Everyone fondly remembers how they met their sweetheart, even if they ended up hating that person in the long run.

My plan was to only have those kinds of interactions. Stick with the good times and forego the inevitable bad ones. I loved first and second dates, but avoided the headaches and heartaches that came with anything beyond that.

"So, do you always work at 7:00 in the morning after studying all night?" I asked as she yawned again.

"Only three days a week," she admitted as she glanced over at the café again. She looked at me in earnest, studying my eyes now for the first time as if trying to read what I was all about.

"Look, I'm going to go home to get some sleep now, but only if we can continue this conversation another day."

She was very direct, that was for sure. I met her stare with a smile and a subtle nod of the head in agreement.

"Of course. You should get some sleep . . . for the patients' sake," I replied.

"You really care about those patients, don't you?" she said just as sarcastically.

"What are you doing tomorrow night?" I asked her with confidence.

"I have the next month blocked off for studying so I think I can squeeze you in," she said. "Why don't you give me a call tomorrow and tell me what you want to do?"

"There's an outdoor concert at Penn's Landing tomorrow," I suggested. "No one spectacular, but there should be a few bands worth hearing."

"Citizen Cope is playing," she responded. "I wanted to go to that. Here, take my number down."

"Why don't you just meet me at the front entrance? 8:00."

She smiled and leaned back away from me slightly. "You don't want my number do you?"

I laughed gently. "It's not that. I just don't have a phone."

"You lost your phone?"

"I don't own a phone."

She looked at me like I had three heads. "Really?"

"I know it sounds crazy but I haven't had one for a while and it is kind of nice to not be tied to it all the time. Liberating, you know?"

"O---K," she said slowly, trying to see if I was serious or just plain strange. "So you've had one before but you don't have one now and this is all by choice," she half-asked, half-stated out loud just to hear how it sounded.

"That's correct, not a big deal at all," I replied, trying to reassure her that I didn't take myself too seriously with all of this. "Would you rather talk to me over the phone or see me again in person? Personally, I like seeing you face to face."

My gaze settled on her for a long moment.

"I can't really argue with that. I'll see you tomorrow at 8:00?"

"You got it."

"My name is Alex, by the way."

"Drew. Great talking to you."

"Tomorrow at 8:00," she said again.

She packed her studying materials pretty quickly and looked over one last time. I gave her a cheesy wave and she gave me her sexiest smile before walking away. This was actually the first time I saw the full picture. She was wearing a pair of soft, comfortable-looking jeans and a pair of black Uggs. Her thin gray shirt hung just to her waist with her hair coming down almost as far.

The jeans weren't skinny jeans like so many of the younger college girls were wearing. I couldn't stand them. Not because I didn't like new fashion on principle. In fact, I had no principles when it came to fashion, largely because I had absolutely zero fashion sense myself. I just knew that skinny jeans were not typically flattering to a woman's body, but the jeans that Alex wore made her ass look smoking hot. She was curvy in all the right ways. It wasn't a shock when I saw several guys do a double take at her on her way past them. If she elicited that kind of a response while wearing a pair of old jeans, God help me when she gets dressed up.

I stayed for a few minutes longer trying to read. My mind was racing though from meeting Alex. She was my kind of girl. I was actually excited about seeing her again. Not that I thought this relationship would go anywhere or even that I wanted it to. I didn't. I was excited because I knew going to the concert with her would be fun. I imagined she knew how to let loose, particularly after spending most nights over the last few months studying for the MCATs. She needed a break and I was in the right place at the right time. Lucky me.

As I sat there staring at my closed book, I briefly thought about the unfortunate parts of the situation: that I'd have to keep conversation surface level when it came to my life; that I'd have to be honest about having no intention of having a long-term relationship if it came to that; and ultimately that I'd get to enjoy her company only another time or two regardless of whether I liked being with her or not. I liked the initial romance but could do without the negative energy that comes with a more established relationship. As with all aspects of my life, I preferred to focus my attention on the positive parts. Simple as that.

I didn't want to think about those things because I had a nice high from my interaction with Alex. I was a pro at blocking out negative thoughts so I instinctively snapped out of my daze, loaded my backpack and walked out of the café thinking only of those jeans, that deadly smile, and the serious head of hair that was practically laying in my lap a few minutes ago.

CHAPTER 7

I just finished eating an apple as I turned off of Walnut down 15ᵗʰ Street toward McGillan's, one of a dozen Irish bars in the downtown area, but easily my favorite. It had great flat screen TVs, a good amount of breathing room at the bar, and bartenders who refused to take money from anyone not drinking alcohol. I guess it was their designated driver policy even though most of their patrons probably walked home from the bar.

I preferred Diet Coke anyway and greatly appreciated their willingness to keep them coming. I was sure not to abuse it. I never went there more than twice in a week, and I always tipped a dollar or two even though they never gave me a bill. In essence, $2 got me unlimited Diet Cokes, a cushy stool in front of multiple TVs airing a variety of games, and a pleasant smoke-free atmosphere. McGillan's typically offered a good looking crowd, too. I didn't usually try to meet women here, though. My eyes were primarily fixed on the games, but it was nice to have other distractions at as well.

"Hey Drew, vodka and tonic?" asked Julie completely straight-faced.

"Sounds good," I replied.

By the time I sat on my stool, Julie had slid a full glass of Diet Coke in front of me, the foam perfectly rising over the glass but not spilling. I was no expert, but Julie was an excellent bartender by every measure. She was very quick with the drinks. I never saw her stumped by an order. She had a presence about her that commanded respect from her customers, but was still friendly and approachable so as not to scare anyone away.

"Lakers coming on?" she asked me.

I looked up at the Sixers game that was on the screen directly in front of me. There were only a few minutes left and the Sixers were up 10. The Lakers game would be coming on next as they were playing the Thunder in the second game of the double header on TNT. Most people didn't take kindly to Lakers fans in this city, and Julie liked to bust my chops about it.

"You know I don't like the Lakers anymore, Julie. I'm a Manu Ginobili fan."

"Yeah, right. You can't desert them now."

I was there a little earlier than on most nights. I usually arrived after 11:00 and caught three quarters of the late NBA game. During college basketball season, I loved watching the West coast games, which often began at 11:30 or midnight on the East coast. Being a Yankee fan, I didn't love West coast baseball but there was always a game on from April through October. Plus, there was always SportsCenter on so I could catch the day's highlights. To me, this beat any living room because you had premium viewing of multiple games at one time, someone to serve you drinks, people to socialize with, and even some good music.

"I know but the only problem is that I can't stand their players. They're all jerks. They've become impossible to root for," I lamented. "I miss Magic."

"Magic's been gone for a long time, maybe you need to come over to the dark side," she said in reference to becoming a Philly fan. Dark, indeed. Never in the history of sports has there been an angrier fan base than Philly fans.

I smiled at her as she walked to the other end of the bar where a few new customers just approached. She had a sixth sense when it came to tending to her bar. I didn't notice her look down there once, but she was on the move before they even had a chance to try to get her attention. She was good at what she did, not to mention she was much admired by most men who came in the place.

Her standard uniform was a black tank top and blue jeans. She had a number of tattoos that were visible and very likely more that were not. Her straight brown hair and naturally dark complexion added to her badass image. Somehow, though, she managed to pull off sexy instead of trashy. It wasn't that I thought most heavily tattooed women were trashy, but accompanied with a certain attitude and clothing choices, it was sometimes the case. Julie was just plain hot though.

The Sixers game ended and the telecast shifted to Los Angeles. I settled in for a few hours of entertaining hoops. I pulled out my notebook in case I had any moments of clarity that I needed to jot down. This never seemed to work. I think my intention was mostly for motivation purposes, like if I had the notebook out I might be more apt to actually write something down.

Instead, I watched Kobe continually force shots and complain to the officials. Inexplicably, I found myself always pulling for him in my heart of hearts, even though I despised his demeanor both on and off the court. I used to dribble around my house at the age of three pretending I was the point guard for the Lakers. My loyalty ran deep, apparently even against my better judgment. I think it was simply the yellow and purple that flowed through my blood that facilitated this strange draw to Kobe and his despicable teammates. They were a polarizing team and I managed somehow to both love them and hate them.

In the middle of the third quarter, a few women walked over to the bar just on the other side of the stool next to me. I had noticed them an hour earlier sitting in the booth along the far wall. Attractive, mid-20s and clearly having a good time. I hadn't paid much attention to them, though, until their proximity forced me to. I glanced over but didn't say anything. I hated being that guy who seemed to be hitting on all of the girls and making them feel uncomfortable in one way or another. It wasn't that I feared rejection. My feelings weren't easily hurt and I had no grand illusions that I would be someone that women just couldn't refuse. I had a nose that clearly had been broken one too many times and a hairline that seemed to creep back a bit every day. I kept it very short with the clippers at the gym just so it wouldn't be so obvious. Plus, I wore the same clothes virtually every other day. I knew that the ladies wouldn't be swooning over that kind of style.

So I kept watching the game with only an ear focused on the women next to me. It was somebody's birthday and what started out as a nice dinner and a drink had apparently turned into an excuse to get a little crazy. They ordered a round of shots and after a quick toast to the birthday girl, down the hatch they went. Before the shot glasses even hit the bar, the tallest one of the three asked Julie for another round. I couldn't help but laugh and take another quick glance over to see what kind of shape they were in after three bottles of wine and then a shot.

The tall woman caught my glance and barked back at me, "What, you don't think we can handle another round?"

"Not at all," I shot back, quickly defending myself. "I just admire the enthusiasm." I turned back to the television chuckling a bit to myself.

"No, you're making fun of us aren't you? You know, we don't get out much so you should be a little nicer to us."

I turned back toward them again. "Nice? I just told you I was impressed. What's not nice about that?"

She tilted her head slightly and gave me a look like she didn't believe a word I said. I turned slightly further to look the birthday girl herself. She was a tiny thing, but cute. No more than 5'2" and maybe 110 pounds. She didn't look overly skinny; she just had a petite build.

"And happy birthday to you. I'm glad you're out having some fun," I said with sincerity.

"Now that's more like it!" the tall woman said encouragingly.

The smaller one just winked at me in response, indicating subtly that she appreciated the gesture but wasn't responsible for her friend's behavior.

"Pour one more for our friend here."

Julie looked at me after she poured the third shot for the women, holding the bottle at an angle over a fourth glass but waiting for my reaction before proceeding.

"No, thank you though. That's very nice of you but my Diet Coke is hitting the spot for me right now."

"Don't be ridiculous," the tall woman continued. "It's her birthday for Christ sake, the least you could do is a shot with us. We're buying."

I raised my hand up in objection but she demanded that Julie pour another shot.

"Sorry Drew," Julie said with a smile while graciously stepping away from the scene like I needed some privacy to deal with this crew.

"Drew, huh? Well I'm Sara, this is Brianna, and the birthday girl is Stacy."

"Nice to meet you guys," I said, fully smiling at that point. I held up my shot and said, "Now that we're all friends here, I want to donate my shot to Stacy. It's only fair that the birthday girl have an extra one."

Much to my surprise, and relief, Stacy reached up, grabbed the shot out of my hand and threw it back. Then she held up her other shot, clinked glasses with the other girls, and downed it.

"To Drew!" she proclaimed.

This made me laugh but I soon realized that this little person had way too much to drink. I had swiveled on the stool to face them more directly. She moved Brianna aside with her hand and took two quick aggressive steps toward me and slid partly between my legs with her body, her left hand resting on my upper thigh. Normally, this move would have been quite welcomed. Instead, I immediately felt guilty for giving her the extra shot. Had I known she was this far gone I would have handled the shot very differently.

"You don't drink?" she asked as she leaned in much closer than necessary for me to hear her. The bar was not particularly loud and I did not have trouble hearing any of them.

"Just not tonight," I replied politely.

"Too bad, our night is just beginning," as she squeezed my thigh deeply and looked me dead in the eye.

I raised my eyebrows in surprise at her while my mind started racing on ways to exit the situation. I looked passed her to her friends who both gave me approving looks which was not exactly the help I was looking for.

"So where are you guys heading next?" I asked in the direction of the other two, hoping to get us all engaged in conversation once again.

"Well, Brianna and I are heading to the bathroom. You and Stacy are going to get to know each other a little bit while we're gone."

"Don't rush!" yelled Stacy after the women. As she said this she stumbled slightly and fell further into me, as if she weren't already on my lap. "Oops, sorry!"

"Not a problem," I said as I grabbed her by the waist to gently hold her back up and push her away from me a bit. For the next few minutes, I defended myself against various lunges, falls and general passes. When the other two returned, I looked at them with eyes begging for some help.

"I like him," Stacy said aloud to her friends fully intending for me to hear. She turned back at me as if she was about to eat me for dinner.

"You're sweet," I said almost sympathetically. "Next time, you guys should come talk to me a few bottles earlier."

I stood up from my stool trying to appear as if I was getting ready to leave. Her friends seemed to finally get the message because they quickly tried to distract Stacy when she asked where I was going. They were trying to convince her to go to another bar down the street for one last drink. Stacy seemed intent on staying close to me, but I excused myself to go the bathroom hoping that they'd be gone when I got back.

When I returned to my seat a few minutes later, I was grateful to see only Julie's teasing grin staring back at me.

"Not you're type?" Julie asked.

"You mean the really drunk I'm going to jump all over the guy I just met type? No, not my favorite."

"Really?" she replied pretending to be surprised. "I thought that didn't matter to guys if a girl was hot enough."

"Come on, Jules. Give us some credit. Jeez." I tried to sound offended.

"Whatever," she said as she walked further down the bar, wiping it with her dishrag.

Julie was great at engaging with her customers, but it never came at the expense of doing work. She was in perpetual motion around the bar. When she wasn't serving drinks, she was cleaning something, anything. She could have a full conversation with someone but never look them in the eye for more than a split second because she literally never stopped working.

"Ah, you're right. The only reason I didn't leave with her is because I couldn't miss the end of this game."

She glanced up at the screen behind her and saw that the Lakers were up 20 points with just a few minutes remaining. She shook her head and walked away. I liked making Julie laugh. I figured if I was going to be a semi-regular and not drink any booze, I better bring something to the table. Goofy humor was all I had to offer.

By the time the game was over and I had finished my last soda, it was a little after 2:00 am. Bars in the city were supposed to close at 2:00 but McGillan's was known to stay open a good bit later and no one ever seemed to enforce the closing time. It was part of why I spent so much time there. I asked Julie for change for a $20 that I pulled out of my pocket. She didn't want money for the soda but I wanted to leave her a few bucks for a tip.

"Here you go, but if you leave me more than $2, it's all coming back to you," she commanded.

"Wouldn't think of it," I said in return while laying down $2. She smiled at my response, probably remembering the fights we had when I tried to leave her $5 a few times. She thought that was too much for someone who was in her words, "no trouble at all."

"Have a good night, Drew."

"Thanks Julie. See you soon."

****

It was about 2:45 am by the time I walked into the locker room. There were a few people there; I assumed doctors or others in the health care field. Being open 24 hours is one of the perks of this gym, and a surprising number of people took advantage of it. I often wondered what brought these people here at such an hour, and I'm sure they thought the same thing about me.

Most of the overnight crew were regulars, although we didn't seem to socialize much. To work out in the middle of the night, you had to have a certain focus, or demon, or secret as the case may be. Something to drive you to fight the circadian rhythms. Of course, there were always a few who liked to share anything and everything about their lives, even at 3:00 in the morning during someone's workout. Those people usually talked amongst themselves, getting the hint from the rest of us that we weren't there at that time of the night looking for conversation.

Headphones helped. I was often the only person in the place without an iPod or iPhone attached to my ears. I refrained out of principle, although I still hadn't worked out what exactly that principle was, other than a manifestation of some subconscious urge to be different. Aside from providing a helpful soundtrack by which to work out, headphones also sent a clear message to everyone else in the gym: don't talk to me!

My approach was to say hello to everyone I passed, headphones or not. I did it in such a way that it was not misconstrued as a stop and chat. I wasn't opening the door for a conversation between the pull up bar and the free weights. I didn't want that anymore than anyone else. I just didn't like how headphones allowed people to slip into their own world without acknowledging that they are among fellow human beings. I understood the need for the escape, I just didn't like that it bred unfriendliness.

As it turned out, these eyes-down, living-in-their-head people actually did say hello back, once they knew that they were not committing to a conversation. A simple smile and acknowledgement did not take away from two things most sacred to gym-goers: time and privacy.

I spent about 45 minutes working out in the weight room area, focusing on back, shoulders and biceps. I had a few different regimens I rotated through each week. I tried to mix it up as much as possible because the concept of muscle confusion seemed to take hold and be pretty effective. The point was still the same. Work out the muscle and then rest to let it build itself back up. But instead of doing the same routine over the period of weeks or months or even years as some did, you work out the muscle doing different exercises or series of exercises. The idea is to prevent the plateau, which is where you see muscle improvement over a period of time but then it seems to stabilize, as if the muscle has built up a tolerance to a particular workout.

I never loved lifting. I refused to do it much when I was younger and could have really used it to help my basketball career. I never cared about getting big. In fact, I was always worried that putting on a lot of muscle would negatively impact my jump shot. What I didn't know was that there was a way to lift to get stronger but not necessarily bigger. That was my goal as an adult and I had to admit that I liked the results. The added strength helped on the court, I felt healthier and leaner, and I thought that skinny, strong people tended to live longer. I figured it couldn't hurt, at least.

So I got through my workouts because I knew they were good for me, not because I was some muscle-head who got off on pumping iron and carrying protein shakes around. By 4:00 am, I had changed out of my shorts and T-shirt and into my swim trunks. I only had one pair of these but there were very few people who ever saw them, considering the hour in which I wore them.

I wasn't a natural swimmer either. I always loved the water but I didn't grow up swimming and I never learned the proper technique. I did something fundamentally wrong because I would be practically hyper-ventilating after every lap, no matter how in shape I was. I had lots of wasted movement and terrible breathing patterns.

I just finished reading a book called, "Total Immersion," which was recommended by one of the guys I played ball with. I had spent the last month overhauling my swim stroke based on the style taught in this book. I was much better than when I started and could even do a flip turn and keep going without dying to reach the other end of the pool. It probably didn't hurt that I swam practically every day, or night really, for the past year. I would never be Michael Phelps, but at least wasn't on the verge of drowning anymore. Plus, it was an outstanding workout. I felt great every time I got out of the pool.

By 5:00 am, I was in the Jacuzzi trying relax and keep my muscles warm after finishing the first two parts of my nightly workout routine. Part 3 was my morning pickup basketball game which officially started at 6:00 sharp. The last game ended by 8:00—plenty of time for the guys to get to work or otherwise start their day. I was usually the first one on the court, taking some shots by 5:30. There were others there at that time but they usually tried to squeeze in a lift before the games started. For about 20 minutes, it was just me, a ball and the hoop. I loved this time of my day above all else. It was my time for peace, clarity and mindless shooting.

The morning pickup game was competitive and fun as usual. Not as much trash talking as the previous day though. Blade and Tony were on opposite teams again but there was a younger player on Blade's team guarding me. He was a nice, quiet kid, so Tony didn't give him a hard time like he did

Blade. Tony and I won three out of the four games we played. I shot the ball well, but tried to get my teammates involved as much as possible.

We had Hank on our team. Hank could shoot well but he was at least 55 years old and had bad knees. He didn't play that often anymore and the last thing he wanted to do was detract from the game—but he did. I liked him a lot and tried to get him open shots, much to the dismay of Tony, who was silently begging me to shoot more and pass to Hank less. As kind-hearted as Tony was, he liked to win. He was not happy when he had to take Hank with his last pick when choosing teams.

I walked to the locker room with Tony after we finished.

"What did you get up to last night, man?" Tony asked me.

"Not much." I replied.

"How's the writing coming along?"

"Terrible. Did meet a nice girl though."

"Of course you did you bastard. What's the deal?"

"I don't know. I'll tell you after tonight."

"You're going out with her? Very nice. Save me the details until tomorrow. I got to run to work a bit early. Big, stupid meeting this morning. Don't they know I have more important things to do like listen to graphic stories of your sexcapades?"

"Alright, man, get going. I give you all the gory details tomorrow."

"Later," said Tony as he took off for the showers.

I hadn't even started to undress yet. I sat down on the bench and realized how tired my body was. Aside for the dip in the hot tub, I had been working out pretty intensely for nearly five hours. I felt great but exhausted. I took my time with my morning routine as all of the other players were very briskly showering, dressing for work and exiting with briefcase in hand. I had the same friendly exchanges as we normally did, and I had the same mixed feelings of pity and envy. They seemed like rats running feverishly on a spinning wheel, but at least they did so with purpose and drive. I knew I had gotten off the wheel some time ago and was better off for it—of that I had no doubt. But I still got a nagging sensation of underachievement when I began to floss after everyone else left for their jobs.

CHAPTER 8

I wasn't in the mood for a sit-down breakfast, so I swung by the Marriott to snag a few muffins, bagels and fresh fruit. I was starving, so I ate an apple and a pear on my walk to the college. Instead of returning to the main library, I walked into the science center and up the stairs to the third floor, which housed a small but very nice science library. Some students came here to do schoolwork. I never saw anyone take a book off the shelf, but that could be said for most libraries in the digital age. I liked this place because no monitor or check-in station existed and it featured a set of comfortable chairs in each of the four corners of the room. I weaved my way to the back left corner to find all four chairs empty. I spun one around toward the window so I could sit with my back to the room and look out over the expansive green below. It created a cozy spot to read, write or sleep—my three favorite daytime activities.

I read the last few chapters of my book before nodding off for an hour. At noon, I left campus and walked a few blocks to the Hyatt where I found an excellent lunch spread. I loaded up mostly on chicken marsala and assorted vegetables. I don't love veggies but know they are good for me so when I found some that looked appetizing, I tried to take advantage of the opportunity. I sat at a table full of people in a discussion about the future of natural gas. I only spoke with the guy next to me from a company called Cabot. I introduced myself as an attorney for a local firm that handles some Energy issues and was attending the conference to stay informed of the latest industry news.

Other than basic small talk, I was left to eat in peace just listening to the group conversation. I actually found the topic interesting but was thankful that I hadn't dedicated my life to working on natural gas issues.

On my way out I grabbed a handful of chocolate chip cookies, my biggest weakness. I threw a few in my bag and began eating as I walked. After changing again in the gym, I walked over the park and went to the first open lawn to the right of the entrance. On the north end of the green were a set of Poplar trees that provided shade. It was a popular spot because finding this oasis did not require walking far into the park. I selected a different spot to rest than I had the previous day so that no one would suspect that I was using the park as my personal bedroom. I settled under a tree next to a few college-age girls. They seemed engrossed in conversation and I was way too sleepy to even attempt to check them out. I got my notebook out but didn't get a chance to open it before I passed out on my backpack.

I had only been asleep for four hours when a Frisbee hit me in the hand and woke me. I tossed it back to a 10-year-old boy who apologized sheepishly. It was only 5:00 pm but I could not fall back asleep. After a long and futile attempt at writing down some thoughts, I packed up and went back to the gym. With a few hours to kill before I had to meet Alex,. I took another shower and put back on the same shorts that I had been wearing. This concert would be outdoors and it looked like we were going to have perfect weather. It was roughly 80 degrees today and the evening wasn't going to be much cooler. Summers in Philly were usually full of warm nights.

I walked over to Penn's Landing early and sat near the front entrance to the amphitheater. The place was buzzing with people and music. The bands scheduled to play brought a diverse crowd. Marc Broussard had a rock/jazz sound that generally attracted those above 30 and Citizen Cope presented a low key rap/folk/rock vibe that was generally popular with those under 30. It looked as though there wasn't going to be a huge teen population in attendance, thank God. Nothing made me more uncomfortable than walking through a crowd of under aged, drunk or high girls dressed in next to nothing at a concert. My last Dave Mathews Band show scarred me for life.

After about 20 minutes, I saw Alex grinning at me as she bounced over to where I was standing to greet me.

"Hi!" she said energetically and stretched up to give me a kiss on the cheek.

"Hey, you seem pretty happy today," I replied.

"I'm just excited to get out and do something fun. Let's go," she urged while grabbing my hand and pulling me toward the entrance. Her aggressiveness surprised me, although I don't know why, considering how I met her last night. She certainly wasn't shy. I liked that, or at least that made things easier for me. There was no need to wonder about what she was thinking or how to move in for the first kiss. She dictated the action which took the edge off in a nice way.

We walked through the opening of a large gate that led into the amphitheater. Since the concert was free, security at the gate was non-existent, but the flow of people was fairly orderly. Alex escorted me to the far side of the lawn section.

"Is this where you want to be or would you rather go down front toward the stage?" I asked.

"I love the lawn. I haven't been here in a few years but I like being up here where I've got room to dance," she said as she held my hand above her head and twirled herself around. She wore a short but flowing black skirt that rose teasingly as she spun. A tight, white tank top accentuated her voluptuous breasts. A tasteful silver cross hung against her dark skin, just above her cleavage. With black sandals on her feet, her style seemed simple yet sexy. You needed a certain kind of body to really pull that off and she had it. I couldn't help but smile and stare.

I didn't know the name of the band on stage as the crowd started to fill in. They sounded a bit like Cake, but I knew it wasn't or they would have been headlining. Some people on the lawn sat on blankets and shared picnics or drinks. Others were on their feet and moving with the music. Alex took off her shoulder bag and took out two small travel size wine bottles before putting the bag on the ground.

"Sorry but I didn't feel like carrying two wine glasses and a corkscrew around all night," she apologized.

"Are you kidding? This is right up my alley," I said as I reached for a bottle and quickly unscrewed the cap. I took a quick swig of the ultra sweet-tasting white wine.

"I'm not any less of a man for drinking this, right?" I asked.

"You're a good sport," she said. "And you are all man to me." She let out a low growl while running her right hand down my chest over my abs.

"Then give me some more," I replied taking another drink. She had another sip of hers too, looking me dead in the eye the whole time. She knew exactly how to use her sex appeal.

"I have to confess that I may have had one of these before I left tonight."

"Just one?"

"OK, two. But I just needed to snap out of studying mode and into fun mode. Is that so wrong?"

"Not at all," I confirmed.

She smiled back at me, took my right hand in hers, and turned to face the stage while wrapping my hand and arm around the front of her. She kept dancing with her body directly in front of mine, pressing back against me. The sway of her hips against my upper thighs and midsection elicited a strong physical reaction from me. If I had any doubt whether I would be attracted to her, it was removed by this simple touch. She was nearly a foot shorter than me so the top of her head nestled nicely below my chin and against my chest. Her hair was as wild as when I first saw it, yet it smelled clean and fresh.

We moved to the music and drank from our mini bottles for the remainder of the opening band. The crowd cheered as the band exited the stage, but Alex turned to face me, her body still attached to mine. She reached up to put her arms around my neck and gently pulled my head toward her lips.

"Thank you for taking me out, Drew," she said as she gently slipped my lower lip between her full sensuous lips. Her tongue slightly brushed the length of my lip. I gripped her by the waist and slowly moved my right hand further down her hip and then slightly onto her left cheek and pulled her even closer to me so she could feel what she was doing to me. I could hear her groan ever so slightly.

"Let's have another one," she said as she sprung away from me and reached into her bag for two more drinks. "This is going to have to do, it's all I brought."

"I think that will be plenty, thank you," I said, with the intensity of that kiss still hanging in the air. "What did you put in these bottles?"

The night continued with more of the same. Good music, undeniable sexual attraction and very little substantive conversation. She said that was exactly what she needed and I was certainly having a good time as well.

She asked me to walk her home just after midnight when the show was over. She held my hand playfully for the entire 10 block walk to her brownstone apartment. There was no awkward moment on her front steps because she never let go of my hand. Instead she pulled me inside after she unlocked and opened the front door. We walked up one flight of stairs to the entrance of her place. Within a minute of walking in the door, she had slid out of her black sandals, grabbed two more bottles of wine and led me into the bedroom.

I didn't make it a habit of sleeping over at women's houses, but when Alex finally fell asleep at 3:00 am, I was exhausted. The thought of going for another workout at that moment was less than appealing. Plus, I had to admit that lying in a bed felt pretty good. I didn't feel one with nature, but it was nice to feel comfort for a change. I just laid back and closed my eyes.

The next time I opened my eyes it was 5:30. I looked over at Alex who was sleeping soundly, her naked body wrapped in a white sheet and still looking beautiful. Part of me wanted to roll over on her and wake her up with everything I had left in me. Another part of me didn't want the trouble that would come along with it. I rolled out of bed on my side and quickly put on my clothes. I walked around the bed to her side and leaned down to give her a kiss. She awoke as my lips neared hers. She kissed me back with a smile.

"I'll see you later?" I asked.

"See you," she replied and nestled down further into her bed.

We both knew that without making specific plans to see each other, there was a chance that we would not connect again. I'm not sure what she was thinking, but it seemed like we both had such a fun, carefree time the night before that we didn't want to ruin it with a conversation about a next time. I appreciated that and took full advantage of leaving it open-ended.

There was a chance that she was just too groggy to comprehend the significance of me walking out the door, but I was OK with that. Perhaps she figured that at least I knew where she lived and if I really wanted to see her again, I knew where to find her. As far as she was concerned, why wouldn't I want to see her again? It was a spectacular night.

Even so, as I walked to the gym for my morning run, I couldn't help but think that was the last I'd see of Alex. Whatever we did next couldn't top what we did on that date. Why ruin a great thing?

CHAPTER 9

"Drew," Tony said as he motioned with his head for me to walk with him to the baseline.

The other guys were already heading into the locker room. Tony eased his way to the ground like every inch of his body was in pain, which may not have been far from the truth. Not many of us took the time to stretch after playing even though our bodies definitely could have used it. Most of the guys had to hustle to get started with the rest of their day. Tony must not have been in a rush today, though, as he was painfully trying to reach for his toes from a sitting position.

"Dude, it's not my fault you lost the coin toss," I said.

"Sit down," he demanded. "I'm not worried about getting my ass kicked for the last two hours. I want to hear the juice from last night."

"Ah, I see." I said as I lay down on the ground next to him. I thought he was bitter because he didn't get the first pick and we ended up on opposite teams. My team won all four games. I was exhausted, even though I got more sleep than usual, with a few hours in an actual bed.

"You look wiped out. Long night?"

"They're all long nights, Tony," I said knowing that he doesn't have a clue about my typical nights.

"She didn't affect your shot though. I don't think you missed all morning. Now let's hear it. Don't make me beg for details."

"What can I say, it was pretty fun," I started.

I generally felt bad for Tony. He openly admitted that he had to live vicariously through me because his life sucked. He loved his wife down deep but they did not have much fun on a daily basis. She annoyed him more than anything else. I hadn't talked to her about it, but I'd bet she'd say the same thing about him. They were so focused on surviving parenthood that they had little time or energy to devote to each other. That took a toll on their relationship after a while.

"Yeah, how fun?" he said, smiling through the pain as he grabbed his left ankle with his left hand and pulled it behind him into the hurdler stretch.

"Tony, this girl was on fire. She was exactly my type: short, dark, full curves. Beautiful. Best of all, she may have been the most forward hot girl I've ever been with. Most girls that aggressive aren't that attractive. And most girls that attractive are a little harder to get. This one was on me from the second we met at the concert."

"Good show?"

"What show? I was so engrossed in her dancing all over me that I couldn't concentrate on the music."

"What?" Tony's mouth dropped.

"It was like she hadn't been out in a while," I continued. "Like a caged animal."

"Caged animal. I'd like to put my wife in a cage for a while and see if she wants to molest me when she gets out."

"Tony, you can't compare. It's not fair. No one is like that in a real relationship."

"Please tell me that you're going to see this girl again?"

"I don't know, probably not. How can I compete with last night?"

"What happened after the concert?"

"We walked straight to her place, straight to her bedroom

and I left there to come straight here. She was incredible."

"How are you still standing? You must not have gotten much sleep in bed with the tiger."

"Very little, but I'm fine." There was a brief pause before Tony started again.

"Drew, you cannot refuse to pursue anyone because the next date won't be as good as the last."

"Why not?"

"You're ridiculous. Why wouldn't you want to do that again?"

"Seriously, what is the point of getting into a long-term relationship if it will just devolve into misery. I'll spend more time plotting my exit strategy than I will enjoying my life. How is that fun? Plus, people get more seriously hurt when they invest that kind of time."

"You *are* serious," he said dejectedly while shaking his head.

"Whenever you're in a relationship, you'll encounter dozens of other women that you'd rather be seeing than your girlfriend. But it's not a relationship with those people that you desire. You don't want to be in the same level of deep unhappiness with them that you're currently in, you just want to flirt and hook up with them guilt free. That's why I keep my dating to a one or two date minimum."

"Commitment-phobe!" Tony accused.

"Unhappiness-phobe is more accurate."

"Semantics."

"Think of your first few hookups with Nikki," I suggested. "Was it fun and exciting? Now picture doing that over and over again, with different hot women. OK, not always hot. But different, which is sometimes more important than hot. You know we're not wired to do this the old-fashioned way."

"Look, don't get me wrong. I think you're onto something. I'm not being at all critical. You're far and away that happiest, most carefree person I know. And I certainly don't want to talk you out of that."

Tony paused, as if deciding whether to continue his thought. He rarely had deep conversations with me and it seemed like he wasn't sure if he was being intrusive.

"Let's hear it," I urged. "I can take it, I promise."

"I guess I just don't want to see you miss out on the sweetest parts of life, which include a bit of misery. On the scale of emotions, you're only scratching the surface. I'll give you that you're tapping into all the positive emotions at a much higher rate than the rest of us, but if you don't get below the surface, you'll never experience the fullness of those emotions."

I was taken aback, not because Tony offended me in any way, but because he showed a vulnerable side that I wasn't sure existed. Before I could respond, he continued.

"A good time with someone new is exciting and fun, no doubt. But a good time with someone you have committed to be with for life is fun and deeply fulfilling in a way that you can't have with a stranger. I'll kill you if you ever utter a word of this to anyone else, but I think what I'm talking about is love. You need it to make the human heart legitimately happy and at peace. Without it, you'll always be searching for a way to fill that deeper void."

"I hear you," I said, fighting the urge to call him Dr. Love. I didn't want to make him regret opening up to me. I appreciated his perspective and actually felt like our own relationship had taken some strides with this breakthrough.

"I know you think it is crap but there's something more to it than just having a good time," he continued. "I can't believe I'm actually saying this," he said, almost to himself. "You're still young but I don't want you to give up on the whole idea. I know I complain about Nikki from time to time, but she is a wonderful woman and a great mother to my kids."

"The thing I'm afraid of," I shared, matching his candidness, "is not having kids of my own. I think I would love being a dad. I know it's incredibly hard, but I can imagine how rewarding that must be. That's the one casualty of my approach that I'm afraid I'll regret."

"Truer than you know."

"I also feel bad that I'm being rude by not pursuing the women I date. I'm not dishonest or misleading in any way, but some of them are great and really deserve to be wanted. Every girl deserves to be wanted. I just feel bad for any sting they feel when I don't choose to see them again."

"I'm sure they're all devastated," Tony joked.

"I don't mean to sound like an ass, but you know what I mean."

"Yeah, you have no intention of having a relationship and the girls you're seeing probably do. And you're not misleading them at all when you seem totally into them one day and you're gone the next."

"Ouch. When you put it like that . . ."

"Not so nice?"

"I like to think I live in the moment. The problem is that not everyone else does."

"Fair enough."

Tony stood up and you could hear his bones crack. He reached his arms up above and over his head and leaned back as far back as he could go. I got to my feet too and suddenly realized how many different muscles were sore and tired. I reached down for my feet once more before letting out an exhausted groan.

"Thanks for sharing, buddy," I said half-jokingly. He

responded by punching my upper arm as punishment for the wisecrack. For the first time, I wished I had shared more about my life with Tony than I had before. We knew each other's personalities very well having played together for so long, but he didn't know much about my life at all. I knew his wife. I knew his kids. I'd been to his house, to birthday parties, to holiday parties. To him and his wife, I was the quirky single friend who always had fun tales to tell. But I never shared with them who I really was. I kept secrets from them and I don't know why.

"That's what friends are for, Drew. To give it to you straight."

I couldn't help but feel like a jerk.

CHAPTER 10

My stomach was gurgling audibly as I approached the buffet. An apple on the walk only served to wake my empty stomach. It was begging to be fed by the time I walked by the sign on the second floor of the Westin that read, "Energy Convention Breakfast."

In some twisted way, I liked feeling hunger pains. I felt like it made me appreciate food a little more than I otherwise would. It also made me feel like I could relate in some small way to those who were chronically hungry. But I knew that was a different animal altogether. Hunger with a capital H didn't stop at a gnawing in the belly. It infested the mind and core of the being as well. I didn't know this from personal experience, just from talking to some people who did.

I overheard a few guys in suits talking about the previous night's activities. I was sure that big oil executives spared no expense when it came to their conventions, and they were known to have some wild times. I didn't pick this spot for breakfast because I thought I'd relate to anyone else there. This decision was based purely on the type of spread these big spenders usually put on. I wasn't disappointed. It was the premium package and I was ready to take full advantage. With plate in hand, I reached for the serving spoon for the eggs but instead gracelessly grabbed a hand that was reaching for the same spoon.

"I'm so sorry," I blurted out, startled to have touched anything other than a spoon.

"No, by all means, if you're that hungry, please go for it," a woman replied with a straight face, but in a tone that was in no way serious.

"Of course not. It doesn't matter that I was here first, and you had to sneak up on me to beat me to the spoon. It's all yours."

"I'm not even supposed to be here," she said looking over her shoulder. "My bush league little breakfast is over there somewhere. Please, you go."

"I'm not supposed to be here either," I said, eager to one up her. "And I don't have a breakfast waiting for me anywhere in the place."

She burst out laughing. I laughed too, surprised at the rare moment of honesty. I reached again for the spoon, scooped up a pile of eggs and plopped it on her plate. "Here you go. You can't get in trouble if someone else gave it to you, right?"

"I guess, but I'm not really that afraid of getting caught, are you?" she asked as she reached for the serving spoon next to the potatoes.

"Obviously not," I replied as I started piling on the ham and bacon.

"I always have the same dilemma when I come to these things," she said. "I always want to try a little of everything because where else can you get this much variety in one sitting. But there's only one or two things I'm really in the mood for, so shouldn't I just load up on those?"

"You happen to be asking the expert. Personally, I think you have to go with what you're in the mood for, but you also need to consider what is good at these buffets and what's not. It also pays to take an inventory of all the options before making your selections. There's nothing worse than filling your plate only to find the thing you wanted most a second too late."

"OK, so how do you know what is good? Just by looks?"

"Looks and experience. I have never been impressed with a pancake I have had at a buffet. Local diner? Delicious. Hotel buffet? Not so much."

"So I should stay away from the pancakes?"

"I'm not saying that. Actually, this place is as good as it gets. But their French toast is legit. If you're up for something sweet, I'd go French toast."

"Now we're talking," she said as she piled two slices of French toast on her already full plate. She poured a disgusting amount of syrup on top, seemingly not concerned that it was seeping into everything else on her plate.

"How can you do that?" I asked.

"What, should I have asked you about the syrup too?" she replied sharply, but still friendly.

"No. It doesn't bother you to have syrup on your eggs and potatoes and meat and everything else?"

"Oh, not at all. I love syrup and it all goes down the same chute, right?"

"I guess. I love my syrup too, but I usually put that on plate number two. And, for the record, you don't have to listen to my advice, you know. I don't know what I'm talking about."

"You can't say you're the expert one minute and a novice the next. A girl isn't going to know what to think," she chided.

"Well, *I* think I'm an expert but that's purely subjective and the only person I consulted about it is me. Just wanted to be completely transparent about that."

"Duly noted, and appreciated. Now I'd appreciate your thoughts on these muffins. They look ridiculously good and unhealthy. How am I supposed to fit these into this mess?"

she asked as she gestured to the heaping pile of food on her oversized plate.

"You take those for later. They aren't hot and they're easy to package so they are prime targets for transporting."

"Brilliant," she said for the first time acknowledging that my insights had real merit.

"They are good and if you were limited to just one item, they'd be up for consideration. But I never eat them here, only to go. Just grab them on your way out."

"Very impressive, I have to admit."

As we reached the end of the buffet table and were no longer distracted by the shoveling of inordinate amounts of food onto our plates, we looked up at each other for the first time. I had been sneaking glances at her throughout our conversation, but I never made eye contact with her. That was one of the beauties of the buffet line. The activity of gathering food was a built-in excuse to not have a formal introduction or any kind of meaningful interaction. Most people wouldn't look you in the eye if they didn't have to. They fear it would invite a more than casual conversation, and no one wants that.

"Where is your name tag, ma'am?" I asked her, instead of asking for her name directly.

"Natalie," I heard a man say as the woman jerked her head in the direction of the voice. "You're in the wrong line. Our food is down there."

"You're kidding?" she laughed, looking back at me. "How embarrassing!"

"Natalie, how could you?" I said, scolding this woman I hadn't yet officially met.

"Don't worry about it," the man wearing a full suit continued, dismissing my comment. "Just follow me, I'll show you where we are."

"I didn't catch *your* name?" Natalie said to me.

"Drew. It was a pleasure meeting you."

"Take it easy on those eggs next time, OK?" she said as she turned to walk away with what looked to be her colleague.

I just smiled after her. It was the first time I could remember that I didn't want a conversation to end with little chance of continuing it ever again. It was also the first time I got a full shot of her. She was beautiful. She was about 5'5", athletically built, and very well dressed in a navy blue business skirt. Her hair was brown, straight and shoulder length. Her skin was tan and I even saw a few adorable freckles scattered across her face—in that brief moment I had to take her in. But those eyes—those eyes were extraordinary. They were blue, yes. And they pretty in shape and color. But that wasn't it. She exuded some rare form of positive energy, and it seemed somehow to flow from her eyes. It was powerful, it was unique, and it was contagious.

As she turned the corner and walked out of sight, I realized that I had been blatantly staring after her with mouth agape. I shook my head to help snap out of it and quickly found a bench along the wide corridor to sit and eat my feast without drawing any more attention to myself.

Jeez, I thought. *How pathetic did I look standing there like an idiot with drool practically pouring out of my mouth?*

I ate much quicker than usual and ended up packing most of it in my bag to eat later. It wasn't that I lost my appetite. I was confused about what just happened and needed to get away from the scene of the crime to gain perspective. With muffins, bagels, assorted pastries and breakfast bars in tow, I left the hotel and headed straight for the park. It was unusually warm for this time of the morning, so I knew I'd be comfortable in the park. My head was spinning too much from the events of the last 12 hours to do anything productive at one of the libraries. I just wanted to lie down and sort out what had transpired.

I went to my favorite spot and set up camp, which merely involved taking out my book, notebook and food so I could rest my head on my backpack containing only soft clothes. I looked up at the underside of the leaves of my trusted Oak tree but didn't feel the immediate peace that I was accustomed to finding. Instead, I could not help dwelling on what in the world possessed me to be so completely honest with a woman I had never met before. I felt like I was having an out-of-body experience from the moment we reached for that spoon. Why in the world was I so strangely consumed by that brief encounter, instead of my spectacular date from the night before with one of the sexiest girls I had ever seen?

I must not be feeling well, I thought. What else could explain it? It was not the first time I had been honest with a woman, after all, and it wasn't like I revealed every strange secret about me. It was just the part about me illegally stealing food from hotel conferences. I didn't feel bad about the food, nor did I fear that she was going to turn me in. It was a fairly safe secret to reveal. Maybe that's why it came out so abruptly. Or was it her candidness that prompted mine? Whatever the reason, it was certainly out of character for me.

I thought back to the women I have dated over the last few years. I didn't always have a maximum number of times I'd go out with someone. That rule was developed over time, for the betterment of all parties.

The first girl I really liked during this phase of my life was Sara. She had all the right qualities: cute, fun, smart and we had pretty good chemistry. We had been seeing each other for nearly a month when I decided it was only fair that I tell her about my lifestyle. She did not take it well. Although I never lied to her, she felt deceived and she was pissed. She assumed

I lived downtown and assumed that I had some type of job that paid the bills. She knew I had been a lawyer but we never really discussed the specifics of my current situation. We had spent most evenings with her cooking at her place so there was no reason for her to question where I lived or whether I had any money.

She did not even ask for any details the night I told her the truth. She ended it right then and there, which actually made me feel better. She was clearly more upset that I had no job and no house than she was interested in learning why. If no explanation would have satisfied her, then the job and house were critical to her. If they were critical to her, then she wasn't right for me. I know it was twisted logic but that was how I rationalized it. Was I wrong for wanting to be liked for who I was and not what I did or what I had?

Then there was Nicole. She was a blonde bombshell with a personality. We connected right from the start and I decided to learn from my mistakes with Sara. Nicole seemed genuine in her feelings for me, so after seeing her for a few weeks I optimistically jumped at the first opportunity to reveal my situation. My instincts were right on. She listened patiently and said all the right things in response.

"Drew," she told me in a calm voice, looking me dead in the eye. "I don't care about material things. I like you and I want to spend time with you. It doesn't matter whether you're the richest man in the world or the poorest."

I think she actually meant it when she said it. She didn't let it bother her for a few weeks afterward either. We continued to enjoy each other's company and spend most of the time at her place for obvious reasons. In time, though, she started making small comments about the future and us. Although she was crafty enough not to come out and say it, the comments implied that my situation was temporary and that I would come around to a more conventional lifestyle eventually. I let her off the hook after a few weeks of passive aggressive pressure and simply put the subject squarely on the table.

"You know, Nicole," I said. "This is a way of life for me, not a passing fad that I'm going to grow out of."

"But Drew, you know you can't go on like this forever. You're going to be sneaking around for food when you're 90?"

I knew I wasn't supposed to laugh but I couldn't help it. The image was too funny and I actually hadn't thought about it before. I was always surprised to be still alive so I never spent much time imagining life as an old man. Nicole did not think it was that funny.

"You're not taking this seriously, Drew. I have been beyond patient with this but it's got to end sometime or I'm not going to stick around for you to figure it out."

"Well, I'm sorry but there's nothing to figure out for me. This is who I am and I had hoped you were OK with that."

"Don't say that like I'm so shallow for expecting you to grow up and get a job sometime."

"I didn't mean that. I'm sorry I'm not going to turn into the person you need me to be. I only know how to be the person I need to be."

"Well then I guess we're both selfish aren't we? I can't spend another minute waiting and hoping for you to come around. I can't do this."

We parted ways amicably, considering the breakup. She really was a special person and I couldn't blame her for wanting more from me. I sure wouldn't date me if I were a woman. I was crazy to think any woman worth her salt would sign up to spend her time indefinitely in my company. For what? The outcome was inevitable.

After Nicole, I scaled back on dating, and I vowed never again to tell a woman about my living habits. I wasn't ashamed of the truth, it was just better to hide it. At first, I didn't date at all and when I did date again, I started ending things before they even started. I knew it still pissed off some women, but it's always easier to deal with the emotional responses after just a date or two. It just made good sense overall to keep a limit on the number of dates I had with a woman. That's when I began to realize that the first few dates were really the best ones anyways. The previous night with Alex was a perfect example.

It took me much longer than usual to fall asleep that morning. I kept fidgeting around on the ground trying to get comfortable and my mind kept replaying the events of the last day over and over in my head. Despite my best attempts at deep breathing meditation and the fact that I was physically exhausted, my mind couldn't shut off its mission to figure out why I needlessly opened up to a complete stranger, and more importantly, why I felt simultaneously unsettled, yet invigorated by my sudden streak of honesty. Was there something special about this woman—Natalie—or was there something refreshing about the truth?

CHAPTER II

"Great work, fellas. Very nice. Now get a drink and listen to me while you catch your breath."

Hakim and KJ jogged over to the sideline and grabbed their water bottles. They had been going hard for about 20 minutes and were sweating profusely. Besides the 100-plus stationary shots they put up during the form shooting warm up, they shot another 200 apiece over 10 different fast-paced drills. Shooting when you're tired takes a high degree of concentration on form so I made sure every workout got their heart rates up.

"OK, listen guys. You can shoot now. It's official. I'm not trying to make your head big. If anything, you know how I feel about the importance of being humble. That's what makes what I'm about to say so tricky, *and* important."

The boys just stared, still too tired to respond.

"When you put the effort into perfecting your shooting form and you put the time into making that motion second nature, then shooting becomes automatic. Getting in the zone happens on a regular basis. When you get in the game and in the flow of the action, you don't have to think through every step of your shot. You let practice take over and just let your body do what now comes naturally."

They nodded, although I could see that they didn't know where I was heading with this.

"The only thing you need in games is the confidence to shoot it. There's no reason to be nervous when you're this good."

The boys finally started to brighten up. "Yeah coach," acknowledged Hakim.

"I'm not just saying that. You guys should think that every shot you take is going in. But here's where it gets tricky, fellas. They don't all go in. KJ, what did LeBron shoot from the field last year?"

"A little over 50%."

"He missed almost every other shot, and guess what, he was in the top 10 in the league in shooting percentage. You know what that means? That means he must have kept shooting even when he missed his last shot. I know it seems simple, but not everybody has the guts, the confidence, to do that. You guys need to. It's what will separate you from all the other little superstars out there."

"I feel you, coach," replied Hakim.

"You need to shoot every shot like the last one just went in, whether it did or not. You're going to miss shots and that's OK, if they are good shots, of course. We're talking about a shooter's mentality here. That does not mean you should jack up any shot you feel like at any time and not care whether it falls or not. That's bad basketball. I'm talking about taking your shots, at the right time of the game, and having supreme confidence in your stroke that it's going to go in. That's what the great ones have: the ability to take the game-winner because they believe it will go in and because they're not afraid of failure."

"We're not afraid, Coach," yelled KJ as he snatched the ball out of my hands and turned and shot a three pointer while Hakim counted down, " . . . 3 . . . 2 . . . 1 . . ."

Swish! The boys went crazy, yelling and running around

the court. As I tilted my head back in laughter, I noticed her, standing at the balcony over the court watching the scene below with a confused smile on her face. Natalie. What was she *doing* here? How long had she been watching? How much of an idiot must I have sounded like to her? I tried to quickly regain my composure, pretending not to have seen her. I did my best to not appear as thrown off by seeing her as I actually was.

"Thanks for the confidence speech," said Hakim, "but we don't lack for belief in ourselves."

"We believe!" yelled KJ.

"Boys!" scolded Keisha from across the gym.

"It's OK, Keisha. This time, it's my fault. I just gave them a talk about shooting with confidence and they certainly have that special quality they are going to need to be great shooters."

I took a quick glance back upstairs to see if Natalie was still there or if it was just an illusion. She was gone. *Great, now I'm seeing things*, I thought. I told the guys to finish up with foul shots and I chatted with Keisha for a few minutes about the workout and how attentive the boys had been.

As the boys finished their final shots and gathered their bags, I saw Natalie walking down the sideline toward a ball lying on the ground. It was all I could do to focus as I said goodbye to the boys and Keisha. As they walked off the court, I grabbed a towel and wiped the sweat off my face and head before turning toward Natalie.

"Show me what you got, coach," she chided, whipping a hard pass at my chest. I had hardly comprehended what she did before I instinctively snatched the ball at the last second before it hit me.

"Easy there, all-star," I replied, walking over to her and handing the ball back to her gently.

"I see that you're expertise goes beyond the buffet line," she said motioning with her eyes back toward the hoop. "Pretty impressive."

"Yes, multi-talented. Did you sneak in here? Was *your* gym not good enough today?"

"No, no, I'm here on legitimate business. No need to call security."

"I won't give you up if you won't give me up."

"Of course."

We started walking slowly down the sideline before veering off into the carpeted hallway that ran parallel with the court.

"Hey Drew, good to see you," said an older man as he passed by us.

"Hi Gus, you too," I replied before turning my attention back to Natalie.

"So, I don't remember seeing you around the Sports Club before," I stated, seeking an explanation for her sudden appearance.

"First time," she said without exactly answering my implied question.

"Drew!" yelled one of the two guys on their way into the court area. "You ballin' with us tonight."

"Love to fellas, but I don't think I could hang with you guys right now," I yelled back, jokingly.

"Yeah, right," the man said as he waived his arm at me dismissively. "Don't want to hurt our feelings, huh?"

"Do you work here?" asked Natalie, still avoiding the explanation I requested.

"It feels like it sometimes, but no. Are you going to tell me why you're here?"

"Do I look out of place or is it that inconceivable that I would be working out?" she asked, trying to look offended.

"No and no. I just mean why here?"

"The Westin's gym is being renovated so they gave us passes to come here."

"And you're staying at the Westin for the conference."

"Correct."

"I got it."

"I'm so glad. Am I allowed to stay?" she asked sarcastically.

"I think so. Can I see some identification?"

"Sorry, I almost never bring my wallet to yoga class," she said, turning toward the yoga room across the corridor from the courts. "Doesn't really fit in my pocket."

At that moment, a woman opened the door to the room and looked at us with a wide smile.

"Hi Drew, are you thinking about coming in? I think you would have a lot of fun," she said in a flirty tone. I just shook my head and blushed slightly. She was a little older than me but very attractive. I wanted to crawl into a hole.

"You could be mayor of this place. Are you sure you don't work here?" pressed Natalie.

"You're joining that class?" I asked, ignoring her comment while looking in the window at the rows of people, mostly women, setting up their mats. For the first time, I realized that she was dressed for yoga, wearing black yoga pants and a yellow light-weight tank top. She wore white Nike running shoes with a yellow swoosh that matched her shirt. She looked so sophisticated in her suit this morning and so sporty in her gym clothes tonight. It was hard to believe it was the same woman, except she had those same penetrating, inspiring eyes that knocked me over once already.

"I am, but I have to show you something first," she said as she walked back onto the court still carrying the basketball. I followed behind her, head spinning from this second surreal encounter with her. She took a few dribbles as she walked from the sideline onto the court and up to the three point line. "How long have you been working with those kids?" she asked.

"Over a year now," I said hesitantly, not knowing where she was going with this. I wondered how long she had been watching the session from the balcony. "They are great kids."

"And they adore you, that's for sure," she said with a smile. I waited for the punch line, but it appeared that she was serious about that.

"Well, I don't know about that," I stammered, "I just teach a little shooting."

"So, all I have to do is believe it will go in, right coach?" she asked, glancing quickly at me before returning her gaze to the hoop.

"Well, it takes more than blind faith . . ."

I no sooner got the words out when she took one final dribble, stepped to the three-point line, and launched the most beautiful shot I had ever seen out of a woman's hands, maybe anyone's hands. Knees bent, elbow under the ball, extension up, follow through perfect. With ideal backspin rotation, the ball floated through the air effortlessly until nestling at home in the bottom of the net. Swish. My jaw dropped and I stared after the ball for a few moments, speechless and motionless.

"Nice running into you again, Drew," she said, walking toward her yoga class, smiling from ear to ear.

"You too, Natalie," my voice trailed as she walked off the court, through the hallway and into the yoga class.

For the second time that day, I found myself watching her walk away from me wondering what just happened. Was it possible that the woman that I already lost sleep over has a better jump shot than I do? Did I just imagine this whole thing? What were the chances that she would end up at the Sports Club at that point in time and happen to look down on the court during one of my shooting sessions? Did I really just let her walk away from me again without making some plan to try to see her again?

If I really wanted to, I could wait an hour until after her class and talk to her then. But that would be pathetic. Since the last thing I wanted to be to Natalie was pathetic, I went straight to the locker room, took a lightning quick shower, got dressed and got out of that gym as fast as I could. I'm not sure what I thought I was running from, but I had an overwhelming desire to get away from the scene—again for the second time today—so I could analyze it rationally from a distance. I could feel some type of mental, physical and emotional paralysis resulting from my interaction from Natalie, so my best bet was to get far away from her and hope the effects eventually would wear off. It was almost as if the gravitational pull toward her grew with time spent with her, so running away was the only way to not get completely sucked in.

CHAPTER 12

My mind was going a million miles an hour, so I don't exactly remember how I got to the library. More precisely, I don't remember actually walking there or even consciously deciding that's where I wanted to go next. Natalie seemed to have that affect on me—where I got so preoccupied with trying to comprehend what just happened that the rest of the world became blurry. Or maybe the world was still clear but I drifted through it as though a dense fog clung to my aura, making outward visibility limited.

I must have been on autopilot because I found myself in front a computer. I had made tentative plans to talk to my sister that night. We always penciled in Thursday nights as potential catch up time, but there were no hard feelings if we ended up having other plans and couldn't connect. It worked out that we IM every other week or so. I loved talking to my sister and I clearly needed to speak with her that night because that's exactly where I ended up in my post-Natalie stupor.

You there sis?? I typed.

Drewsy Poosy! Devin responded after a few minutes. That was the annoying yet affectionate name she called me since we were kids. She knew better than to utter those words in public, but I have to admit there was something sweet about it when it was just the two of us.

What's up with you?

Nothing too much.

How's Bradley? He went by Brad but I liked to call him by his full name, just to be a pain the butt. It must have been a little brother thing. I had no reason not to like him. Brad was her husband of three years and he and Devin were great together. He wasn't exactly my kind of guy, but he made my sister happy and that was more than enough for me.

BRAD is fine, thank you very much.

Are you guys watching the Bachelorette tonight?

It's on Mondays, stupid.

Idol?

Nice try. Actually we got hooked on the Wire recently. We're on Season 2 already. Awesome show!

I actually heard that was great. I hadn't watched much TV, other than sports, for a few years. I was clearly out of touch, but I at least paid attention to pop culture even if only from my strange vantage point.

It's a nice break from Glee, she wrote self-mockingly.

Please tell me Bradley doesn't watch Glee with you.

You'd be surprised how many Gleeks there are out there.

Oh my God. My sister and I had a rule when it came to instant messaging. We insisted on using full words and correct punctuation. The culture of abbreviations bothered us both. It wasn't like we had to use perfect English, we weren't grammar Nazis after all. We just committed to respecting the English language. Call us old school, or just plain old.

What's new in the big city?

Oh a little of this, a little of that.

Come on, give me something better than that. I got to have something to tell mom and dad when they ask about their baby.

Well in that case, let me tell you about some juicy sex I've been having.

95

Gross.

Not gross at all.

Change of topic, please.

Fine. Things are good. I'm not sure if I've ever been happier actually. I was telling the truth.

Really?

Is that so hard to believe?

No. That's awesome. Have you made progress on your book?

No. Not really. I'm just happy doing what I'm doing.

Playing a lot of basketball?

Yes.

Any romantic interests I should know about, minus the sex stories?

I've been dating but nothing serious.

Is that a permanent state?

I hope so. I think it's the key to my happiness!

Staying out of love is the key to happiness. Ugh. That is one depressing statement.

I didn't say that exactly, although I guess it's pretty close to accurate.

This was not a new topic for Devin and me. She has been concerned about my lack of love life for several years. She was so happy and secure in her relationship with Brad that the concept of not wanting that was completely foreign to her. They had dated for five years before getting married and the relationship never seemed to go through any major ups and downs.

So, are you back in the job market?

Is this one for mom and dad?

For me too.

No, I'm still focusing on other parts of my life right now.

Like your writing?

Like basketball.

Are you serious?

Of course. And my writing. And my reading. And my connection with the community. And my appreciation of life.

Oh, Lord. I don't know how you get by.

By the seat of my pants and an insane amount of luck.

I'm going to come see you.

Excuse me?

I miss you and I want to see for myself this happy existence that you've created for yourself.

It's always easier for me to come out to see you guys. I should be able to come out in the next few weeks.

Nope. It's my turn to come down there. I haven't seen you in the city for years. It's time.

It's really not that exciting.

Stop trying to discourage me. I'm coming. I'll come down for dinner and stay over at your place and then head back to dear old suburbia. I think it will be good for me.

I paused a long time before responding. I was not sure if there was any way to persuade her from coming, at least right now.

Is there any way I can talk you out of this?

Stop. Don't you miss me? Plus, I've got some stories for you.

Do tell!

They can wait until I see you. Now what's a good day? I guess we have to plan now since I'm assuming you still don't own a cell phone?

Next Sunday? I suggested, hoping that would be enough time for something to come up that would cause us to cancel. I wanted to see Devin but certainly not in the city and certainly not if she was expecting to stay at my place.

Perfect! What's your address?

Let's meet at Rittenhouse Square for dinner and then we can go from there. That will be easier.

OK. Whatever you say. I'm psyched!
No one has said psyched since you were in 8th grade.
Jerk.
That either.
OK, we're all set then? Sunday at 4:00 at Rittenhouse Square?
Yep. Bradley coming too?
Just me. See you then!
Love you sis.
Love you too.

CHAPTER 13

The only upside of my conversation with Devin is that it momentarily took my mind off of Natalie. I immediately started obsessing about Devin's upcoming visit and her intention to stay at what she referred to as "my place." How was I going to pull this off?

The reprieve only lasted a few minutes, however, because my mind started wander back toward the Natalie debacle at the gym. I acted like a child meeting a movie star. Why was it so hard to formulate sentences around her? Why did it seem like I always end up gawking at her while she walks off into the sunset? I was a mess around her.

For the next 12 hours, I wasn't sure which haunted me more: the fact that I let Natalie walk out of my life without making any impression whatsoever, or the fact that my sister was coming to visit me in a week and I would no longer have the luxury of distance to hide her from the truth. So I did what I do best, I started to rationalize the situations.

First, why did I care about meeting Natalie? I wouldn't want to go on more than a date or two anyway, so what was the point of being all sorts of disappointed? Was it the thrill of the challenge? Was I more attracted to her than others? Why would I have such a strong reaction to seeing her for the brief moments that I'd seen her? That's the part that got under my skin so much. Why was I experiencing such internal upheaval when, practically speaking, there was no reason to get excited at all?

Second, a visit from Devin wasn't the end of the world. There was a high percentage chance that she could bail before even coming. Or I could bail. That would be a temporary solution, but would be effective. Even if she came, we could always stay out talking all night and not even have to deal with my living arrangement. Or, I could just tell her. What's the big deal? She would have to swear to not tell mom and dad but we've kept secrets from them before. I would trust her. I think she could handle it, couldn't she?

Thank God it was Friday. After the events of the previous few days, I was beyond confused and restless and nothing centered me more than spending a few hours at St. Paul's soup kitchen. The place did more for me than I did for it—that was for certain.

"Good morning, Myron," I said, as I walked behind the serving counter.

"Right on time, Drew. Great to see you. Can you help me with some boxes in the back?"

"Of course! What's on the menu, today?"

"The same thing as every Friday, buddy. Turkey and assorted slop. Nothing ever changes around here."

"I would hardly call this food slop, Myron. I know the chef and he has too much pride to make slop."

"Pride can't overcome ingredients, man. There's only so much I can do."

"Hey, the soup is good and you make enough gravy to smother everything else so it tastes as good as the gravy, which is pretty darn delicious."

He grabbed a box of milk and motioned for me to grab another. We carried them out to the serving area and installed them into the milk dispensers, one for whole milk and one for skim. It was 11:00 am when I arrived and the kitchen opened its doors for lunch at 11:30. Myron typically started cooking at 10:00 with the goal of bringing the food out fresh at about 11:15.

We spent the next 15 minutes bringing out dish after dish to the cafeteria-style counter. Along with a massive amount of sliced turkey, we brought mashed potatoes, baked beans, string beans, broccoli, peas, chicken noodle soup and an assortment of cookies. One thing Myron believed in wholeheartedly was that a person should have food choices, no matter how bad his or her situation.

He prided himself in providing an array of foods for the guests at St. Paul's. He felt like it contributed to their self-respect to be able to choose what food they were in the mood for as opposed to being forced to eat anything put in front of them. *Just because you're hungry, doesn't mean you like peas*, he always said.

"Hi Regina," I said, as a woman came through the swinging doors from the back.

"What's up good lookin'?" she barked.

"You look younger every time I see you."

"Flattery will get you everywhere with me, sugar. You know my weakness, don't you?"

"Enough nonsense, you two," interrupted Myron. "We've got some work to do."

"Don't start with me Mr. Myron. You know I've been busting my big rump since early this morning."

Myron smiled at me and rolled his eyes in Regina's direction, clearly intended for her to see. We all cracked up laughing. Myron and Regina had been running St. Paul's for nearly 10 years and they were a great team. They brought energy and enthusiasm with them every day, no matter how discouraging the homeless and hunger problems in the city could be.

They had two strict rules that everyone knew and abided by: all patrons must be fully clothed and must be respectful of staff and other patrons. They provided shirts, pants and socks to those who truly didn't have any, and they promised there would be enough food to go around, so there was no reason whatsoever to fight during meals. Everyone was there for a shared purpose and any disputes could be resolved outside the doors of St. Paul's.

I admired these two, as well as the rest of the staff. The injection of spirit into the patrons was almost as critical as the food and drink provided. I was honored to be a part of this effort and was inspired by their energy from the moment I walk through the door.

"OK, we have a group of volunteers in the back ready to help us today, Drew," said Regina. "We won't run you ragged like we normally do."

"That's OK, I'm up for anything. Just plug me in where you need me."

"Well, I'm going back now to give them the pre-game speech, maybe you can help facilitate their participation today," Regina suggested. "I only saw them for a second, but they strike me as one of those corporate types eager to get their hands dirty for once in their lives."

"You got it." I came on Fridays specifically because that was a down day for outside volunteers. The kitchen did a great job with recruiting volunteer groups from companies, as well as schools and churches. Most companies and schools came from Monday through Thursday and most church groups came on the weekends. Friday was often the only day without a group volunteering.. I figured that I could contribute the most on Fridays when they needed it the most.

"All right Drew, I'll send them up in a few minutes and you can get them situated. There are about 10 of them so it might get a little crowded. Make sure they all feel like they participated."

Regina knew that the key to getting return visits was to provide a good experience for the group where they truly felt like they made a difference. If too many people are standing around with nothing to do, they would be less likely to come back and do that again, choosing instead another cause where they feel like they could contribute.

Myron and I finished bringing the other dishes out with a few minutes to spare. Once Regina provided an overview of St. Paul's and its mission, she sent the group up front to meet with Myron and me.

"Good morning, folks, come right in," he said as they started to file into the serving area from the swinging doors. "Slide down so everyone can come in and we'll get you situated before the doors open. We have less than five minutes so let's get ready to have some fun and feed some hungry people!"

Just as Myron was about to give his welcoming remarks, the final two volunteers walked through the doors together in mid-conversation, stopping abruptly when they realized we were about to start. I glanced once at the pair and then looked back at Myron. Then I quickly looked again because I was certain I saw something that couldn't be real. When I looked away the second time, my mind ran through quickly where I was, what I was doing there, why a group of volunteers were there at that time and whether I could possibly be dreaming. The human brain seems to run this automatic reality check in a fraction of a second when it experiences something that is completely out of place. My brain determined that I was indeed awake and, as serendipitous as it seemed, that it could possibly be her standing in the back. I completed my triple take by holding my gaze long enough to see Natalie mouth to herself, "Oh my God!"

If anyone happened to be watching me at that moment, they must have thought I had seen a ghost. Not that I looked scared, but I must have looked completely stunned. The only thing that kept me from flat out fainting was the fact that Natalie began to smile at me, a genuine happy-to-see-me smile that somehow put me at ease even though I felt like I was having an out-of-body experience. I hadn't been exactly listening to Myron for the previous 30 seconds or so when he typically outlined the flow of food and patron traffic. The first thing I remember hearing Myron say was, "and now I'll leave you in the capable hands of Drew who will coordinate your assignments and make sure this whole thing goes off without a hitch."

To snap out of my now familiar Natalie stupor, I shook my head rather violently like I was trying to get water out of my ears. "Ah, yes, thank you Myron, and ah, welcome folks," I managed to stammer.

"OK, Drew, where do you want us and what do we do?" said Natalie as she stepped forward, clapped her hands together and began rubbing them rapidly indicating that she and the group were ready to work.

"All right, now that is the spirit," I said smiling in return, regaining the full capacity of my senses. It didn't look like Natalie was the leader of this group, particularly because she was one of, if not the youngest in the crowd. But she certainly stepped up at that moment and, judging by the expressions on most of the other faces, it was because she was the only one comfortable handling what was about to happen—over a hundred hungry people filing through the door over the next few hours. Or maybe she spoke up because she could tell that I was virtually speechless and she knew it was her fault. Either way, it broke the ice nicely, so I was able to begin placing people at different stations.

We needed four servers for the eight menu items. We needed two people to help bus the tables and keep the eating area clean. The system required that patrons throw away their own trash and put the trays and silverware in the designated containers, but we always needed people to facilitate that process as it didn't always go smoothly. We needed two people to wash the dishes. We needed the final two people to greet folks at the door, guide them through the line, and let me, Myron or Regina know if anything went wrong.

Once I explained the options, Natalie spoke up first to claim her spot.

"I'll serve," she volunteered.

"Great, you get post position serving the turkey and stuffing. Best spot in the house."

"I'll serve too," said the woman who had been standing with Natalie.

"I'll bus the tables," said a middle-aged man toward the front of the line-up. "I can't screw that up for you."

"You got it," I said encouragingly. The rest of the group followed suit until all the positions were filled in a matter of seconds.

"Servers, grab your gloves from the table behind you," I said. "Cleaners, the brooms and mops are in the back just inside the door. You'll need them at some point. Your dishrags and soap are above the sink over on the right side of the room. Dishwashers, you can help serve until the first round of patrons are finished. Then you can team up to wash and dry in the back as our table cleaners bring you the dishes."

Everyone took their positions. The scared and intimidated looks that were on some of the faces seemed to have dissipated once their roles were established. It can be a little overwhelming at first, but I've never seen anyone not be able to handle it, and feel completely rewarded by the end of serving a meal.

"OK, I'm going to open the doors now," I continued. "Remember, we are not only serving these people today, but we are treating them with the respect and dignity that they may not get elsewhere in their lives. Let's do this with the passion it deserves!"

With that, I opened the doors to a long but remarkably organized line of people ready to enter St. Paul's. Myron and Regina had been doing this so long that nearly all of the patrons knew to line up before entering the doors. They knew that there would be enough food for everyone so there was no real rush to be first. That didn't mean some people didn't still clamor to be in the front or wait there for more than 30 minutes just to be one of the first inside. Many of these people were legitimately hungry and only ate the food provided by St. Paul's. Others were a little better off, but needed one good meal a day at St. Paul's for their families to get some semblance of nutritional balance. Still others had serious mental issues and were more difficult to manage. Most had been around long enough that they had become accustomed to the routine and assimilated very well considering their overall state.

"Good morning, folks," I greeted. "Come right in, we've got a great menu for you today."

"Thank you," said a familiar older man in a low voice as he walked past first.

"Hi Marvin, good to see you," I said to another man a few people back. I tried to learn as many names as I could, although not everyone was willing or able to talk. I had a good relationship with a few of the regulars but others were more distrusting. I didn't take it personally and it didn't stop me from trying to communicate from time to time. Typically, it wasn't just me who they didn't trust. They didn't trust anyone. It was just who they were. Others didn't talk to me but would light up around Myron or Regina. A few seemed to actually prefer me to them. I guess it was no different than any other area of life. Some people just clicked with some folks but not others.

I usually greeted the first patrons and ushered them toward the serving line for a few minutes to show the greeters generally what we needed from them. After the first 20 people or so had entered, I settled back into the serving area to field any questions that the servers might have. This group seemed to be doing fine and, of course, there was one standout.

"Thank you for coming in today, would you like some turkey?" Natalie said as the patrons approached the serving line.

Her smile elicited more smiles in the first 15 minutes than I received in a few years of working at the kitchen. She exhibited such genuine emotion and warmth that it was difficult not to respond to it with warmth of your own. Watching her interact with these people from a distance made me understand clearly why I had been so moved by my previous interactions with her. It wasn't just her instant rapport with the patrons, it was the natural charm that emanated from every pore of her being. I realized then that I was in big trouble.

"Drew, how do I know how much is the right amount?" a man asked as he scooped some mashed potatoes for the next guest.

"You're doing great. One good scoop is perfect. No need to ration it, but we limit it to just one scoop for the sake of being fair."

"Sounds good."

"OK, gang, just let me know when you start running low on anything. We have plenty more of everything waiting in the back."

Things ran rather smoothly and the volunteers seemed to open up as the lunch went on, which was not unusual. Once the first dozen or so people came through, even the quiet ones started to get friendlier and became more vocal.

There is usually an initial shock to see the condition of some of the patrons, whether it's their clothes or physical and mental health. Most volunteers respond well and overcome their fears enough to interact. But you can tell that there is some profound internal processing going on as they try to get their heads around the depressing facts that hunger and homelessness exist in the city where they work, play and live so comfortably.

It is a hard pill to swallow, especially when you see the families come in. The children are always the most difficult. They brighten your day and break your heart all at the same time. Under a certain age, you wouldn't be able to tell if they were at St. Paul's or a local restaurant. They seemed carefree and actually happy. Most of them know nothing different.

There was a steady flow of traffic in and out of the kitchen. I helped bring some of the dishes to the sink basin in the back and got the dish washers started. Then I jumped back to the serving area to make sure the others were OK without the other two volunteers. The servers were fine though since they had exactly enough people to cover it as long as everyone scooped two different foods. I had just replenished the mashed potatoes and the green beans when I heard a yell from the far end of the serving counter.

"Coach Drew, we're running a little low on the turkey . . . when you have a second."

"I'm on it, ma'am," I returned Natalie's smile.

I returned a few moments later with a hot tray of sliced turkey. I set it down partially on the counter next to the tray in front of Natalie. "OK, be careful. This is a little hot. Now can you grab the rest and put them on top of these," I said motioning from the few slices left on her tray to mine.

"You got it, coach," she said as she snatched the remaining slices in her tongs and laid them on top of the turkey in my tray.

"Nice. Now can you pull that tray out for me?"

"Of course."

I dropped the full tray into the slot using the oven mitts. Then I reached over Natalie to grab the handles on the other tray. It was the closest I had ever stood to her and it immediately made my heart race. She managed to smell like fresh flowers even though the room was filled with notorious odors such as cafeteria-style food and dozens of infrequently-bathed bodies. I was racking my brain for something witty to say when I was saved by the next person in line, a regular with whom I happen to have a good rapport.

"Drew, get out of this nice young lady's way, please," ordered Mrs. Curley. "Can't you see she's trying to give us some turkey?"

"My apologies, Mrs. Curley, but this nice young lady keeps turning up everywhere I go," I replied in jest.

"You should be so lucky, young man. She is clearly out of your league."

"Indeed she is," I replied quickly and honestly.

"Listen to her," snapped Natalie as she smacked me on the shoulder. "This is one sharp woman." Natalie turned with a wink toward Mrs. Curley. I felt like I was 12 years old. I could do nothing but giggle, blush and walk away.

I took advantage of having so much help and tried to mingle more with the diners than I usually do. I made a point to say hello and offer help to those who sat alone or appeared to be isolated from the others. I received mixed responses as usual. Some people appreciated the gesture, others resented it and sat apart for a reason. But as much as I tried to focus on engaging with the diners, I continually found myself glancing, sometimes even staring, in Natalie's direction. I was mesmerized by the ease with which she interacted with everyone around her. She met every person with a ready smile and sparkling eyes, which meant to me that she was absolutely fearless. Being thrust into such an environment almost always intimidated most people, men and women alike. But she did not blink.

It wasn't just the diners who felt her electricity. Her vibe spread to the others in her group, breeding an atmosphere of lighthearted fun which you could see visibly relax the group, in turn, allowing them to engage more comfortably with those being served. I caught her eye once from across the room, which elicited a non-cheesy wink and a smile from her. She was clearly not doing this for my benefit. This was no act to impress anyone. This was Natalie, and it was awesome.

One o'clock came along more quickly than I would have liked. After checking the street for any late-comers, the greeters and I closed the entrance door. Thanks to the dishwashers and the bus boys, there wasn't much to do once lunch finished. We packaged the remaining food in the refrigerator and lined up trays for a final wash. Myron had the place so well-organized that every piece of equipment belonged in a designated spot. Within 15 minutes, we completed the cleanup and the group was ready to go. Sometimes groups would stay and eat after lunch but this group intentionally ate before arriving so that they would not take away any food from St. Paul's. We had enough to go around, but understood their logic.

"On behalf of St. Paul's soup kitchen," Myron addressed the group, "we want to thank you so much for your help today. Without volunteers like yourselves, this kitchen would not serve the hundreds of hungry folks in this city that you saw today. You have no idea the impact you have on these people by providing something as simple as a hot meal and smile. Please keep us in mind in the future as we rely on your generosity to survive. Have a great rest of your conference and thank you again for choosing to work with St. Paul's."

We all began to exchange handshakes as Regina led them through the back where their mini-bus was parked. I moved toward Natalie as we all walked to the back together. A few conversations broke off so it wasn't noticeable to the rest of them when I pulled Natalie aside the second we walked outside.

"I don't know where to begin with you," I stammered, hoping to find some eloquence in the next half a second. "Three is my lucky number and I just can't take the chance that I'll magically run into you again a fourth time."

I paused, still looking her in the eyes. She stared back encouragingly.

"I would love to see you again," I continued. "Maybe have a chance to talk a bit longer than we have so far."

"I would like that too," she replied.

"Do you want to have dinner tomorrow night here in the city?"

"Sure."

"Have you ever been to Luigi's?"

"No, but I have heard of it."

"Do you like Italian?"

"Of course. Tell me what time and I'll meet you there."

"7:30?"

"OK, coach. I'll see you at 7:30."

With that, she started walking toward the bus, turning one last time to flash me her smile, as if it wasn't completely ingrained in my mind already. I simply smiled after her, feeling that all too familiar Natalie haze creeping over me. This time it was not so unsettling. This time the haze didn't bring confusion. It brought excitement. I was going to see her again.

CHAPTER 14

I walked slowly south down Walnut toward 15th street Saturday evening. The temperature was warm so the breeze was a godsend. I wasn't a heavy sweater and I had layered on the deodorant before leaving the gym, but I still feared I would start dripping profusely if I walked even at my normal pace. I was nervous. I had been on literally a hundred dates over the last few years and I did not have so much as one butterfly for any of them. I had been excited before. I had been unsure of what to expect before. But never had I been downright queasy and afraid I might pass out.

I was sure that Natalie would like Luigi's. It was a classic, small, hole-in-the-wall, authentic Italian restaurant where you are skeptical when you walk in and minutes later feel like you're a welcomed guest at someone's home. The setting was romantic but the atmosphere so lively and energized that the intimacy was not overbearing. The staff was extraordinarily friendly—following the lead of Big John I'm sure—but it was the quality of the food that made Luigi's stand out among the other restaurants in town.

"Big John, are you going to be at the restaurant tonight?" I asked him that morning after basketball.

"Of course!" Big John responded. "Please tell me you are going to come join me."

"I know it is Saturday night so if you guys are all booked I completely understand . . ."

"Stop!" Big John interrupted me. "Say no more. We always have room for you Drew. I will have a special table reserved for you and . . . will you be joined by anyone in particular?"

"Actually, yes. I'll be with a woman named Natalie." I had no idea why I started smiling and I hoped to God that I had not started blushing. I took a quick glance toward the other guys in the locker room to see if anyone noticed my bizarre behavior.

"Ah, Natalie," said Big John as if recording to his memory. "Natalie will have a wonderful time tonight, I guarantee it Drew."

"And John . . ."

"Don't even think about bringing your wallet tonight either," he preempted me. "I will be offended if you even mention it."

As much as that hurt my pride, I appreciated the opportunity to have a nice proper meal out without having to deplete my minimal cash supply.

As I turned onto 15th Street, I began to wonder if Natalie would be less impressed because I was not paying for our meal. Then I began to wonder if she would be impressed at all considering I had nothing impressive to offer on any level. We couldn't talk about my job. We couldn't talk about my home. We couldn't talk about the book that I was too scared or too stupid to start writing. As I saw it, the only thing we could talk about that wouldn't expose me as a loser was her.

That was it. I would simply dedicate the entire conversation to finding out all about her. I couldn't wait to learn more anyway so that was a completely natural approach to this date. *Who doesn't like to talk about themselves*, I thought.

I arrived at Luigi's about 15 minutes early. Not only did I want to be sure to be there before Natalie, but I thought it might give me a chance to cool off in case my efforts to prevent sweating were ineffective. There was a bench along the street just a few houses down from the restaurant so I took a seat and drew a deep cleansing breath. Just as I raised my left leg to cross it over my right knee, the wardrobe crisis I had been having all day struck again. I sat there looking at my khakis wondering whether Natalie will realize I'm wearing the exact same clothes as I was the first time she saw me. *Of course she will*, I thought. *This is what girls do innately. They recognize stuff like that.*

I had already rationalized that I could only be myself. The fact that I don't care what I'm wearing, or don't have many options of what to wear, is just a part of me. If Natalie or anyone else took issue with that, then it was their problem. I wouldn't want any part of them.

Even so, I was bothered by the possibility of being judged negatively by Natalie. I could not deny caring, even though on principle I should not have cared at all. I guess that was why I dreaded the date almost as much as I was excited for it. That probably explained the uninvited butterflies. Revealing myself in almost any way guaranteed rejection by a woman who thus far deservedly stood upon a pedestal in my mind.

Thank God Natalie arrived just a few minutes later, forcing me to get out of my own head and back into the reality that was walking toward me with a big goofy smile.

"What are you laughing at?" I asked.

"It is almost more surprising to see you when we have plans to meet," she replied. "I just got used to simply seeing you around."

"Do you want me to go hide and you can try to find me?"

"That actually sounds like fun, but I'm afraid if you're too good at that game we'll never eat."

"I take it you're hungry?"

"I didn't mean it like that, but yes, I'm pretty hungry."

"You look stunning, Natalie. Let's eat"

She smiled up at me and looped her arm in mine and we walked toward Luigi's. She wore a white sun dress with a red and purple floral pattern on the bottom half. It was a completely different look than the other three times I saw her. She was smart-sexy in her business suit. She was sporty-sexy in her yoga outfit. She somehow pulled off grungy-sexy in her jeans and T-shirt at the soup kitchen. But tonight, she was simply natural-sexy. Her nicely tanned skin looked silky smooth next to the cotton dress. A delicate necklace with a small cross hung from her neck.

"This place is packed," she said to me when she realized that the handful of people lingering on the sidewalk were actually waiting for a seat at Luigi's.

"Yes, and these guys actually have reservations. It's worth the wait though," I said as I passed by the crowd, stepped up the small flight of stairs and opened the door for Natalie.

"Thank you," she said as she let go of my arm to walk past me and into the restaurant.

I hadn't even set foot inside when I heard Big John call out from the back of the seating area, which wasn't more than 30 feet from the door.

"Drew, Natalie! Great to see you!"

I waved hello, but decided against yelling back at him since we were in a small restaurant. Natalie looked back at me wide-eyed as if asking me why this monster of a man was yelling her name across a crowded restaurant. Before I could address her, Big John was shaking her hand feverishly with both of his oversized paws.

"Ms. Natalie. It is truly a pleasure to meet you. What a beautiful woman you are. Any friend of Drew's is a friend to Big John. You are welcome here anytime. We are so happy that you could join us tonight."

He didn't even look at me. I couldn't blame him.

"What a lovely restaurant you have here," Natalie responded, matching Big John's charm. "Thank you so much for having me. Drew said it's the best in town."

"Oh, too kind, too kind, Drew. But I sure hope you enjoy it. Now let me take you to your table. Dominic!" he yelled in a friendly tone to a waiter carrying a pitcher. "Follow me with that water."

Big John seated us at a table for two along the window at the front of the restaurant—clearly the best spot in the place. Within 30 seconds, we had water in our glasses, hot bread in a basket on the table next to plate of freshly poured oil and ground pepper and menus in our laps.

"Wow, that was some entrance," she said, sounding both impressed and slightly embarrassed by the commotion we caused.

"There's no containing Big John as you may have noticed."

"He sure loves you."

"He loves everybody," as I motioned over to him at another table laughing with the guests. "That's what makes him so amazing."

Another waiter came over to tell us the specials and take our drink orders. Although it was a BYOB, he offered a number of house wines if we were interested. Natalie just ordered a soda and I followed suit. Each waiter's heavy Italian accent made us feel like we'd been transported overseas where the food is better and no one is in hurry to do anything but sit and enjoy.

"Gnocchi?" Natalie asked after we ordered.

"I love it," I explained. "No matter how good the other options sound, I just can't pass it up. The red sauce here is ridiculous."

"I like it too, but that sea bass sounded awesome."

"You'll have to try some of mine, just so you don't think I'm crazy."

There was a pause in the conversation. She was looking at me smiling but this time I couldn't interpret what the smile meant. I just smiled back hoping she would give me a clue about what she was thinking. The silence was strangely comfortable and I didn't mind letting it linger a bit.

"Thank you for taking me out tonight," she said finally.

"Can you believe this week?" I said leaning in toward her as if sharing a secret between us.

"Yeah, the weather was just beautiful."

I sat up straight, with mouth agape, wondering the best way to backtrack. Clearly she didn't see this whole ordeal as pure serendipity like I did.

"I'm kidding," she said mercifully. "This week was crazy! The gym? OK, I could see that. But the soup kitchen too? That put me over the top."

"You put me over the top at the buffet line, but I understand what you're saying."

"Funny. I half expected you to show up tonight in green tights and tell me you're actually Robin Hood."

"What!" I laughed out loud. "You don't want to see me in green tights."

"I don't know," she said unconvinced, pretending to look me up and down.

"Natalie, you were incredible at St. Paul's yesterday."

"That was a really powerful experience for us. We so appreciated the opportunity to help feed those people."

"Well you did more than just feed them. You lifted some spirits in there too."

"I don't know. I think they did more for me than I did for them. I was so scared walking in there because it's so new and different than what I see and live every day. But they are the brave ones to walk through that door and be served by a bunch of complete strangers who I'm sure they don't trust. Yet for the most part they were kind and gracious in ways I didn't expect. I can't imagine how hard that is to do."

"I totally agree. It's inspiring. And if you were scared, then it certainly didn't show."

"How often are you there?"

"I go every Friday."

"That is so great. I walked out of there kicking myself for not doing something like that more often. I have no excuse either. I just haven't made it a priority."

I was taken aback by her honest self-assessment, while at the same time felt significantly more at ease about the date than I did before it started. Why fear judgment by someone who would so willingly share her own faults, I thought. It was a refreshing surprise.

"Do you guys always do charity work during your annual meeting?"

"Yes, but that's what is so pathetic. The only reason I even did that yesterday is because the firm made it a priority."

"Well I think that is great that the firm builds that into your meetings."

"You're kind, but I'm not going to feel better about this. I'm sorry for dumping this on you before we even get our appetizers."

"Natalie, you're talking to someone who steals food from hotel conferences. I won't try to make you feel better if you promise not to try to make me feel better."

"Deal, but you're still my hero for the food stealing thing."

"Robin Hood took cooler things than blueberry muffins."

"I bet he took muffins too. He just didn't get the publicity for that. If you're going to take money, you're not going to have a problem taking some baked goods too."

"Just to be clear, it doesn't work in reverse. I don't take money, just food."

"Of course!"

"Just in time," I said as our calamari arrived. I made her take the first scoop and the first bite before I dug in.

"Do you want me to ask for more marinara sauce," she chided after I buried my first piece in so much sauce the calamari was unrecognizable.

"I told you I like the red sauce here."

"So, when you're not stealing from the rich, giving to the poor or coaching kids, where can I find you?"

"Truthfully, I love playing basketball. I like coaching, but I wasn't born to do it. Playing on the other hand . . ."

"So you were a gym rat growing up?" she guessed correctly.

"Still am," I admitted. "How's that for pathetic?"

"There's nothing wrong with that. I grew up playing ball myself. It was big with my dad so my brother and I spent more than enough time on the court."

Could she get any better? I gave myself a quick pinch to make sure I didn't just slip into a dream, even though my dreams usually exposed my worst fears instead of my ultimate wishes.

"Well, I could certainly tell, judging by your shooting stroke. Jeez."

"Lucky shot," she said referring to the three-pointer she drained right in front of me earlier in the week.

"Right. You looked like you really closed your eyes on that one."

"So is that your game? Outside shooter?"

"Pretty much."

"That's good because you're not the tallest basketball player I ever met."

"Thanks a lot."

"So, do you do a lot of coaching or just those boys?"

"Just the boys right now, actually. I've done some shooting with others but they are it for now."

"You like working with the boys, but if you had to choose you'd rather play, is that right?"

"You got it."

My plan of focusing the conversation on her was failing miserably. She was much quicker at firing the questions than I was. I actually didn't mind sharing with her because she was so easy to talk to, but I still tried to redirect the conversation the next chance I had.

"So who wins when you and your brother play one on one?"

She laughed out loud.

"We haven't exactly played one on one in a long time."

"Is he older or younger than you?"

"Younger. Is that step one of your attempt to figure out how old I am?"

"Not at all, but if you want to give me some hints I can start guessing if you'd like."

"That's quite all right. It's a lose-lose proposition for you."

"How so?"

"Because even if you guess it on the nose, you're in essence telling me that I look my age which no girl wants to hear. If you guess too young, then I'll just assume you'll be disappointed when you find out I'm actually older than that because who doesn't prefer a younger woman."

"Huh?"

"And if you guess older, forget about it! If I have to explain that one at all, you're in big trouble."

"You can't be serious."

"Not at all about the being in trouble part, but the rest of it? Consider that a free peek into a woman's psyche. And if you think that was ugly, you should know that most women are far crazier than me."

"So I won't be guessing your age."

"Ha. I'm 27. My brother is 25. We are pretty tight. My dad is 50 and my mom is 49."

"So young. I never would have guessed."

She reached across the table to smack me but I scolded her for her poor table manners.

"I'll tell Big John if you don't start to behave," I said to her.

We took a break from our conversation for a minute to enjoy the remainder of the calamari. It was the kind that I liked; very lightly breaded and no tentacles. I couldn't stand when half of your serving of calamari was the overly chewy dregs.

"Did you like it?" I asked.

"Did you see me wolf it down?"

"Sure, but I thought you might have been trying to be polite."

"Do I strike you as polite?"

"Well you're not to me, specifically, but you seem very well mannered with everyone else."

I'm not sure why we so freely gave each other such a hard time, but it probably had something to do with our first conversation. We just naturally fell into this level of comfort in teasing each other, which was both fun and flirty. She was funny, sharp and sweet all at the same time. You had to be on your toes to keep up with her, yet conversations flowed naturally and comfortably.

We were looking out the window at the people waiting for a table and others passing by when the entrées arrived. She had a lot of questions about the city. She did not spend a lot of time there even though she lived less than 30 minutes away in the western suburbs. Natalie was fascinated by how many small restaurants were nestled along these residential streets, which were mostly full of beautiful, old brownstone homes. She was right. There were many hidden gems in the downtown area that you would easily miss if you did not know what you were looking for.

"I'm not going to lie to you," Natalie started, "I made the right choice with this sea bass. It's incredible."

"But you haven't tried the gnocchi yet."

"Here, have some." She cut off a small portion and put it on my plate despite my urging to the contrary. The fish practically melted in my mouth. I could not imagine liking fish more than this, but it is not fair to compare fish to a pasta dish. It's just a matter of what you're in the mood for. It's rare that something piques my interest enough to actually turn down a good gnocchi.

"What do you think?" she asked.

"It is incredible. It's just not better than my gnocchi." I plopped a hefty spoonful on a clean portion of her plate, not giving her an opportunity to protest.

"OK, this is pretty good, I have to admit," she said reluctantly.

"Pretty good?" I asked. "Come on."

Natalie flashed that deadly smile. She was so different than anyone else I had talked to before. Flirty banter was not unusual. That was what I enjoyed most on my endless cycle of first and second dates. There was something deeper about this interaction though. Unforced and meaningful. Small talk and big talk infused into one easy conversation. I didn't have time to figure it out during dinner but simply noted that it was happening and that I'd have to make heads or tails of it later.

"So, what do you like to do now that your gym rat days are over?" I probed.

"To be clear, I was never a rat. I just played because that's what we did."

"Understood."

"I don't know, I guess I like to do a lot of things. I still spend a lot of time with my family. I spend a lot of time with my friends. I like to read but I have a major reality TV addiction. I love to travel. I'm a pretty big sports fan. I like good food. I like to cook. I love to eat. I don't know, are these too cliché? I'm not good at this game."

"You did great. How often do you see your family?"

"Uh, all the time. I live about five minutes away so I see them some nights after work. My mom makes a Sunday dinner which I always go to as long as I'm in town."

"Your brother too?"

"Yep. He's a sucker for mom's cooking too."

"That is awesome." I really meant that. My relationship with my family was very much my own doing, but I always had a twinge of regret for not being in better touch.

"Are you not tight with your family?" asked Natalie, apparently reading my expression well.

"We are tight, but I don't see them on a regular basis." I paused as if about to add more context.

"Are you happy about that?" she asked encouragingly.

"You know, I am, but I have to wonder if I'd be happier seeing them more."

"What is stopping you?"

"Nothing, really. I see them as much as I allow I guess."

"Allow yourself to see them, or allow them to see you?"

"Both. They live out in the country a few hours out of the city. I don't venture home too much, and I don't really invite them here either. I guess I like seeing them on my terms, but boy that sounds selfish when I say it out loud."

"Mom, dad, brothers and sisters?"

"Mom, dad and sister."

"Do you guys get along?"

"Yes . . ."

"Yes, but?"

"Yes, but I have always kept a distance from them as an adult."

"For a reason?"

"I think it is just easier. Mothers worry. Fathers judge. Sisters meddle. They all are well intentioned but it's just easier to not deal with it. By regulating the information they receive and the visits, I keep things on my terms and don't give them the chance to get worked up over my life."

"That makes sense," Natalie replied matter-of-factly.

"I don't think I've ever said that out loud. I think I sound like a heartless monster. I really love my family. I do. But it sure sounds calculated, doesn't it?"

"I've heard of much stranger and less healthy relationships than that. Sounds like the distance gives you some necessary space that allows you to live the life that you want, without your family all over you. I can't say that doesn't sound appealing to me."

"But you just said how you love spending time with your family so much."

"I do, but that doesn't mean I wish they didn't smother me half the time. But I guess I thought that's just what family is. Never thought to extract myself from it before."

"Well I'm not recommending it."

"And I could never do it. I'd die of heartache, if the guilt didn't kill me first."

"Guilt, yes. I spend most of my days rationalizing my way around that persistent little creature."

We took a break as the waiter cleared our plates and showed us the dessert tray. We ordered some Cannoli even though I was dying for the wild berry gelato. As much as I liked the gnocchi, I could live off the Luigi's gelato alone. I spent a week in Italy back in college and I swear I had gelato three times a day. It seemed like there were a dozen places in every town square we visited. I went through withdrawal when I first came back, but I eventually found the few places in the area that sold it. I didn't want to force it on Natalie though, considering her excited reaction when she saw the Cannoli.

"You know, you might be the least judgmental person I've ever talked to," I started again after savoring a few bites.

"That's funny. I guess everyone has their opinions, right?"

"And they're usually not shy about sharing them."

"Maybe I'm just being shy," she said jokingly. Although the conversation had been heavy, the tone remained remarkably light.

"No. I don't think that's it. And it's not like you don't have opinions. You seem like you've thought through things very well. It just seems like you don't apply your opinions or positions to me. That's what I like."

"Do you do that?"

"I try not to, but it's hard. Most people do it instinctively."

"You think?"

"My family does," my candidness continued.

"They judge you."

"Well, they would if I gave them the chance."

"So what don't they know about their prodigal son? It can't be as bad as it is in your head. You're a saint in my book."

" . . . A thieving saint."

"I think most saints had some shadiness in their past, so that's not necessarily an oxymoron."

"They don't know what I do or where I live. They know I play basketball but that's probably it."

"And there's no point in giving them a chance to not judge?"

"They couldn't handle it. Parents worry, it comes with the job. And to worry means to judge that something is not going as it should."

"You're screwed either way, though, right? If you let them into your life, they'll worry and judge based on the facts. If you don't let them in, they'll worry and judge based on pure speculation, which can be worse than the truth."

"You think their imagination is running wild?" I asked with a smile.

"Mine is!" she said excitedly.

"I don't work," I replied without hesitation. "I quit my job almost three years ago and have been living on next to nothing ever since. I don't need money for rent or a mortgage because I don't live anywhere. I just live. I pretend to write but I rarely put pen to paper. I play a lot of hoops and work out every day. I read a lot. I volunteer. I just try to do the things that are important to me and that make me happy."

"Wow," she uttered with eyebrows raised after a few seconds of silence.

"If I told my parents that, they would drop dead on the spot."

"They would be shocked that you workout every day?"

I laughed out loud. Leave it to Natalie to disarm such an intense moment of confession. I was shaking on the inside so badly that it must have been visible on the outside. True to form, the words had stumbled out of my mouth uncontrollably as if Natalie had a magnetic force designed to draw out my innermost secrets.

"Hey, do you want to go for a walk around town?" I asked, not intending to change the subject, just the setting. "Maybe get some ice cream?"

"Dessert for our dessert? Sounds great!"

As if sensing that we were ready to move on, Big John came over to our table to see if we wanted anything else. I was impressed with his display of hospitality without being too much in our space throughout dinner. He was not only a gentle giant, he had exceptional intuition when it came to interacting with people.

"Well, thank you so much for coming in tonight," he said after we turned down several attempts by him to give us an after-dinner expresso. Big John loved his expresso.

"Thank you so much for such a wonderful dinner," said Natalie.

"Please, it was my pleasure. You are welcome here anytime, with or without this handsome young man."

As I started to get up, Natalie looked alarmed. "Drew, we didn't get our check yet," she said in a rather low voice through gritted teeth, indicating that she did not desire for Big John to hear her.

"Miss Natalie, Drew knows that his money is no good here. He was being polite not to ask me about it because he has offended me too many times in the past." He shot a look of disapproval toward me.

"Thank you," she said hesitantly.

"Thank you so much, John," I said as I wrapped my arms around his massive torso and gave him a few quick pats on the back. "This will always be my favorite restaurant. The food and the service are unbeatable."

"Come again, Drew. And not a year from now, you hear?"

"Of course."

We walked out the door and Natalie immediately looped her arm through mine again, looked me in the eyes with both understanding and enthusiasm.

"Let's go live, Drew."

CHAPTER 15

We walked several blocks northeast to the historic district of the city. I didn't want to get ice cream straight away since we just had some dessert. I gave an amateur's tour of the area, pointing out the main buildings and providing as much information as I could remember. She had visited this area not that long ago but was still interested in my random stories, both historic and personal.

Strolling arm in arm with Natalie evoked feelings of peace and comfort, even though my head and stomach continued to spin. Never before had I experienced a sense of unease while at the same time being absolutely sure that I was doing what I was supposed to be doing at that time. How was it possible to be so sure and confused at the same time?

Our conversation continued to be dynamic. Flirtatious without effort. Challenging without accusation. Deep yet light.

"What do you pretend to write?" she asked as we walked slowly down a cobblestone street.

"Garbage," I replied with disgust. "I don't try to write garbage but that's the only thing that seems to come out."

"I see," she replied with eyebrows raised exaggeratedly, reacting humorously to my negativity.

"Well, I have lots of ideas on topics and I used to actually get something written. But the problem is that I have to read what I write and I just can't take it."

"You don't like the ideas or the writing?"

"Both, I guess," I said after thinking for a second. "My writing annoys me to death. I get so embarrassed the minute I read my own voice. I read the classics, but write like a third grader."

"Think you're a little harsh on yourself?"

"And the ideas are worse. What makes sense to me one day is obsolete the next. Either my perspective evolves pretty quickly or I'm more wishy-washy than your average politician. How do I dare write something that I won't believe tomorrow?"

"Well, I hate to burst your self-deprecating bubble but I don't think that's an unusual phenomenon. I'm no writer, believe me, but can't you solve that dilemma by not being definitive? I'm not saying don't ever take a position on something, but writing should be about sharing perspectives. It should be a fluid process."

"I agree with you. I just don't know when to take a position and when to just provide some thoughts and perspectives. Instead of working through it, I just get paralyzed by the uncertainty . . . and mostly by the fear of sounding like an idiot."

"I see. I don't know the first thing about writing something original. I can write the hell out of an appellate brief, but my audience is pretty limited and my creativity is bound by case law. I'm the last person to talk to about this."

"Actually, you're the first person I have talked to about this. And believe it or not, I feel a little better already."

"Really? I was not at all helpful."

"Something about admitting this stuff out loud helps."

"Sorry. Last question. Why do you want to write if it causes such struggle? Seems to go against your motto."

"Ha, my motto. I'm not exactly sure what that is, but I get your point. I suppose that's why I end up reading a whole lot more than writing. I just don't deal with it. The struggle just sits there in the back of my mind, gnawing at me. But it doesn't actually affect my daily life much. I ignore it and repress my failure to my subconscious. Sound healthy?"

"Yikes," she replied, taking my cue that it was OK to be unimpressed by that peek into my psyche. "Sounds like you still have some latent desire to write though. Guess that's not going away."

"Yeah, that's hard to put a finger on. I think it has something to do with what you said earlier, originality. I feel like writing is one of my only opportunities to be different. Among other things, that's part of what drove me to leave my job a while ago."

"Because you wanted to be different?"

"More like I didn't like being the same as everyone else."

"What, were you a lawyer or something?"

"Yep!" I said with a huge grin.

"Oh God, so I must sound like everyone else you know, huh?"

"You're not like anyone in the world, Natalie. And that's not fair suggesting that I would judge you like that. I would never. I'm the crazy one. Sane people figure out better ways to deal with their issues."

"I am just teasing. So you were a lawyer and just dropped everything?"

"Yes, but it was more than the being different thing."

"Go on," she said encouragingly. We had walked through the historic section and were heading back south toward Walnut again. The weather was perfect for an evening stroll. Still warm, but with a light breeze. The city could be stifling at times in the summer, but the wind prevented any unwanted sweating.

"Alright, but can we get some ice cream first?" I asked.

"Of course!"

"There's an Italian gelato place around the corner. I'm in the mood for it after Luigi's. Is that OK with you?"

"Sounds delicious."

I ordered the strawberry and Natalie got the chocolate. There was a decent line out front so it took a few minutes before we got the gelatos. I wondered if people could tell if we were on a first date. I considered myself an expert at this game but I'm not sure if I could have spotted us. We didn't have the awkward and forced small talk. We were comfortable going for periods without talking, particularly with interesting people watching to be done as was the case in the gelato line.

Our smiles seemed permanently planted as we looked around and at each other. If she was like me, she was thinking about our revealing conversations and wondering how in the world we found ourselves in the position we were in at that moment. That's what made me smile at least. That and the fact that being in Natalie's presence just generally made me happy.

The only downside of eating my gelato—which I did as slowly as possible to savor every drop—was that Natalie was no longer touching my arm. Besides the obvious connection we had in conversation, I felt a strong physical chemistry with her too, even if just by linking arms with her. Touching her felt so electric that I didn't think I was far off in my theory that she had a magnetic field. It not only drew words out of my mouth, but also sent shockwaves through my body upon contact.

"I quit my job because I started to make money," I started, knowing that I'd probably have to elaborate.

"OK . . ."

"I worked for a year or so at a big firm until my loans were paid off. I didn't owe anyone any money, so what I made actually went to just me and I didn't like it."

"You didn't like having money?"

"Not really. I mean I like doing certain things. Travelling is great but I didn't have a real need for it. I didn't have a need for any of the things I could buy with my money."

"You only wanted it if you had a need for it."

"Well, I guess it was just that. I didn't want to *need* it."

"I'm dense, please explain."

"You're not dense," I defended her. "I'm just an idiot. I had no problems making money when it went to paying off my debts. But once the money was fully at my disposal, I could see how it could become a driving force in life. It starts with eating better food, living in better places. Then accumulating more material, more clothes, more waste. Next thing you know you are beholden to the paycheck to keep up with this new standard of living. The more you make the higher the standard of living gets. I saw it as a vicious cycle."

"That makes a lot of sense. And you don't think you could have maintained a low standard of living, or whatever standard you wanted?"

"Maybe, but it would be very challenging. Then you have a different problem though. You start accumulating money and for what purpose. With people starving every day, what am I going to do with cash in the bank?"

"So it's partly an issue with wealth in general?"

"Yes. At the time, I think it bothered me to have money while others had nothing. Why was that fair? Just because I had something that could be monetized, which, by the way, was nothing more than a brain and a law degree. It wasn't anything tangible and it wasn't anything that other people could have, necessarily. A lot of people out there simply don't have the brains or the physical capacity to have a skill that can be monetized. Should they be banished to a shitty life because of what God did or didn't give them at birth?"

"So why not just give it away?"

"I guess I never felt right earning it in the first place. And I don't think I would have been happy busting my ass at the firm just to give away every dime. That's another reason why I decided to reprioritize my life to align with the things that made me happy. I could still positively impact the poor through volunteering, as opposed to providing cash, and I could spend my time shooting baskets instead of doing legal research for cases that are ridiculous in the first place."

"I see. Pretty complicated."

"Well, truthfully, it stemmed from a Catholic maxim that was always in the back of my mind."

"Easier for a camel to fit through the eye of a needle than a rich man to enter the gates of heaven?" Natalie guessed.

My jaw dropped. I guess I shouldn't have been surprised considering the context of our conversation, but I was still shocked to hear her repeat this line that used to keep me up at night.

"Now that was impressive," I said to her.

"I didn't go to Catholic school for nothing," she replied, acting proud of herself.

"Well, you nailed it. I guess I'm becoming obvious. I should shut up soon."

"Please," she said disapprovingly.

"In a world of haves and have-nots, I didn't want to be a have."

"So you dropped everything and began preaching the Gospel?"

"Not exactly. I can't stand preachy people. My vow was to have a positive impact on the world through action, not through mere words."

"Sounds great."

"The only hitch is that it's not the year 33 A.D. and not everyone just feeds you when you knock on the door. Calls the police, yes. Offers food, no."

"So . . . you took to stealing from hotels . . . because the food is extra anyway . . . and it harms no one," she said slowly as if a light bulb began shining brighter with every thought. "Genius!"

"Not genius. Just selective stealing. It works on a one-off basis, but can't really be a way of life for us all, now can it?"

She shook her head. She stopped with the questions as if she got to the bottom of a mystery and wanted to ruminate on it for a bit before moving on. She asked questions like a trained lawyer but without the pushiness. I knew our conversation had been terribly one-sided but that I'd get my chance for some friendly interrogation soon enough. I guess it just felt so good to get all of that junk off my chest that I didn't want to stop it.

"Thank you," I finally said to her after a long pause. We had walked a block without saying a word after throwing out our empty cups and spoons.

"You're welcome," she said hesitantly, clearly not knowing what deserved the thanks but was kind enough to not force me to explain it.

I pulled her arm a little tighter under mine. After wandering rather aimlessly around the entire Center City area, we found ourselves walking toward the Art museum. The museum was one of my favorite spots in the city. Besides being impressive to look at in its own right, the view of the city from on top of the entrance steps was breathtaking. No matter what a city looked like up close and personal, a view from above and afar always allowed me to see the beauty not otherwise recognized.

I offered to race her up the steps, but she claimed that the double dessert would slow her down too much. When we reached the top of the steps, we turned around to take in the late-night skyline. The standing clock at the head of the Parkway showed it was slightly after midnight. I wasn't sure how the time had slipped by, but I didn't want the night to end.

I asked if she wanted to sit for a while and she plopped herself down on the top step without even responding. Judging by the sigh, her legs were as tired as mine, and perhaps her head too. No matter how many miles I could run or how many hours I could play basketball, walking always made my legs tired. Shopping was the worst, but strolling around the city was no better. Sitting felt great.

Natalie grabbed my arm again as she had when we were walking. This time she leaned her head and part of her body on my shoulder. This was really late morning for me but she must have been getting very tired. I was just about to ask if she wanted to go home when she questioned if I was a Phillies fan.

"Why?" I responded. "Do I seem miserable?"

She lifted her head long enough to give me a backhand across my shoulder.

"You're probably a Yankees fan," she muttered under her breath.

"A very proud one," I said, head held high.

We spent what seemed like hours talking sports. Why were Philly fans so angry, regardless of the sport? Why were New York fans so obnoxious? Why did I like all the best teams when I didn't grow up close to any of them? She knew what she was talking about and I did my best to keep up. It was nice to talk about something both interesting and mindless like sports—a welcomed break from the heavy topics we got into earlier.

After a few hours, we forced ourselves to get up and start walking back toward Center City, not because we ran out of conversation but because our butts had fallen asleep from sitting so long. Natalie asked me if I wanted to come to her house for dinner during the week. We made plans for me to visit her Wednesday, after I warned her that I didn't have a cell phone. She said that would be a topic for another day.

Four days seemed like an eternity to wait to see her again, but I refrained from telling her that. I didn't want to scare her by sharing that I was worried about going through Natalie withdrawal. In truth, I could use the time to sort out my thoughts and feelings. I obsessed for hours over my shortest of encounters with Natalie. How was I going to digest an entire evening?

When we arrived at her car, I opened her door and told her that I would see her at 7:00 on Wednesday in the burbs. She smiled up at me and then reached up with her right hand and gently grabbed the back of my neck. She rose up on her tiptoes and leaned in to plant a sure but gentle, lingering kiss on my lips. Eyes closed and lips locked, I lost myself in this brief, timeless moment, hoping it would never end. Although my butterflies were awake and kicking in my stomach, it was the beating of my heart that made me feel more alive than I had ever felt before. When she released me from the power of her kiss, I said nothing, but simply opened my eyes and smiled. She got in the car, started it up and pulled away with a wave. For the fourth time, I just stared after her, speechless, as she vanished from sight.

CHAPTER 16

As most of the guys walked off the court toward the locker room, I gradually let myself fall to a heap on the floor along the baseline. I let out an audible groan and began stretching my legs. Tony sat down and started in on me right away.

"Struggling a little bit today, Drew?"

"What makes you say that, the fact that I couldn't hit a shot?"

"Nah, everybody has an off day, buddy. Your legs just looked a little shaky. Anything happen?"

I knew he was fishing for a story. I had one for him but it probably wasn't what he was expecting.

"You been talking to Big John by any chance?"

"C'mon Drew. You know nothing gets by me. Let's hear it!"

"Well, what did he say?"

"Nothing . . . other than that you looked like a little puppy dog around this girl last night. What's the deal? She was so fine she had you tripping over yourself?"

"No. It's nothing like that."

"What do you mean? She's not hot?"

"I'm not saying that. She's beautiful. It's just . . . I don't know. It's just different with Natalie, that's all."

"Natalie, huh? I don't remember you coughing up names that easily before."

139

"What? I'm sure I've told you names before. Now you're making stuff up."

"So, dinner at Luigi's . . ." Tony urged.

I usually made him work for information. I wasn't exactly the kiss and tell type. But I also took pleasure in being elusive with Tony. He was always starving for a juicy story and I liked to make him suffer as much as possible. I usually ended up giving him what he wanted because he wouldn't quit until he got details.

"Yeah, it was really nice. John really hooked us up. Great meal, great conversation. Then just walked around the city talking. I . . . let me put it this way. It was all I could do to keep up with her."

"Fast walker?" Tony asked with brow furrowed, misinterpreting what I said.

"No. I mean she's smart. She's funny. I'm talking quick witted and legitimately funny. She knows sports. She's deep. She's sweet. She gave me a rash of shit on every topic we discussed, but did so without an ounce of negativity. I just like being around her."

"Whoa, what did you do with Drew?"

I laughed a little but had to admit internally that I have been asking myself that question too. I didn't intend to rave about her like that to Tony but it was how I actually felt. I think my filter has been malfunctioning since I met Natalie.

"So," Tony continued, "it sounds like you have seen her before?"

"I guess you could say that I've bumped into her before."

"Does she live around here?"

"No. In the 'burbs."

"She sounds awesome. Why will this one fizzle like all the others?"

"Ouch."

"Oh, don't play hurt. You never get serious with anyone. I'm just wondering what you will find this time to make an early exit."

"Tony, I'm not trying to marry every girl I meet. I thought you were in support of my single lifestyle."

"I am. I just wonder why you wouldn't want to actually try to stick with one who you actually like."

"Well, I'm not saying I wouldn't want to stick with someone. I enjoy spending time with Natalie, so I can see myself doing more of that in the future."

"So you just want the benefits but not the pain of a relationship. Sounds like a good plan. Good luck with that."

"No. I'm not talking about a no-strings-attached set up. I don't even know what I'm talking about. My first date isn't even 12 hours old so I think this conversation might be a little premature."

"Hey, you're the one who said you want to see her more."

"I guess you're right. I just like being with her. That's all I know."

"Did you guys go back to your place?"

I knew he'd eventually want to hear the juice. It was only a matter of time.

"No. I told you, we walked around the city."

"All night? Get out of here."

"That's why my legs failed me this morning. Too much slow strolling."

"Pathetic. You should not have told me that. I would have just assumed that it was too much sex."

"I didn't want to give the wrong impression. Last night was completely PG."

"Bullshit. You went back to her place. I don't get it. Why don't you ever take girls back to your place? Every story for the last two years ends up at some girl's place. What is the deal?"

141

"First of all, last night ended at her car where I happily said goodbye as she drove back to the suburbs. Second of all, I don't invite girls to my place because I don't have any place to invite them to."

I looked up as I said this to see Tony's reaction. He turned his head slightly, looking at me out of the corner of his eye as if trying to figure out what exactly I had just said. I'm not sure what possessed me to blurt this out other than that I felt so liberated when I got everything off of my chest to Natalie. I hadn't thought through the repercussions of revealing this to Tony. It just fell out of my mouth.

"What do you mean? You don't like your place?"

"It's not that I don't like it. It's that . . . well, it doesn't exist."

"Do you live with your parents and you never told me?" Tony asked as he started to laugh.

"No. I mean I don't live anywhere. I don't have a place for myself. Strange, I know."

"Where do you sleep?"

"Uh, anywhere I guess. The park. The gym. The library. I don't sleep a ton at one time and it's usually during the day."

"You're kidding," Tony replied in complete disbelief. He was no longer laughing. He actually had a blank expression, like he wasn't sure how to react. This was the first time I've ever seen him speechless.

"It's not a big deal. I just like my freedom."

"It's not a big deal? You tell me you're homeless after all the years that I've known you and you think it's not a big deal."

"I'm not homeless like that. I just choose not to have a house or apartment to call my own."

"So you have the money but choose not to get a place?"

"Well, I don't really have the money, but that was a choice too. I chose this lifestyle."

"I'm not familiar with this lifestyle. The one where you

chose not to have any money or a place to sleep. Please explain."

"I'm not sure if it's common. I mean most people without a home are in that situation because of circumstances, not because they are following a path they chose. I just like living this way."

"Where's all of your stuff?"

"Uh, in my locker," I said laughing. "I don't have much."

Tony didn't laugh. He slowly turned away from me as the concept sunk in for him. I could see the wheels turning in his head going through all of the basic amenities that a home provides, and how I could survive without them. He did not say a word for a full minute.

"You use the gym as home base. That's why it seems like you're here all the time. Shower. Bathroom. Laundry. Exercise. TVs."

I just shook my head in agreement. There was no one else nearby and we weren't talking loudly. I knew I could trust Tony not to blow my cover, not that there was anything illegal about my use of the gym. Everything I did there was appropriate. I just wouldn't want anyone to know that I essentially lived there.

"What do you do in the winter?" Tony asked with furrowed brow, still trying to wrap his head around this news. "Or if it rains?"

"If it's really cold or wet, I'll sleep in the library. The last two winters were really mild, so it hasn't been much of an issue so far. Might have to take this gig down south after a while. Sleeping during the day helps though. Sweatpants and sweatshirt do the trick. It gets way colder at night."

"Well, I have to hand it to you," Tony finally said after another long pause. "I didn't see that coming. I just don't know why you never told me that before. Did you think I was going to rat you out, or judge you or something?"

"No," I responded quickly, understanding now that he was actually upset about my revelation.

"I mean we've been through a lot together," he continued before I could respond with more. "You've been to my house a dozen times. You helped me move for Christ's sake. You've been there for the birth of my child, birthday parties, family barbecues. I thought we were tight enough that you could tell me anything, even something like this."

"Tony, it's not that I kept a secret from you that involved our friendship. This is just a silly fact about my life that I don't share with anyone really."

"Did you tell Natalie?"

"Well, yes, but that's complicated."

"I've heard enough for now," Tony said as he got up off the floor. "We are going to talk about this later. I'm not through with you yet."

He gave me a long stare and a threatening point of his finger. He looked like he was joking but I could tell he was legitimately hurt. This took me completely by surprise. I hadn't given it much thought before, but I never would have guessed that he would take it so personally. He was such a clown most of the time that I wasn't sure if there were any real feelings inside of him at all.

"Tony."

He looked back at me and said nothing.

"I'm sorry I didn't tell you before."

He just continued to shake his head as he walked off the court and headed to the locker room. I decided to just lay there a while until everyone had cleared out of the locker room. I just wanted some time to myself to sort out the events of the last day. My conversation with Tony made me feel bad and I needed to figure out why.

After 20 more minutes of alternating lying and stretching, I finally gathered my strength to leave the court. My morning routine took a little longer than usual as my mind was clearly elsewhere. I was still buzzing from my night with Natalie, but something deep inside was eating at me after talking to Tony.

My body felt great in the hot shower since I had been on the go for the last 10 hours straight, and even though I had plenty of more important life-changing things to think about, I couldn't help but wonder why I had shot so poorly during the games. I've had tired legs before and I typically just focused on bending my knees a little extra to compensate. I tried that today but to no avail. I stifled some conspiracy theories before they even developed. *It's just one bad shooting day*, I told myself.

I didn't arrive at the park until 10:30. I had a fairly light breakfast at the Hilton and ended up bringing most of the food with me in my backpack. I was more tired than hungry, so I ate a few bites of hot food and then loaded up my bag with bagels and muffins. Since it was late and I was tired, I decided that I'd skip the library and any other stop I might typically make.

So why was Tony so hurt? I asked myself as I finally lay my head on my bag. I knew he'd be surprised and even a little pissed that he didn't figure out my big secret before I told him. But actually hurt? I did not see that coming. I had a few reasons why I kept the secret in the first place. There were some people who I didn't want to worry. There were others who wouldn't understand. And there were others where it just made life easier not to tell. I guess plenty of people fit into several or all of those categories. But the one consistent fact was that I primarily kept the secret from people for their own good. I guess that's why I assumed no one would ever be hurt by it.

Now that I saw Tony's reaction, I started to run through the reactions of everyone else. I had played this out in my head before but concluded nothing beyond the fact that it would blow their minds. When I conducted this exercise now, just hours after my interaction with Tony, I started to come to different conclusions. My parents would be hurt too. The fact that I wasn't willing to confide in them would probably devastate them more than the news itself. My sister? Forget about it. She would question how thick blood really is. They wouldn't disown me, but their hurt feelings would be exponentially greater than Tony's.

There were others in my life who worried me too. The impact on Hakim and Kijana would have serious negative ramifications. All this time I had been worried about telling them about my lifestyle because I didn't want to be a bad influence on them. But in reality, I was teaching a more harmful lesson in how I had handled my choices. I kept a secret from them and my loved ones about something integral to the person I am. Would the message be that I was too ashamed of the truth or that I did not care enough about the feelings of those around me to share with them such critical facts? Either way, I would have failed them as a coach and mentor.

I started getting that sick sinking feeling I got when I realize that something bad has happened and it's too late to stop it. Like the damage was already done. It didn't happen often, but it was memorable. It happened when I heard about the deaths of my grandparents and some friends when I was younger. It happened when I lost a big game. It happened when I finished a test that I bombed because I didn't study hard enough. These instances are not created equally by any means, but the feeling of helplessness was the same. I hated that feeling. Particularly when my decisions created it.

With my sister visiting on the upcoming Sunday, I started to feel anxiety about how I would handle our conversation. I had no intentions of revealing anything to her at that point in time, but I had to at least think about if it was the right thing to do. How had my life gotten so complicated so quickly when my whole goal was to keep things simple and enjoyable? This must have been Natalie's fault, I thought. Then I couldn't help but laugh at myself. I noticed then that I was actually smiling while I was lying there. With all the dreadful thoughts that ran through my head for the last 30 minutes, just the mere inkling of Natalie made me smile. Wow, was I in trouble.

I allowed myself to relive the previous night in my head: the dinner, the walk, the conversations, the ice cream, the museum and the kiss. It was perfect. I had no idea where it was heading with Natalie, but I knew I had to see her again or I'd go crazy. I knew that she captured something inside me that hadn't been touched before. I knew that she effortlessly made me become a complete open book despite being so secretive with everyone else in my life. Without intending, she opened my eyes to things in my life that I couldn't see clearly. Simply put, she turned my life upside down.

But despite that Natalie caused such discomfort in so many areas of my life, I don't remember anyone making me fall asleep with a smile that wide.

CHAPTER 17

We were all sitting in a booth in the back of the café sipping our strawberry milkshakes when the oldest boy looked up to me and said, "Dad, I'm going to be a fireman when I grow up!"

"Really, buddy?" I responded. "That's awesome."

"Me Spid'man!" yelled the younger one, trying his best to join the conversation.

"Spiderman!" I yelled back to him pretending to shoot him with webs coming out of my wrists.

The three of us laughed heartily, although I noticed out of the corner of my eye that the woman next to me did not seem amused.

"I want to be a fireman just like you, daddy," the older boy said with undeniable pride in his voice. He held his head up high.

"Like me?" I asked him.

"Yeah, Grandpa said that you were a fireman just like we see on TV."

"He said that I . . ." I started to ask until the woman next to me nudged me under that table hard enough to stop me from finishing my thought.

I shot her a brief glance before turning back to my boys. The older one noticed that something was off and a slight look of disappointment flashed across his face.

"You are a fireman, right dad? Grandpa said so."

My heart sunk. I didn't know what to say. Their Grandpa must have made this up so the boys had something—or someone—to look up to, even if untrue. It was a cruel lie in a sense, but not nearly as cruel as a dad who was too selfish to be a good role model for his children. I stared back at the older boy, searching for the right thing to say. I didn't want to perpetuate the lie but I didn't have the guts to tell him the truth. I was speechless. Motionless. My eyes turned toward the little one who was painstakingly trying to fold two fingers on each hand into his palms so that he could shoot spider webs back at me.

What injustice! Two beautiful, innocent little people with their whole lives in front of them deserved better from their father.

"Dad?" the older one asked in response to my silence.

"Let's go guys, time to go to Grandpa's with Mommy," the woman said as she got up from the table, ending the painful, awkward silence.

I was devastated. I felt sorrow for my boys and hatred toward myself. I was so pathetic that I had to be bailed out of a *conversation about what my kids wanted to be when they grew up. Worse yet, their mother had to take them away from me and to their grandparents' house because I had nothing to offer them. Literally nothing.*

I couldn't move as she cleaned them up and got them ready to go. I was frozen in my seat. Before walking away, the older boy waved weakly at me and quietly said, "Bye dad."

The little one just started to cry. He didn't want to leave and he didn't understand why his father never went with them at night. As the door closed behind them, I was suddenly free to move, but all I wanted to do was to bury my head in my arms on the table and cry. And so I did.

CHAPTER 18

I was not nervous until I turned onto Natalie's block. The houses weren't McMansions like I had seen crop up in other wealthy neighborhoods. They were all older homes of varying sizes with fully-grown trees lining the road side and littering the front yards. Her street was very wide with sidewalks along both sides, consisting of large imperfectly shaped and fitted stone with grass growing in between. It was such an idyllic setting that it dawned on me for the first time just how different her life was than mine. Until that point, I was just plain excited about seeing her. When it hit me how ridiculous I must have seemed to her, with my unique version of an alternative lifestyle, I started to get anxious and significantly less confident than I had been seconds before.

From my perspective, it would have been better if she lived in a brand new development with perfectly manicured grounds. I wouldn't have been as discouraged by that. At least then I could have convinced myself that the environment was just pretty on the outside and that there wasn't much substance or history on the inside. If that were the case, then her lifestyle would be more temporary and perhaps she wouldn't be completely put off by my way of life. Instead, her neighborhood spoke of good old-fashioned values with deep roots and history. It looked like one of those neighborhoods in a wholesome, family movie like "Father of the Bride." It spoke of tradition. My life was legitimately void of tradition.

I stood in front of her place for a few minutes before venturing down the path to her front door. Her house was white, with black shutters and a red door. It was one of the smallest on the block, but still good-sized for a single woman in her 20s. It was cute and suited her perfectly. Rather than standing on her front step all night, I forced myself to ring the doorbell. In just a few seconds, the door swung open and Natalie started ushering me in immediately. I had spent time preparing for when I saw her. I hadn't planned on what to say exactly or anything like that. I just visualized the event a few hundred times so I wouldn't be so floored by seeing her like I had been every other time.

When I laid eyes on her standing in her doorway, I only felt a quick bolt in my chest. It was not because I was getting used to seeing her. The shock lasted only a second because Natalie assured me that she was going to burn down the house with her cooking if we didn't immediately run to the kitchen. She closed the door behind me and practically sprinted through the dining room. I walked behind her, taking it all in. She wore a pair of blue shorts that showed off her amazing legs and a relatively snug red shirt that accentuated her athletic, yet curved figure. It was probably good that she didn't give me a tour right then because I knew I would find it hard to focus on anything but her, at least during those first few minutes.

She went out of sight into the kitchen from which I could see the steam billowing before I even entered. The place smelled a bit like chicken fajitas, but she had a back door open so most of the odor was rolling out through the screen door.

"I'm sorry it seems like such a wreck in here, but I thought I could get the chicken done before you got here."

"Am I early? I'm sorry."

"Of course not, you could have come anytime. I just didn't

want you to have to witness me making a fool of myself like this."

"Well in that case, I'm glad I showed up when I did."

Actually, I wished I had been a few minutes earlier. I noticed that her hair was still wet, meaning that she probably got out of the shower right before she started to sauté the chicken. She turned down the stove and the noise and steam subsided. I noticed that she had a few other pots on the stove.

"Very funny," she replied. "OK, I think we're no longer in danger of a fire. It will just be a few minutes before everything is ready."

"Sounds great. I'm in no hurry at all. What can I do to help?"

"Don't be ridiculous. I didn't invite you all the way out here so you could cook for me."

"I'm so glad to hear you say that you invited me. I've had this bad feeling that I invited myself."

"What?" she asked, laughing. "Of course I invited you . . . out of pity, you know. Not because I really wanted to hang out with you again."

"I'll take it any way I can get it. I was just afraid that without any way to reach me, you didn't have any way to back out if you really didn't want me here."

"Jeez, enough fishing. How many times do I need to say that I wanted you to come before you'll feel better about it?"

"Maybe one more," I said with a smirk, egging her on while acknowledging that I had been feeling insecure about the dinner.

"Well, I'm glad you are here, and I'll say it as many times as you need me to, OK?"

"Alright. And although you don't need to hear it as much as I apparently did," continuing to make fun of myself, "I am really happy to be here."

She reached into her cherry cabinets and pulled out two plates and two salad bowls. I met her as she turned around and grabbed the dishes from her. Together we set the small counter-height bistro table in her kitchen. She had a longer formal table in her dining room that I'm sure she used sparingly. There wasn't room to fit all of the serving dishes on the table so we just grabbed our plates and served ourselves from the stove top.

"You don't waste any time do you?" I asked. Our plates were loaded within 10 minutes of when I walked through the door. "I might be in and out in under a half an hour at this rate."

"I just thought you might be hungry, you know, in case you got banned from the hotels."

"I deserved that, I guess."

"Seriously, I actually just hate when you get invited to a dinner party at 7:00 and you get there and the hosts haven't even begun making dinner yet. I know that cooking the meal can be social in and of itself, but it sucks when you arrive hungry. I always found that to be inconsiderate for some reason."

"I can see that."

"We'll have plenty of time to be social later, on a full stomach."

"Spoken like a true Italian."

The fajitas were hot and delicious, better than what I typically consumed for sure. She provided warm soft tortillas, along with the classic accoutrements for fajitas like tomatoes, onions, avocado and sour cream. If that wasn't enough, she offered a side of antipasto, a broccoli and cheese concoction, and a fruit plate with every berry and melon imaginable. She clearly hadn't whipped this meal together in the last 20 minutes.

154

"This is awesome, Natalie," I said sincerely. "And thank you for having me over."

"I'm glad you like it," she replied with a sweet smile. "So, what's it like being out of the hood?"

This made me laugh because I clearly didn't live in the hood, if it could be said that I lived anywhere.

"Just like home," I said in return. She knew that there was some culture shock for me coming out to the suburbs, probably because she had the reverse shock when she came to the city.

"You know, there was a time when this would have been actually urban to me," I added.

For the rest of dinner, we swapped stories about growing up in the country versus growing up in the suburbs. Neither one of us could have imagined being raised in the city. Even though I preferred spending my time there as an adult, it still seemed like a strange place to raise kids. Natalie had a true neighborhood experience as a child, while I had to ride my bike miles in order play with other kids my age.

When I was sure she was done picking at the food on her plate, I jumped up and grabbed it away from her before she had a chance to object. I cleared the table and started doing the dishes, all the while still talking about life as a kid on the dirt road. She filled glass containers with the extra food and brought the empty pots and pans over to the sink for me. Within 20 minutes, we had the dishes washed, dried and put away. The table was wiped clean and if you couldn't identify the smell of fajitas in the air, you would never have known that we just eaten a five-course dinner.

"Do you want a tour now or should we just relax on the back porch for a few minutes first?"

"You deserve a break," I replied, correctly reading into her question. As we sat down together on the porch swing,

I noticed the picture frames on the coffee table against the wall of the house. Every picture reflected the beaming smiles of a happy family. I was sure Natalie's family must have had their share of drama, like everyone else, but there was no mistaking how much they enjoyed being with each other.

"That's the gang," she said, noticing me staring at the photos.

"How in the world is a woman like you not married?" I blurted out. I knew as soon as I said it that it bordered on inappropriate and maybe even offensive. I certainly didn't intend it that way and I hoped I could recover with a little explanation. I just never understood how someone so wonderful had not been snatched up earlier in life. I had been thinking it ever since the first day I met her when I noticed she wasn't wearing a ring. But seeing her in her own house with pictures of her family and the scents of a home-cooked meal in the air was too much for my weakening filter to contain any longer.

"Knowing you, I think I'm supposed to take that as a compliment, right?" she said kindly.

"Yes of course . . ." I quickly replied before she continued.

"That can be taken another way, you know."

"I simply meant that you are such an incredible catch that you must have had your pick of the boys over the years."

"Ah, yes, flattery will dig you out of most holes."

"Well, I mean it and that wasn't flattery just for the sake of flattery. I know a wanted woman when I see one."

"I don't know about all that," she started. "I guess you could say that I was off the market for quite some time."

"How long is quite some time?" I asked, pushing for more information. *Finally*, I thought, I was going to get the scoop on how I could be so lucky to have a chance with a girl like this.

"I guess about 10 years, give or take," she replied sheepishly, and looked closely at me for my reaction.

I just nodded my head, intentionally trying to take it in stride. I swear a dozen questions popped into my head in less than a second. How old was she when she started this dating streak? Was it one person or had she been a serial monogamist? If it was one person, what happened? Did he end it? Did she end it? Is he alive? How long has it been over? How over is it? Thankfully, she didn't make me wait long to satisfy my curiosity.

"OK, so I dated the same guy since junior year of high school," she continued. "Off and on, that is. We had a break or two during college, but I never considered myself really ever *on* the market. I know. Very cliché. Stayed with my high school sweetheart for all those years."

"That's sweet," I said, trying to stay neutral as best as I could.

"Yeah, real sweet. Didn't end very sweet, that's for sure."

"For him or for you?" I asked, while shamelessly praying that he didn't die a hero's death, thus making her heartbroken for eternity.

"For either of us, I guess. But probably worse for him." She grimaced as she said this. She clearly did not delight in his unhappiness. "I ended it. I actually ended it a few times but I ended it for good this spring."

"Heartbreaker," I said trying to keep it light and not showing that my heart sunk when she said *this spring*.

"Oh don't call me that. I can't begin to describe my guilt. It makes me sick just thinking about it."

"Don't feel like you need to talk about this if your dinner is going to come back up as a result."

"Thanks. I don't mind talking about it. And just because I still feel very bad about the whole thing doesn't mean I haven't moved past it. In fact, how good I have felt since ending it is part of what makes me feel so guilty about the whole thing in the first place. It was something I should have had the strength to do a long time ago, and as a result, I inflicted a lot more pain than I should have. And now I feel like the weight of the world has been lifted off my shoulders."

"I see. You're happier, but you feel bad because he's miserable now. I think I get that."

"I'm not saying he's never going to recover. I'm not that conceited! I just know that he's hurting now."

"Not that I can even begin to weigh in here, but he'll be better off in the long run. I mean . . ." I started to scramble. "Not better off without you. Just better off without you if you didn't want to be with him, if you know what I mean."

"I know. No one should be with someone who doesn't want to be with them. I can't think of anything worse."

It was probably best to keep my mouth shut in this conversation, but I couldn't help but share my thoughts. It was Natalie, after all. Words always spilled out of my mouth when I was around her.

"Lots of people probably fake their way through relationships," I said. Natalie looked at me like I accused her of murder, so I quickly tried to recover.

"I'm not suggesting you did that at all. I just mean some people don't have the strength or the necessary motivation to end a relationship even though they have decided it should be over. You know, why prolong something that is destined not to work out? That's not what you're describing though."

I wasn't sure if I dug myself out or just a deeper hole, so I just kept rambling on.

"Plenty of people have had on again off again relationships like you. That doesn't mean anyone was faking anything.

Love ebbs and flows in some relationships and all you can do is make the best decisions you can at that point in time and follow your heart. That doesn't always lead to the best results but this isn't a perfect world, is it?"

"No, you're right. I guess I just feel bad I didn't make the final decision sooner and put us both out of our misery."

"Totally understand, and I don't mean to pretend like I know what I'm talking about. I'm the last person . . ."

"I shouldn't say misery," she corrected herself. "That was part of the problem actually. We were perfectly compatible and got along great 99 percent of the time. We were never unhappy with each other. I just always felt that there was something missing. Because of our history and because I loved him, I kept holding out in the hopes of finding that missing piece. And at times I just pretended like I didn't need it. I guess after 10 years, I finally realized it just wasn't going to be there, and I needed more."

"Well, no one can say you didn't give it a fair chance," I said with a flinch, half expecting to get smacked in the arm as was prone to happen with my wiseass comments. I hoped she was OK with joking about this sensitive topic.

"That is for sure!" she responded. "I don't know. Some people say that you just *know* when it's right."

"You don't believe that?" I asked without offering my position on it.

"I'd like to but I always worried that I wouldn't know it when I saw it or when it happened. I just *know* I never got that feeling with . . . with my ex."

"Does ex have a name?"

"William."

"Good. It's not nice to call him ex for the rest of your life."

"So, loverboy, do you think you'll just *know* when the time comes?"

"Jeez, I don't know the answer to that. I think it happens differently for different people. Some people need time to get close and develop deep feelings that might lead to *knowing* that it's the real deal. Other people seem to get it right away and never waver from that point. Both have their successes and failures I think."

"Are you speaking from experience here?" she started to probe.

"I'm just talking very generally. There are lots of failed marriages out there and I'm willing to bet there are plenty of people who just *knew*, then when the shit hit the fan they realized they didn't *know* anything."

"Yikes . . . a little cynical, don't you think?" Natalie teased.

"I don't mean to be at all. It's just that a 50 percent success rate for marriage can't be ignored. I don't plan on contributing to that statistic, but I'll take it as a cautionary tale if I were ever to take that plunge."

Natalie jumped out of the swing and grabbed one of the family pictures off of the end table. Judging by this abrupt move, I figured I must have pissed her off with this conversation, which stemmed from her sharing her relationship history. But she acted like nothing was wrong and brought the frame back to the swing to show me who was in the picture. It was taken at a family picnic last year and although there was apparently more than 50 people in attendance, this photo contained just her grandparents, parents and brother. I was about to start asking about her family in hopes of changing the subject, but Natalie wasn't done yet.

"Maybe you're right about only being able to make decisions based on what you know at the time. No one has a crystal ball. Maybe people just think they *know* at a certain point in time, but then when they get to know someone better, the warts start to come out and people aren't who you thought they were originally."

"That is true for every relationship," I replied. "To make it work, you almost have to commit to sticking it out no matter how ugly the warts might get."

"And if both people are committed to making it work," Natalie added, "then you can get through almost anything."

"True. But I wonder if that is truly love though. It's almost like you are in love with the commitment to each other and how that makes you feel. Like the comfort you get from knowing . . . from being loved unconditionally."

"So you're saying it doesn't really matter who it is, it's just the feeling of being loved that makes us happy." She said this with curiosity, not with accusation.

"I don't know if I'm saying that," I said, now certain that I had gone too far. "I'm just running my mouth, that's all."

"I think it matters who it is. I spent 10 years being loved unconditionally and it never made me happy enough to want to get married. There has to be more."

"For you. For others, that might have been enough."

"I guess," she conceded.

"Did William ever propose to you?"

"Yes, twice actually. Once five years ago, and once again this spring."

"And what did you say?"

"Um, I said not yet the first time, and not ever the second time."

"Wow, harsh."

"Well I didn't say it just like that, but that was the message I guess. See why I feel so bad?"

"You shouldn't feel bad for giving that much effort into a relationship to make it work."

"That's just it. It was no effort at all. It came easy and

naturally for us. It just wasn't enough."

"So love and commitment wasn't enough to make it last?"

"It would have been enough to make it last, but it wouldn't have made me happy in the way that I think I should be happy, does that make sense?"

"Absolutely. It sounds like you think there might be someone else out there who makes you happy in a way that William couldn't."

Natalie looked away from me before answering, more out of shyness than awkwardness.

"I feel terrible but I hope so. He wasn't the one for me, I guess. I didn't used to believe that there was one true person for each of us. But after going through everything with William, I think there might be something to it."

"You need more than just love and commitment. You need love and commitment with the right person," I said in attempt to understand her position.

"That's right!"

"So is there more than one right person for each of us?" I pressed on.

"I'm not sure, that gets into some deep shit that I don't know if I can handle without a few glasses of wine. Are you thirsty?"

"Of course," I said, happy to leave it at that.

We walked back into the kitchen and she poured two glasses of white wine. She walked me through the rest of the first floor as the tour began. The house must have been at least 40 years old but the hardwood floors were in excellent condition and must have been redone very recently. There were pictures everywhere of family and friends. I didn't see any pictures of someone who could have been William though. I couldn't help think about how odd it must be to spend 10 years with someone and feel the need to erase his presence from your life entirely. I understood it. It was surely healthy for her healing process. It was surely healthy too for any new male visitors to the house like me. But it was still odd.

The upstairs had a thick neutral carpet and brightly-colored walls. There were three bedrooms and two bathrooms. All the rooms were small but had a warm, coziness. Somehow the house itself felt as cheery as Natalie did. I wasn't sure whether Natalie's presence had rubbed off on the house, or if she just created an environment that mirrored her personality. Either way, I felt comfortable being there just as I always felt comfortable being around Natalie, regardless of what we were doing or talking about.

I reluctantly followed her out of her bedroom over to the stairs. We had been so engrossed in dinner and dishes and conversation that I had been distracted from just how stunning Natalie was physically. How was it possible that my sexual attraction to her actually got overshadowed at times by her other features? As she turned to me before descending down the stairs, I had to once again deliberately shake my head to snap out of the daydream I was having of her jumping into my arms and onto the bed.

She must have read my thoughts. "Are you still with me, Drew?" she said smiling wryly.

"Of course!" I said, pretending that my mind hadn't gone in another direction.

She held out her hand. I reached out and grabbed it before walking down the stairs together.

"This place is you, Natalie."

"Do you like it?" she said, intending the double meaning.

I laughed and smiled at her in response. I liked her and the house, indeed. I liked her more every second that I spent with her. I couldn't imagine ever getting sick of her. I knew you didn't always see the warts at first, but this woman seemed beyond warts. That wasn't what I liked about her. I liked her spirit and everything that came with it. If she had a hundred warts and that same spirit, I would have liked her just as much.

"Natalie, this has been great," I said, as we settled down onto the couch in the living room, clutching our second glasses of wine.

"I agree," she responded.

"I was really nervous when I got here, but you have a way of making me just feel lucky to be with you. You are so comfortable in your own skin that it's almost contagious."

"You? Nervous? I'm not sure if I believe you."

"Well, it's true."

"Well, it never shows. You carry yourself with such confidence but without any cockiness. That's a rare combo."

"Thanks?"

"Seriously Drew, you have really inspired me. The way you live your life. Your focus on what is important to you. The goodness in your heart. I don't see it every day. I mean I know other good people, but none that have committed their lives to it like you."

I looked at her with my mouth agape, in disbelief that I could have affected her a fraction of how much she affected me.

"You've changed me," she said.

"Don't tell me that!" I exclaimed. "I'll never forgive myself. I am completely blown away by you, so you better change back to Natalie right now!" I pretended to order her.

She laughed and took another sip of her wine.

What am I going to do with you? I thought.

"You are so different from what I am used to," Natalie started again. "I think I spent so long trying to make something work with William because he was perfect on paper. I know you don't want to hear this."

"I don't care, honestly."

"It's just that I think I was using the wrong standard. I think I was using my parents' standard. Society's standard. But not my own. I never gave it enough original thought to know what I truly liked. Nice. Funny. Responsible. Close to family. These were attributes that seemed to comprise the perfect guy, but that doesn't make someone perfect for *me*.

"He knew me well. He treated me well. We had fun together. But he didn't challenge my thoughts and ideas. He didn't inspire me to become a better person. He was a great guy, but that's not the essence of what makes me happy."

"Natalie, you are the one who has turned my life upside down."

"How so?" she asked skeptically.

"Well, you are all I can think about. I went from completely at peace in my head and heart to not knowing whether I'm coming or going."

"Don't tell me that!" she said mimicking my comment to her. "Why do we like spending time with each other if we're causing such internal turmoil?"

"It's not bad turmoil. It's actually exciting turmoil. I literally can't get enough. I get so excited just thinking about what might happen next."

"You know what I like most about you, Drew? I love that you don't have a phone. It means you're not distracted by the frivolous things in life, and it forces you to make specific plans to meet people. It's so old school that I love it."

"You don't want me to text you my feelings tomorrow?" I said facetiously.

"Exactly! That's what most people do these days. The hard and meaningful conversations happen that way now."

"I agree," I said. "I think real personal relationship growth occurs in person, not through texts and emails and tweets and whatever other social media nonsense is out there now."

"Totally agree," she responded.

"So, with that said, do you want to hang out on Saturday night?"

"Sure," she replied, enthusiastically.

"I was thinking that we had a long talk about life the other night, and a long talk about love tonight. Let's just go have some fun Saturday night."

"I'm game!"

"OK. Meet me in the city anytime you want in the afternoon, but come dressed up. We're going to a party, OK?"

"That's all you're telling me, a party?"

"That's all you get. Just be ready to have a good time."

"Sounds perfect."

With that, she grabbed my glass of wine out of my hand and leaned over me to place it on the end table on my side of the couch. Instead of retreating to where she was sitting, she stopped on my lap, with her face just inches from mine. Her sweet scent overwhelmed me. I wrapped my arms around her body and pulled her even closer to me. Our lips met once again, yet this time there was no quick ending. They lingered on top of each other until she parted hers slightly, leaning forward taking in my upper lip softly but confidently. If sleep did not overtake us some five hours later, that kiss might never have ended.

CHAPTER 19

It was 4:00 pm by the time I got into the shower at the gym on Saturday. I hadn't wasted a minute all day. After playing basketball in the morning, I showered and got ready to go straight to the park to sleep instead of eating in one of the hotels. I had loaded up on bagels and muffins the previous day so I would be prepared. I had a bagel, a muffin, an apple and a pear before falling asleep under my tree. It was a perfect day for sleeping outside: warm with a steady breeze. I slept for about six hours in the park before heading back to the gym early to get ready.

Now that it was less than an hour from meeting Natalie, I started to get really excited. For the last few days, I vacillated between the high—brought upon by my feelings for Natalie—and the low that resulted from my embarrassingly poor handling of the other relationships in my life. I concluded that I had spent so much of my focus and energy on living my life the way I wanted that I had completely undermined my relationships.

On the surface, they appeared normal and even healthy. But keeping a major secret like I had, even one that could be justified on privacy grounds, prevented the cultivation of any depth and actually made a mockery of it all because trust and openness are at the heart of any good relationship.

I had been beating myself up ever since I told Tony the truth. He and I still hadn't had another heart to heart about it, but I knew we needed one. His reaction opened my eyes to how others would probably handle the news. The problem: I hadn't thought anyone could handle all the facts about my life. What started out as an effort to protect others turned into a subconscious effort to protect myself. What I hadn't realized before was that this effort was backfiring, hurting, rather than protecting the ones I loved.

Even with these thoughts weighing me down, I still got a dose of adrenaline as I continued to prepare for my night with Natalie. She was going to meet me outside the gym at 5:00. I quickly went through my entire routine of flossing, brushing, cleaning my ears, trimming any unseemly hairs, applying deodorant and lotion. I dressed in my only khakis and sports coat. I know this wasn't quite as dressy as it should have been for the night, but it would have to do. I didn't have a button down shirt or a tie, so I was doing the best I could. I actually wasn't worried that Natalie has already seen me in this outfit. Being completely honest with her made everything easier. I didn't have to worry about what she knew or didn't know or could find out. Honesty was liberating.

I walked outside of the gym a few minutes before 5:00. I normally would wait until the last second so I didn't start sweating through my clothes, but the breeze allowed me to stay outside for a few extra minutes. I also wanted to be there when Natalie arrived, not for any strategic reason, like showing her that I was responsible or timely. I wanted to be there first so I didn't miss a moment of being with her.

When I saw Natalie turn the corner, I was more excited than I had even anticipated. I had seen her in a number of different outfits, but never in a stunning, sexy blue dress like she was wearing now. As usual, she was laughing at me before she was even close enough for us to say hello. There was plenty about me that could make her laugh from a distance but I assumed it was because I was wearing the very same outfit as the last time we went out in the city. I really knew how to dress to impress.

"Good to see you too," I said, referring to the fact that she was laughing at me.

"What? I'm just laughing at your face. You make wearing this dress even more fun."

"Well, I hope my amazement was that obvious," I replied. "You look unbelievable."

"Thank you," she said, blushing.

"Here's where you say you've never seen such a stunning khaki/blazer combo in your life."

"Vaguely familiar. I think I saw it in a catalog recently. You have exquisite taste."

I tried not to squeeze her too hard as I gave her a hug. I couldn't resist lifting her slightly off the ground though. She held on tight and didn't put up a fight. Once she landed, I took a good long look at her and told her again that she was beautiful. It was hard not to compliment her continuously. Thankfully, she had a knack for moving the conversation along so as to deflect such attention.

"Alright, enough with the suspense, where are we going?"

"We're going to walk down this street," I replied knowing that she was expecting more detail than that. I held out my arm and she grabbed on as we started walking west down Walnut. She pestered me for more information as we walked, but I didn't have to hold her off for long. We stopped at the entrance to the Hyatt just three blocks into our walk.

"Here we are," I said.

"Are you taking me to a conference?" she said jokingly, but with a tinge of disappointment in her voice.

"Of course not! You have to have more faith in me than that, Natalie."

"OK. I just know how you like to operate," she said giving me a squeeze.

We walked in the entrance to a buzzing lobby. There were people everywhere, many of them in formal attire, but they didn't appear to be all together. Saturdays were often this chaotic at the city's bigger hotels, especially in the summer. I led her through the lobby over to the escalators on the right. There were signs everywhere indicating which party was in which room, but I knew where we were going and we didn't linger long enough to read any of them.

We got off the escalator on the second floor and followed a few other couples down the wide hallway that led to a number of ballrooms. The area outside the final ballroom was set up for a wedding cocktail hour. I noticed off to the right a large table that housed the table cards and a series of pictures of the bride and groom and their families. I instinctively walked away from that display and directly toward the food, acting like we belonged there.

"What are we doing?" Natalie said through gritted teeth and gripping my arm with all of her might.

"Oh, look honey, here's some fruit," I said to her as we approached the first table of food. I grabbed a grape, turned to look at her, raised my eyebrows and popped it into my mouth. She started to shake at her head at me in disbelief and for a second, I thought this might be a bad idea.

"Do you think they'll bring around any of those little crab cakes or scallops wrapped in bacon?" she asked excitedly. "I love the scallops and bacon!"

I was relieved by her reaction. I knew right then we were going to have a lot of fun.

We made our way to one of the three bars set up in this makeshift cocktail area. I rarely drank but I found that it helped me take the edge off in these types of awkward situations. Besides, I needed to be a little tipsy in order to bust a move on the dance floor. I was beyond stiff without something to loosen me up. I'm sure I was no better after a few drinks, but at least I was smoother in my own mind.

"I might need something stronger," Natalie said when I asked the bartender what kind of wine they had.

"Totally agree," I said to Natalie. "I'll have a Stoli and Red Bull, and she'll have . . ." I said turning from the bartender back to Natalie.

"The same!"

Although I didn't drink often, I drank quickly. By the time we walked over to the antipasti table, I had nearly finished my first glass.

"Are you more nervous than me?" she asked, motioning toward my glass.

"It's a wedding, Natalie, we're supposed to celebrate," I replied.

"Well, let's party!" she said tipping back her glass.

"I smell bacon," I said eyeing a waitress coming our way. Sure enough, the tray contained a heaping amount of scallops wrapped in bacon.

"I called that one!" exclaimed Natalie.

"Impressive. So, can you believe that ceremony? Absolutely beautiful," I said with a raised voice, pretending to want to be overheard.

"So lovely," Natalie forced, embarrassed by my obnoxiousness.

"So, what do you think the bride and groom will do coming in? Are they going to be all fired up with a choreographed dance routine, or are they going to be complete duds?"

"I'm kind of impressed with the spread here and the bar selection, I have a good feeling about this party. I think they're the type to be fired up."

The area had really filled up and it was clearly a younger crowd. The doors to the reception hall opened and we could see many tables, enough to seat at least 300 people. There were food stations along the sides of the wall and one corner dedicated to desserts. Some people started to filter into the room, but we stayed outside observing the action. Natalie shared my love for people-watching and there was really no better place than a wedding reception for pure stranger entertainment.

"You guys don't want to go in either?" said a guy who walked up next to us with his date.

"Nah, we're just taking it all in," I replied on behalf of Natalie and me.

"We were just saying," he continued, "that we wished the cocktail hour went on all night. The food's great and booze always flows a little quicker."

"I agree!" chimed in Natalie. "I could eat these little things all night and not feel like a pig." She reached over and grabbed another cracker with cheese and tossed it into her mouth.

"The only problem is I'm feeling more than a buzz already," I added, laughing a little giddily.

"That's the point," said the woman who stepped forward with hand extended toward me. "I'm Amy and this is Jeremy." She motioned toward her date.

"I'm Drew and this is Natalie," I said putting my arm around Natalie's shoulders and pulling her toward me.

"Are you guys friends with Casey or Brian?" she asked us.

"Brian . . . from a long time ago," I lied.

"How about you guys?" asked Natalie, like she had been doing this all of her life.

"Oh, I work with Casey. I actually don't know Brian well at all. I don't think Jeremy has even met him, have you?"

"Nope," said Jeremy. "But I'm going to enjoy the hell out of this party anyway."

He raised his glass and finished the contents, which looked like a Jack and Coke. He set that glass down on a tray nearby, but had another full glass in his other hand ready to go.

"I don't know if I'll recognize him myself," I joked. "It's been a little while."

Natalie smacked me. "Of course you will."

Just then, a few of the waiters walked through the cocktail area ringing some bells which signaled that it was time to wrap it up and enter the hall. Those of us who were still lingering outside the ballroom were not particularly moved by these bells. We all paused long enough to recognize what we were supposed to do, but most of us just continued our conversations and didn't make a move in that direction.

"What do you say," I turned to Natalie, "one more Red Bull and vodka for the trip to dinner?"

"Let's do it before they close up shop," she replied.

"We'll see you guys inside," said Jeremy. "I guess we've got to find our seat."

Natalie had a death grip on my arm as we walked in the opposite direction from our new friends. I could hear her stifling a squeal under her breath. I could tell at that point that she wasn't as calm as she came across. When we were well out of earshot, she exhaled deeply as if she had been holding her breath for the last three minutes.

"Oh my God!"

"What? You handled that like a champ," I said encouragingly.

"I can't take the stress. We didn't have a game plan for that at all."

"That's what made it so much fun," I replied. "Sometimes it's more stressful to remember what the plan is than it is to just wing it altogether."

"I don't know. You're the expert here, but it seems like agreeing to some of the basics would be pretty helpful."

"I'm not the expert. I've only crashed alone. You're my first date. I've only had to keep track of my own stories before."

Once we had our third Red Bull and vodkas in hand, we started to drift toward the reception entrance. There were only a few stragglers left, as there were no waitresses offering trays of food any longer, and the bars looked like they were closed for the time being. Members of the wedding party were milling around a few feet from the cocktail area. The bride and groom likely had just arrived and would be making their way into the reception shortly.

"I never understood why the bride and groom miss out on their own cocktail hour," I said to Natalie.

"I don't think the day ever goes completely as planned," she replied.

"I understand but I would make sure I built in enough time to make it to my own party. Like Amy said, it's the best part."

"So, you're planning your wedding now?" she asked. "Is there something you want to tell me?"

"I'm just saying . . ."

At that moment a few other bridesmaids were walking toward the crowd, followed by a number of groomsmen. The time was getting close and we didn't want to be caught out there by ourselves. We walked into the reception hall for the first time and noticed numbers on each of the tables. We assumed they corresponded to the name tags that were placed on the table in the cocktail area. Luckily there were still a lot of people mingling with each other throughout the room, so it wouldn't be noticeable if we didn't find a seat right away.

If I were on my own, I would have left the area at that time without being noticed by the incoming wedding party and returned once people started to go through the buffet to get their dinners. But it was a little trickier to walk out with Natalie. Plus, I didn't want to shortchange her from the whole experience.

"Shouldn't we take a walk now and just come back later when the festivities heat up?" she suggested. "Then we wouldn't stick out nearly as much as we're about to."

"That's actually what I usually do, but I figured why not try to really live it up tonight."

"You're ridiculous. Do you think it's too late?"

As she said this, we both turned toward the open door behind us only to find the wedding party congregating right outside the door getting organized to make their entrance. We turned back toward each other.

"Guess so," I said.

We took one last look back at the scene before getting ready to get lost among the people in the reception. But this last look made me do a double take. Actually, it made us both do a double take as I could see Natalie jerk her head along with mine out of my peripheral vision. Two men were walking in the door and I could not believe what I was seeing. Both of them walked directly toward us, which wasn't much off course since we were still standing just a few feet inside the doorway.

"What are you doing here?" asked both men at exactly the same time with the same accusatory tone.

Natalie and I both looked at them, stunned. Realizing that they just asked the same question of us, Natalie and I turned toward each other and asked in unison, "you know him?"

"I'm so confused," said Tony. "Can someone tell me what the hell is going on?"

"Tony, this is Natalie," I said.

"Ah, Natalie," he said knowingly. Tony and Natalie shook hands.

"How are you doing, my name is Drew," I said holding my hand out to the man with Tony, not waiting for an introduction.

"William," he said in reply.

"How *are* you?" Natalie asked him, hesitantly.

"So, you guys know each other too?" Tony asked, slowly piecing it all together.

"You could say that," replied William. "I'm good Natalie, a little surprised to see you here."

"Yeah," Tony continued the thought, "do you guys know Brian or Casey?"

As if choreographed, Natalie said "Brian" at the exact time I said "Casey."

We both started backtracking immediately. I started saying that I know Brian too, but that I knew Casey first, while at the same time, Natalie said that she hopes to get to know Casey better tonight but that she felt closer to Brian thus far. None of it made sense and all of it made us look like we were bumbling idiots trying to hide something. It didn't take Tony more than a second to figure it out.

"You guys don't know them at all, do you?" he asked with a cross between a smile as a scowl. "Oh my God, what are you doing?" he asked, directed at me.

"Natalie? Is that true?" William looked completely bewildered.

Before Natalie could respond, the emcee barked, "Ladies and gentlemen, it is time to introduce the wedding party!"

Loud hip hop began to play and the whole room broke into a cheer and everyone turned toward the door. At that moment, the door to the room swung open not ten feet away from us with a pair of grandparents holding hands and staring back at the crowd. I could not help but burst into laughter at the absurdity of the scene as I quickly stepped out of the pathway and against the wall. Natalie, Tony and William took an extra second to comprehend what was transpiring, but joined me by the wall a moment later.

"They looked psyched to walk out to Beyoncé, don't they?" I joked, making it clear that the awkwardness of our meeting wasn't going to stop me from having a good time. Tony just shook his head at me, Natalie tried to stifle a giggle, and William stared in general disbelief at Natalie.

The emcee introduced two sets of grandparents followed by two sets of parents. The wedding party came next. As predicted, each pair in the wedding party did a little routine before walking through the crowd.

When the third couple did a synchronized running man before breaking into walking stride, Tony turned to us and said, "That's my wife!"

Nikki walked past without noticing us, thank God. I hadn't had time to think about her reaction to me crashing this wedding reception. I was sure she would give me a hard time, and rightfully so. I imagined how strange this must look to the average person, let alone a member of the wedding party.

The fourth couple did a risqué version of the sprinkler in unison. As they started to walk into the crowd, the woman spotted us and waved flirtatiously in our direction. Whether as a result of her seductive dancing or her bridesmaid dress, she looked incredible. I know women always say that they hate their bridesmaid dresses, but I was always a sucker for them. This one was blue, cut just below the knee and light and flowing: the kind that rose teasingly upon movement.

"That's my date," said William, for the first time taking his eyes off Natalie. Tony and I nodded at him secretly, acknowledging our approval of her level of hotness, as if men abided by some unspoken code in these situations. Natalie looked at him with sheer surprise.

That's when it dawned on me that this was William. Natalie's William. Not just some ordinary William. I don't know why I hadn't figure it out before. I guess the chaos of the moment clouded my observation skills. It suddenly made perfect sense why they had such a strong reaction to seeing each other and why William couldn't seem to stop staring.

Immediately, I felt bad for Natalie. She didn't exactly sign up for any of this, particularly not a chance run-in with her longtime ex-boyfriend. I also felt a little bad for me. Spending time with someone like William, who knew Natalie so much better than I did, wasn't exactly what I had in mind either. I had no one to blame but myself, of course, so I decided that I had no other choice than to make the best of it.

"Do you hate me yet?" I asked into Natalie's ear with the music still blaring and the best man and maid of honor walking onto the dance floor to join the other members of the wedding party.

She looked up at me, winked and said, "Not yet."

Within a few minutes, the bride and groom had been introduced and were swaying happily in their first dance. The emcee asked the rest of the wedding party to join about halfway through the song. With the focus of attention shifted to the front of the room, we no longer had to cling to the wall.

"So, where are you two wise guys going to sit," asked Tony of Natalie and me. Tony put his arm around my neck and pulled me roughly but playfully into him.

"We might take your seats if you're not careful," replied Natalie.

"I wouldn't put anything past you, that's for sure," Tony responded, smiling for the first time since he saw us.

"I think we might go for a little walk until this party heats up a bit," I chimed in. "We'll be back to eat, don't you worry."

"I don't get it," said William. "You guys seriously don't have a seat? You really weren't invited?"

"It's called a wedding crash, didn't you see the movie?" asked Natalie jokingly.

"Yes, with you. I didn't actually think people did this in real life. I don't even know what to say."

"No need to say anything," Natalie continued. "Just enjoy your dinner and we'll see you guys on the dance floor in a little bit. I want to see if Tony's running man is half as good as his wife's."

Natalie grabbed me by the hand and led me out of the room, leaving both of them shaking their heads again. When we were safely on the other side of the door, we broke into laughter and ran down the hall as if we were escaping. I wasn't sure how Natalie was going to respond to what just happened. Actually, I wasn't sure how I was going to respond either. This wedding was turning out to be a lot more fun than we bargained for.

"I can't believe that just happened," said Natalie still giggling in excitement.

"That was pretty wild," I responded.

I pulled her over to a set of double doors that led to an outdoor terrace overlooking Walnut Street. We walked to the balcony before turning to each other. Natalie immediately gave me a bear hug, burying her head in my chest. I wasn't sure if she did that to make me feel better or herself. Or perhaps the she just needed to release some of the energy generated by the extreme awkwardness of the previous hour, particularly the last 15 minutes.

"You OK?" I asked quietly.

"Yes! I think. I mean that was absolutely exhilarating. Bizarre and almost out-of-body, but somehow really fun."

"Good," I said, sounding relieved.

"What about you? That must have been a little strange even to you, right?"

"Ah, yeah, completely crazy. It all happened so fast I don't know if I'm in a state of shock or if it really was just too fun to get bothered by."

"So, that was William."

"Thanks."

"And apparently his new girlfriend."

"I know, are you pissed?"

"No, why would I be pissed?"

"I don't know. Some girls would be pissed because she was hot. Others would be pissed that she existed at all."

"*I* left *him*, remember."

"I remember, but there's still an adjustment to seeing someone you love with someone else."

I actually chose my words carefully because I wanted to let her know that I didn't expect her to simply drop all feelings for this guy who was such a large part of her life. I knew that just because you fall out of love with someone doesn't mean you necessarily stop loving them. I wanted Natalie to know that was OK and that I understood. Of course, she fought it nonetheless.

"I don't love William."

"You know what I mean."

"I guess. It was strange seeing him in that setting and with another girl."

"Do I sense an ounce of jealousy?"

"No, I don't think so," she said with a little too much honesty. "It's just . . . different. I don't think I've ever seen him with someone else. Ever."

"I see."

She paused, clearly trying to decipher her thoughts and feelings.

"Are you freaked out?" She looked at me, suddenly concerned.

"No," I replied with some hesitancy. "I don't think I have the right to be. I think it's something you guys will have to confront at some point and you're either OK with it or you're not."

"Why are you so level-headed?"

"I'm crying on the inside."

"Sure you are. Tony sure looked surprised to see you."

"He sure did. I think he might have been more surprised I was with you than that we were crashing the wedding."

"And why would that be?" Natalie asked accusatorily.

"No. Nothing negative about you. Just the opposite actually. He gives me a hard time about . . . oh, never mind."

"Drew Kelley. You better finish that sentence right now. Considering the level of disclosure we have with each other so far, you best be willing to tell me anything now."

"I am, don't worry. Let me put it this way, he'll be proud of me for seeing you again."

"Not good enough. Sorry."

"He knows how much I like you and he has been known to encourage me to actually spend time with someone that I like . . . like you."

"Well, that was before he knew I was the wedding crasher type. I'm sure he wouldn't be so proud now."

"He is, trust me. But I don't care if he is. I'm proud of me and that's what counts."

I picked Natalie up and spun her around. The spinning didn't sit well with either of us, so I quickly put her down. I knew I was pretty tipsy and I figured Natalie must have been feeling the same or worse. We each had three cocktails in under an hour, and neither one of us were accustomed to that kind of binge.

"Wow, are you still spinning me?" she asked seconds after I had put her down.

"I think we better eat some more, I am really feeling it."

"OK, do you think it's safe to go back in?"

"Of course, what else could go wrong?"

When we walked back toward the reception, we could see that the doors were propped open and that people were freely walking in and out. The bars in the cocktail area were reopened and the little formality there was to this reception appeared to be over. It was a perfect time for us to drift back in and assimilate into the crowd. There were small lines at most of the buffet stations but it looked like all of the tables had an opportunity to get their food.

We took a walk by each of the stations to see what the options were before settling on a buffet station with a short line. After filling our plates, we grabbed extra utensils that were placed at the end of one of the serving tables. I didn't want to take anyone's place setting and I definitely didn't want to sit down at one of the tables where people already were sitting. Instead, we walked back toward the entrance that the wedding party used when joining the reception. Without obviously hiding against the wall, we stood out of the main pathway just enough to not be in the way or noticed for hiding in the corner. The food was delicious and I immediately felt my head returning to normal. I wasn't done drinking for the night, that was for sure, but I at least wanted some food in my stomach so I didn't get sick or lose the ability to function.

By the time we finished, the music had started and people began to descend upon the dance floor. We set our plates down on an abandoned table and went out to the bar for another drink. With Red Bull and vodka in tow, we joined the mob that had begun dancing.

For the first 25 years of my life, I was too shy to dance. That doesn't mean I never did it. It just means that I did it rarely and not very well. To enjoy it and do a halfway decent job of it, you have to lose your inhibitions and just live in the moment. I used to have record amounts of inhibitions, but thankfully they slowly started to fade as I got older. I began to care less of what people thought of me and more about doing things that made me happy. Dancing, as it turned out, could be downright fun if done with the right people and in the right setting.

Since Natalie was virtually kryptonite to my remaining inhibitions, dancing with her was extraordinarily fun. It was at once goofy, sexy, and borderline reckless. I'm sure it was not a pretty sight, but I felt like I could pull off any move imaginable. The vodka helped more than a little.

"I'm not going to let you have all the fun!" Tony yelled in my ear as he cut in between Natalie and me to bust a move of his own. I wasn't surprised that Tony was a good dancer, significantly smoother than I could ever be. He brought out the sexy side of Natalie as easily as I had brought out the goofy side.

"Hi Nikki," I said leaning in for a hug and a kiss.

"I hope you saved some of those moves for me," she replied disarmingly. I'm sure she thought I was nuts for being there, but she didn't act like it as she grabbed my hand, raised it in the air and spun herself around underneath my arm.

"Of course!"

We spent the next 30 minutes moving with the music, along with what seemed like the entire crowd. I usually liked a packed dance floor because it was fun to float between the attractive women in the crowd. But on this occasion, I solely focused on Natalie. I was aware of the crowd around us, but they were nothing more than background noise compared to her.

Eventually the music stopped and the emcee announced that it was time for the father-daughter dance, which meant it was time for us to step outside to get some air. Nikki had to be the good bridesmaid and watch the dance, but Tony walked out with us. When we walked through the doors, I noticed William's girlfriend walking in, probably to watch the special dance, too. I looked in the direction from which she came and spotted William standing by the bar alone. I turned to Natalie and knew she saw the same thing. I could tell by her expression that she was considering how to handle the situation.

"Why don't you go catch up for a bit?" I suggested. "Tony and I will take a walk outside on the balcony."

"You think?" she asked, not seeking my permission as much as wondering out loud whether it was a good idea.

"Of course. It will be good for both of you to talk."

"Thanks," she said as she walked toward William.

I wrapped my arm around Tony's neck and pulled him down the hall toward the doors to the balcony. He waited until we got outside before he gave me a hard time.

"What have you gotten yourself into, man?"

"Aw, come on. It's been fun, right?"

"I guess," he said, not able to prevent himself from laughing at me. "I didn't know you could let your hair down like that, you're not that much of a stiff after all."

"Gee, thanks. What a compliment."

"I'd say stick to shooting, but I don't want to discourage you. You actually looked like you were enjoying yourself."

"She's great, isn't she?" I asked, cutting to the chase.

"She seems it. I have to question her judgment to willingly come here with you though."

"That wasn't her fault. This was sort of a surprise."

"Then I just have to question your judgment I guess. You thought this was going to win her over?"

"I think I was right. Scary, huh?"

"I don't get it."

"Which part?"

"Any of it."

"Hey, I thought you were the one encouraging me to go on more than just one date with a girl."

"I was. I was. Actually, you guys seem great together. You know Nikki will insist on you guys coming over to spend some normal quality time with us."

"We would love that."

"I'm happy for you buddy. I don't know how this hot girl is still talking to you after knowing that you live in the gym. But I got to hand it to you. You duped her somehow."

"Charmed. Can we use charmed instead? Look. I'm not getting married tomorrow. I just like spending time with her in a way that I never have before. She's real. She's honest. She's fun. And she brings out the best in me . . . and she still likes me."

"Speaking of the devil," Tony said looking over my shoulder as Natalie approached us.

"Boys," she said. "I hope you had something more exciting to talk about than me."

"Um, not really," replied Tony.

"Well, I can leave you to it if you want to continue," she pretended to turn around to walk away.

"No, we covered it already," said Tony. "I got to get back to attend to my lovely wife. You, my dear, will have to spend some time with us in the very near future."

"I would love that," said Natalie.

"Hi," I said to her after Tony walked away. I didn't want to ask about William if she didn't want to talk about it, or if she had any bad news for me.

"That went surprisingly well, thanks for encouraging me to talk to him."

"That's great," I said, fighting the urge to push for more information.

"He actually seems . . . happy."

"Are you disappointed about that?" I asked teasingly.

"No. Just surprised. It seems like he has come to terms with things in a different way than ever before."

"So, he's over you and you're not upset?"

"I don't know. I guess. I mean I guess he's over me. I'm definitely not upset. It's just strange. I've gotten so accustomed to seeing him in pain that it's weird to see something different."

"Was it awkward?"

"Not really. A little awkward trying to explain the wedding crasher part, but he even handled that well. I think he's in a good place."

"Cool."

"You know, I think I'm acting so weird because I have been living with guilt for so long. I don't know how I'm supposed to feel if he's actually fine now."

"Maybe you're supposed to let it go," I suggested.

"I'm sure you're right," she agreed. "Want to dance?"

"Sure, do you?"

"I really do. Let's have some fun!"

We spent the rest of the night on the dance floor in our own little world. We had connected on so many levels during our first few encounters. I wanted to see if we could just let ourselves go and have fun together—and I had my answer.

CHAPTER 20

It was just after 4:30 when I awoke. I wanted badly to keep sleeping, but I was supposed to meet my sister Devin for dinner at 5:30 and I needed to shower and change first. I should have been well rested, considering I got seven hours of sleep, several hours more than usual. I had gone straight to the park after basketball, skipping my breakfast routine. I wasn't as hungry as I normally would have been anyway because of the wedding feast the night before. Plus I knew I would have a good meal for dinner. Big sisters were good at feeding little brothers. But I was still exhausted. Maybe the wedding crash was more emotionally and physically draining than I thought.

As I walked toward the gym to get ready, I started to get excited about seeing Devin. Although we often went months between visits, we always seemed to pick up just where we left off. She had been my best friend since the day I was born. Even though she was three years older, we did a lot of things together growing up. I wanted to do everything she did and go everywhere she went. Luckily she liked having a shadow.

As adults, we remained tight, but we didn't live in the same city and we weren't exactly at the same points in our lives. She moved back to our hometown a few years ago, got married to my brother-in-law Bradley, and hangs out with my parents on a regular basis. In contrast, I have lived the single, city life and have avoided my parents as much as possible. Devin and I still loved each other but our lives were completely foreign to one another. I don't know how she did it—never really moving on from the life she grew up with—and she didn't understand why I didn't want to move back and recreate that life for myself. She didn't know the half of it of course.

Despite the anticipation of seeing Devin, my mind kept returning to the events of the wedding. The whole experience seemed so surreal. What were the chances of seeing Tony and William like that? Did Natalie still have feelings for William, or more accurately, what was the nature of her feelings? As bizarre as the scene was, there was something completely peaceful about drifting in and out of sleep all night with Natalie wrapped in my arms while laying on a college library sofa. It was one of the spontaneous, fun, quirky nights that you never forget. It was the perfect date. We passed the fun test with flying colors.

I walked out of the gym onto the street right at 5:30. Devin agreed to meet me at the gym since most of the restaurants were within a few blocks of this spot. She had suggested meeting at my place but I convinced her of this alternative for obvious reasons. Devin did not know the details about my lifestyle and I didn't plan on divulging that kind of information anytime soon.

There were multiple parking garages in the vicinity of the gym, so I wasn't sure from which direction Devin would come. I was looking westward when I heard footsteps quickly approaching me from the east. I turned just in time to see my sister running toward me and lunge at me. She was sprinting so fast that I think she was trying to tackle me to the ground. I staggered back but caught her and gave her a long hug. She was happy to see me and had her unique way to show it.

"Aw, I missed you little bro!"

"Hey Dev, great to see you!"

"Have you gotten bigger? I think I was able knock you over last time I saw you."

"No, just a little more alert to your attacks, that's all."

"Whatever, I could have snuck up on you if I'd really wanted to."

"So, what's up? Did you find a place to park alright?"

"Yeah, no problem. You think I can't handle this little city of yours."

"You're not in Kansas anymore, Dorothy."

"Ah, I've never been to Kansas and you can just call me Devin."

"Whatever, it's good to have you here."

I gave her another hug and quickly studied her face. It has been awhile since we saw each other and I wanted to get a good look at her. Something was different about her but I couldn't immediately identify it. She had the same perfect smile as always, and her eyes were exactly the same shade of blue as mine. Her hair was still blonde, even though it was naturally a shade or two darker. In typical Devin fashion, she wore a pair of stylish jeans and a fairly plain-looking shirt. She had always been well dressed, but never quite on the cutting edge. Not that I had any fashion sense of my own—I wore virtually the same clothes every day for God's sakes—but I could tell that she lagged behind the most current styles you'd see in the city.

"Well it's great to be here. Even if I have to trek down to the hood to see you."

Devin was much tougher than she seemed. I joked with her about being a country bumpkin, but she actually went to college in a much more urban area than where I attended. She prefers the burbs now but she could more than handle the city if she wanted to.

189

"Are you hungry?" I asked.

"Sure, are you?"

"Yeah, where do you want to eat? What are you in the mood for?"

"I don't care. Why don't you pick. I'm taking you out."

"No, then you should pick. Pasta, steak, fish, burger, salad . . . you tell me that and I'll find you the right place."

"I'm in the mood for a burger. Is that bad? I should eat better, but I can't help what I like, right?"

"Of course. Let's go to *Rouge*. It's cool, it's got great outdoor seating, and it's known for its burgers."

"Perfect."

"OK, this way," I said leading her west along Walnut.

We arrived early enough that we were immediately seated outdoors along the sidewalk. Any later and we would have been waiting at least 30 minutes, even on a Sunday night. The weather was perfect, still warm but not as muggy as earlier in the day. It was a great spot to eat, overlooking the square. I passed by *Rouge* almost every day, but I had only eaten there a time or two over the years. It wasn't cheap.

Devin caught me up on our parents and what was new in Flemington. I wasn't completely out of touch, but Devin always had a different perspective on things than my parents did, especially on my parents themselves. Devin thought they were good overall but said they wished I came around more often. That always hurt to hear, but I had my reasons and felt everyone was better off with a little distance.

"OK, enough about Mom and Dad and Flemington," said Devin. "What's going on with you? Anything new and exciting in your life?"

I was so accustomed to not sharing anything personal with anyone that I assumed that some nonsense would naturally flow out of my mouth along the lines of *same old same old.* Much to my surprise, however, and completely unintentionally, I began to smile and could not look up at Devin. I'm not sure who was more surprised by that reaction, me or Devin.

"Are you blushing?" Devin practically yelled. "What happened?"

"No, nothing," I stammered.

"Something happened or you wouldn't be acting so strangely."

"Nothing happened, I'm only smiling because I knew you'd ask about my love life."

"I didn't ask about your love life. I just asked what is new and exciting, but I think I have my answer. Drew! Do tell!"

Now laughing, I replied, "I have no explanation for that reaction. I have been spending time with someone new but . . . but . . . was I really blushing?"

"Bright red!"

"Ugh, that's not good."

"Listen, you little punk. You better give me every last detail or I'm going to pull it out of your throat, word by word," she said threateningly.

"Her name is Natalie. I met her a few weeks ago. We went on a few dates and she's . . . well . . . she's pretty great."

"Oh-kay. Let's hear some details."

"Well, she's, she's not like anyone I've ever met."

"Where did you meet?"

"Uh, here in the city. I met her just randomly. Actually, I met her just randomly three different times in the course of three days. Even I knew enough to read the signs at that point."

"That's cute. Completely random?"

"Yes. I didn't want to leave it up to chance any longer, so we made plans to go to dinner."

"Go on . . ."

"Dinner was awesome. We had great conversations. She loves ice cream. It was perfect."

Devin stared at me in disbelief, partly because I was sharing, and partly because it was taking me so long to get out the details of the story. She was always frustrated by how slow I told a story, let alone one that I hadn't intended to tell at all. I knew I had no choice but to continue.

"She invited me out to her house for dinner a few nights later. She lives in the burbs in a great little neighborhood. She cooked. I ate. We laughed. It was great."

"Continue please," ordered Devin, clearly annoyed with me, but not wanting to protest too much in fear that I might stop altogether.

"Our third date was last night. We went to a wedding together and it was a blast. Crazy and wild, but a blast."

"Really? Who got married?"

"Ah, you don't know them . . . and I really don't either."

"That doesn't make sense, but I don't really care about that right now. What do you like about her?"

"Well, she has a number of amazing qualities, one of which is that she brings out a side of me that I haven't seen in a long time, maybe ever."

"She found your dark side?" Devin asked, laughing because she always complains that I'm overly optimistic in life.

"No," I replied laughing as well, "more like . . . the honest side."

"Are you dishonest?" Devin asked with a quizzical look on her face.

"No, I just don't feel the need to divulge details of my personal life or opinions as much as the normal person."

"Are you talking about your aversion to Facebook again?"

"No . . . well . . . it's related I guess. It's more serious than that. I just tend to be coy about who I am and what I do with my time and with Natalie, everything just spills out of my mouth beyond my control."

"Wow! That is a great power!"

"I know. Not unlike a super power, I agree!"

"I'm serious. That is certainly unique. I know how you are and how you like to keep a certain distance, with everyone except me of course, right?"

"Right. And Natalie I guess. I'm not really doing her justice either. She's smart, beautiful, funny, fun. All the great qualities you want in a person. Plus there's this special piece of her personality that draws people to her. She infectious . . . but she doesn't have any diseases if you know what I mean."

"I know what you mean, Drew. Not to worry."

"So, that's it. That's all that's new and exciting with me. Your turn."

"Well, what a great answer. I'm very happy for you. I have another hundred questions but I don't want to annoy you any more than I already have."

"For some reason, I don't think I could get sick of talking about her. I definitely don't get sick of thinking about her. Or seeing her, or . . . sorry, are you still here?"

"That is awesome. What do you think will happen next? Where is this going?"

"I hope it goes exactly as it has been going. I hope this doesn't change in any way."

"Just indefinitely?"

"Well, yeah, if possible. Look, I know nothing beats the first few dates, that's why I usually end things right then. But I think this one could work beyond that. She gets me and I think I get her."

"Drew, no girl, no matter how cool, wants to spend time with someone if it's destined to go nowhere."

"I don't know if that's true. I mean, I think it's possible. I've dated girls like you're describing. Even though they say they don't want anything, they eventually do."

"Exactly!"

"But I think Natalie is different. She accepts me for who I am. More than accepts, she appreciates. She doesn't want to change me. She enjoys spending time with me now. I can't see her all of a sudden not enjoying it because our relationship hasn't changed or progressed in some old-fashioned manner. In fact, she's been there and it wasn't all that great."

"She's been in an 'old-fashioned' relationship?" Devin asked, mocking me with her air quotes. "You mean she's had an actual boyfriend and tried to make it work and it turned out that they broke up?"

Devin didn't give me a chance to respond.

"That's not an affront to all relationships," she continued. "That's just life. Some things work out and some things don't. It doesn't mean it's not worth trying."

"When it comes to relationships, I think it actually isn't worth trying."

"Oh Lord, you've lost your mind."

"You think I'm crazy but it's a fact. Most relationships are destined to fail, either by break up or by hidden unhappiness."

"No, you're crazy because you think this amazing woman you just described believes that."

"I didn't say *she* believes that."

"You think she's OK with the fact that *you* believe that, is that what you're saying?"

"I guess so. Did I just win that argument or lose it?"

"You never win against your big sister, you know that."

We both laughed because we both knew that was true. It wasn't the first time a conversation with Devin left me more confused when it was over than when it started. She was calling into question whether my relationship with Natalie—I hadn't officially committed to that word relationship yet either—could continue as it was without progressing into something deeper. I knew that we would get closer over time; there was no disputing that fact. But to consider where it was "going" seemed artificial to me and not the essence of our relationship in the first place. Natalie admired my theory of putting happiness first and letting that guide your actions. Not doing it the other way around.

As I sat there sifting through my French Fries without really eating them, I began to wonder if Devin had a legitimate point. What she described was actually the very reason I rarely went beyond date number two with anyone. I hadn't made an exception to that rule in over two years. Why did I think it would be different with Natalie? In truth, until Devin started asking about it, I don't think I had really thought it through. I tried to defend why this situation with Natalie might be different, but I hadn't considered that in advance. I just kept seeing her because I really wanted to keep seeing her. Why was that? Did the happiness of seeing her outweigh the future unhappiness that inevitably comes with an ongoing relationship?

"Well, I can see that I at least gave you something to think about," Devin said, referencing the fact that I had been lost in my own head for a few moments.

"I don't know what you're talking about," I said playfully.

"Well, you're going to have to figure that mess out later. I have something to tell you."

"You're moving back in with Mom and Dad?" I guessed, sarcastically.

"I'm pregnant!"

"What?" I yelled a little too loud. "Congratulations!"

"Thank you Drew," Devin replied, now beaming.

"I can't believe you waited until we downed two burgers before you told me that!" I scolded her.

"Sorry, I couldn't keep it in any longer." She literally looked like she was about to burst.

"Devin," I said gravely. "Whose baby is it?"

"Brad's you idiot," she said throwing her napkin across the table at me. I got up and walked around the table to give her a hug. She clung on to me even tighter than she did when she arrived a few hours earlier. She was a happy woman. I sat back down shaking my head in disbelief. Now I understood what looked different about her. She wasn't showing at all but she had that unmistakable glow that comes with pregnancy, especially a first one.

"Are you actually surprised?" Devin asked.

"Yes! I guess I shouldn't have been?" I asked back.

"No. I'm 30 and have been married for almost three years. These things tend to happen you know."

"I guess I still picture us as kids, pretending to be in the real world. Even your wedding seemed like you were just acting. Not that you didn't mean it, I just mean it seemed more like a fairy tale than it did like real life."

"This is real, the doctor said the baby is healthy and I'm due in February."

"Do you know if it's a boy or a girl yet?"

"We will find out next month, but I think it's a girl."

"What are you talking about? Did she whisper that to you or something?"

"No, mothers just know these things."

"Oh my God, you're going to be a mother. That's insane!"

"Gee thanks."

"No I mean I can't believe you're actually going to have another being pop out of your body."

"Drew," she said looking me deep in the eyes, "I've never

been so happy in my life. This is the most exciting thing I've ever experienced. I have a little person growing inside me. I don't know what she's going to look like or sound like or what she's going to want to be when she grows up. She's going to be part me and part Brad. Every day is going to bring something new and precious to our lives. We actually created this little being, with a little help from God, of course. I am so excited I can't even describe it. Drew, you're going to be singing this tiny person to sleep one day."

Devin started to cry. Then I started to cry. It finally hit me what this meant to my sister: how much she was going to love nurturing and caring for her own child; how she was going to be an incredible mother; how her child was so incredibly lucky to be born into Devin's family and to be loved like she was going to be loved. I don't know if I had ever been so happy for someone before.

"Thank you for being the best brother, Drew," Devin said through a steady stream of tears. "It means so much to me that you are happy for me."

"Of course, Devin. I always want the best for you and this is the absolute greatest thing I've ever heard."

"I know!" Devin exclaimed, somehow managing a huge smile while the tears kept streaming.

Then something else hit me. Something I didn't see coming. For just a brief moment, I saw Natalie sitting across me crying with joy the same way Devin was. What a beautiful sight it is when someone you care that much about is that happy. This vision struck a chord deep in my heart. I immediately wanted nothing more than for Natalie to experience the greatest joy a woman could have, just like Devin.

The thought of Natalie beaming with happiness was exhilarating. I started to cry harder. That's when I became overwhelmed by the thought that I could never offer that to

Natalie. I realized that as long as I was involved with Natalie, she would not be experiencing this ultimate joy. The fact that I hadn't cried a drop in years made it all the more powerful that tears began pouring out of my eyes. I wasn't sobbing. I didn't make a sound. I just had a wave of emotions running through me that caused what seemed like a faucet to turn on. What started as happy tears became tears of disappointment and sadness.

"What is wrong with you?" Natalie said, rightfully concerned.

"Nothing. I'm so sorry. I am so happy for you. And so happy for Bradley."

"I know you are, but something else is going on."

"No, no. I'm just a little overwhelmed is all."

"You can tell me. Does this make you sad? Did I do something . . ."

"No!" I cut her off. "Please don't say that. I am truly happy for you."

I reached across the table and grabbed her hands and looked her in the eyes so she understood my sincerity.

"Drew, please tell me why you're still crying," Natalie begged.

I breathed a deep sigh and try to get a hold of myself. It all happened so fast that I had not sorted out this emotional outburst yet. What I said next was completely unfiltered.

"Devin, I've never seen you so moved and happy in all of my life. For some reason, I started to think that I wanted that kind of happiness for Natalie. I know that sounds crazy but I guess I feel so strongly about her. The problem is that I know I can't provide that kind of happiness for her."

"What are you talking about?" asked Devin incredulously.

"She deserves the very best. She deserves what you have. And I can't give her that."

"Can't or won't? You need to get over yourself. You don't need to commit tomorrow but to block yourself off from ever going there isn't fair to yourself."

"There's more to it than that," I said, knowing that she was not getting the full picture.

"I don't think there is," Devin challenged.

"Devin, trust me. It's more than a small case of commitment phobia. Creating a family is impossible with the way I live my life."

"Why?" she asked.

I could feel the truth about to leap from my lips and something about my emotional state fought off my usual instinct to keep in the truth. I simply let it out.

"Well, let's see. I don't have a job and therefore I have no money. I don't have a house, or an apartment or any place to call my own. I have nearly no belongings aside from the clothes on my back. I just live. I love my life. I love that I play basketball every single day. I love that I can do whatever makes me happy on any given day at any given moment. I love the freedom that comes with not living by the rules of society."

"Drew, are you homeless?"

"No, no, not at all. And don't for a second feel sorry for me because this is the way I live entirely by choice. I had plenty of money. I quit my job. I chose to get rid of my junk and only keep the bare minimum. I have never felt so good about where I am in life."

"Where do you sleep?" Her eyes looked both concerned and hurt. I knew it would offend her to some degree that I had never confided in her and that she had never been given a chance to help.

"I sleep in the park most days, at the college on colder days."

"That's being homeless."

"No, I sleep there during the day while others are playing or picnicking. I sleep under a tree in the shade. It's actually awesome. I spend my nights doing things like going to bookstores or cafés. But most of the night I spend at the gym."

"You're kidding."

"No. The gym is open 24/7. I work out from 3:00 until about 5:00 or so. Take a break in the sauna or Jacuzzi and then we play basketball starting at 6:00. It works out great."

"OK, then how do you eat if you have no money?"

"Well, that's a little less cute."

"Let's hear it." For the first time, I sensed slight amusement in Devin's voice.

"You know how most hotels downtown have a steady stream of conferences or conventions? Well, they do and they always provide huge amounts of food in the hallways outside the conference rooms. They have three times as much food as the attendees could possibly eat. The rest of it literally goes to waste. Straight in the garbage."

"So you pick it out of the garbage?" she said, almost hopefully.

"One step ahead. I just pretend like I'm attending the conference and help myself to the food. I know I might go to hell but seriously, no one is worse off for it. Not one bit."

"Oh my God," she said quietly.

"Are you going to disown me?"

"No. I'm pissed that you never told me this, of course, but I think my intrigue is outweighing that for the moment. I'm fascinated that you've pulled this off. How long has this been going on?"

"A few years now. Obviously no one knows. Except Natalie. And now my friend Tony. I confessed to him the other day too. I'm telling you she has surgically removed my filter. I don't know how she did it."

"So you shower and take care of all of your hygiene at the gym. You steal your food. You play all night and sleep all day. There's no need for any money. Wait! How do you pay for the gym?"

"I worked out a deal where I ref a few basketball games for the league there and they give me a free membership. Not a bad gig, huh?"

"Oh my God," she said again.

"You keep saying that."

"I can't believe you. Wait 'til I tell mom and dad this one."

She burst out laughing before I had a chance to protest. It was a good sign that she was already able to joke about this. I felt like another enormous weight was lifted off my shoulders after having told her this.

"Now you see why I can't have a family. I didn't mean to ruin your moment. I hope I didn't and that you understand how happy I am for you. I just couldn't help but think about Natalie and obviously I'm disappointed that my lifestyle isn't conducive to making her happy like that. I can never provide for a family."

"Drew, you are an amazing person and you can make anyone happy if you feel like it. I want you to know that I am proud of you for living the life you want to lead, whether that makes you sad or happy in the long run, it doesn't matter. You are you and that's what counts. I love you."

"I love you too, sis!"

CHAPTER 21

Most people would probably assume it was difficult to live as I did: sleeping on the ground, wearing the same clothes day after day, having nothing to call my own, and never knowing exactly where I was going to get my next meal. But I always thought of it as fun, like it was a game. It was a challenge that I enjoyed, relished actually. I liked being off the grid, relatively speaking at least. I liked being self-reliant, or at least a form of it, considering I hypocritically relied upon conference food for sustenance. I just liked doing my own thing at any point in time, answering to no one but myself. The relationships in my life clearly suffered as a result of this philosophy, but I established my happiness as my number one priority and I followed my heart each and every day to attain that happiness.

From my perspective, life was actually easy for me. The most difficult decisions I faced each day was whether to have the pancakes or the French toast, to pass or to shoot, to read or to write. Sure there were the occasional challenges of dealing with my family but those were truly few and far between.

So as I sat on Natalie's front porch watching a few children play in the yard across the street, I was struck by how heavy I felt. I wasn't sure if the weight was bearing down on my shoulders or on my heart. I just knew that I had made the most difficult decision I remembered ever making.

I didn't know what time Natalie got home from work on a typical day. She had recently made an effort to get home earlier than she used to, a result of a recent priority shift she attributed to me. I got there at 5:00 pm, assuming that I might be there a while before she arrived. I just wanted to be sure to catch her as soon as I could, for her sake and mine. I needed to tell her what I had decided and why. Whether it would make sense to her or not was another story.

I had not scripted exactly what I wanted to say to Natalie. I figured I would just speak from the heart since that is what happened when I spoke to her anyway. The only thing I worried about was getting her to understand that my decision was driven by selfless motives rather than for my typical selfish reasons. I was also worried about hurting her. I had broken my golden rule by dating her as long as I did— even though it was only three dates—and I had a feeling I was about to pay the price.

When I saw Natalie's car turn into her driveway just after 5:00, my heart sank. I wished I had more time to rehearse. I was overcome with a feeling of dread that this wasn't going to go well and that I had made, or was about to make, a huge mistake.

She got out of her car and smiled at me, but didn't have her usual bounce in her step as she walked over to me. I smiled at her, but remained sitting, partly because I didn't want to seem overly enthusiastic about seeing her because of the reason for my visit. But mostly I didn't move because I was paralyzed by a combination of nervousness, fear and utter lack of confidence.

"Are you lost?" Natalie called out to me as she walked down the pathway that led from the driveway to her front steps. She looked at me inquisitively, gauging my body language for a sign of why I showed up unexpectedly.

"I always hang out on this stoop when you're at work, I didn't realize you'd be home so soon." I replied.

"Yeah, I've been leaving more work on my desk for the next day than I used to," she said as she sat down on the step next to me. "I learned that skill from a wise young man that I know."

She did not greet me with a kiss or hug or even a touch on the arm. With instincts like hers, it was no surprise that she sensed some negative energy coming from me. She could read my feelings from a mile away.

"I don't know about that. He's probably as far from wise as they come."

She smiled at me and took an obvious, deep breath. "What's up, Drew?" she asked in a quiet voice.

"I don't know Natalie. I think I'm losing my mind. I don't know how to say this . . ."

"Just tell me what's on your mind," she said calmly. There was a long pause as I struggled to find the words.

"We've never had problems sharing before," she said encouragingly.

"Look, Natalie, I'm crazy about you. I can't get enough of you. You're all I think about and the last few weeks have been incredible. My sister told me last night that she's pregnant. I've never seen someone so happy in my life. She is truly blessed with a wonderful husband and a baby in her belly who will change her life forever. As overwhelmed as I was for her happiness, I was equally devastated at the thought that you might miss out on that if you spend your life slumming it with me.

"I know, I know," I continued. "You never said anything about spending your life with me and I'm not that full of myself to think you would ever consider doing so. It's just that any time you spend with me is time diverting you from the path toward experiencing the greatest joys in the world—the joys of motherhood.

"It crushes me that in essence I'm no good for you. And it crushes me more that I simply can't provide for you those joys. You, more than anyone I've ever met in my life, deserve those joys. I saw it so clearly last night by the look in my sister's eyes when she told me she was pregnant."

I stopped. Something about what I said did not feel right, but I knew it made sense in my head. I couldn't make her happy the way she deserves, and I certainly wasn't going to deprive the greatest person I had ever met from experiencing life's most precious moments.

Natalie did not respond or have any physical reaction to these comments. She just stared out at the same children across the street that had drawn my eye as well. After about a minute, she turned to me and asked, "Do you want to finish your thoughts?"

I didn't. I knew why I stopped talking when I did. It was all well and good to explain the rationale behind my decision. It was something different altogether to actually articulate what we should do about it. I was unprepared to utter the words. Closing my eyes and blurting them out would be the only way I could do it.

"I guess I'm saying that we shouldn't see each other anymore."

I wanted to say a lot more. I wanted to tell her how that broke my heart. How much I cared about her. How much I loved her. But I knew that wouldn't help her. I knew that wouldn't come across as genuine and sincere as those feelings really were. It would come across as empty and even condescending. No one wants to hear that when someone is telling them that a relationship is over.

Natalie remained composed. After giving this a few moments of thought, she asked just one question. "Is this what your heart is telling you, Drew?"

It was such a sweet and understanding question. It epitomized Natalie's graciousness and spirit. Her tone suggested that she could live with this decision as long as it truly came from my heart, as if to say that my heart was pure enough to make choices like this, even ones that hurt her. I felt like she was entrusting me to get this right. There was only one correct answer to her question. It was because I loved her that I was doing this. It was her happiness that I wanted to preserve and that came from the heart.

"Yes, it is," I replied.

After another brief pause, Natalie turned to me and said very succinctly, "Hearing you say that is heartbreaking. I had not given the distant future with you much thought yet. I was just focused on trying to live in the moment. But I have learned that it's never worth trying to persuade someone to do something against what their heart is telling them to do. I've been on the other end of this exchange and it's a lost cause. I'm not going to try to convince you that you're making a mistake, if you are truly following your heart."

I nodded my head to show her that I was following.

"I have loved every minute spent with you, Drew, and I'm truly blessed to have had you in my life even for this brief amount of time."

She leaned in and gave me a kiss on my cheek, then got up and promptly went in the house. I sat there for a minute in shock. How could she remain so eloquent, so sweet and sincere, even as tears welled up in her eyes? I wanted to follow her inside but it seemed like the conversation was over and that she preferred to be alone to deal with what transpired. I thought it would be best if I just left. It took all of my strength to lift my heavy body and soul off the steps and start walking down the street. It felt like I was an imposter in my own body when I turned to look at Natalie's house one last time. Why did I feel so confident in the logic behind my decision while at the same time feel like this was all wrong? I felt like an actor in a play following the script that says to walk away, but the ending didn't seem right at all.

CHAPTER 22

I walked into a familiar café and immediately heard my two boys laughing like crazy at a table near the window. Their mother, facing away from the doorway where I stood, attempted to calm them down. I sneaked over to the table to surprise the boys, but when I jumped in front of the table, they just looked at me blankly. They didn't recognize me. They weren't scared of me; rather, they simply didn't know who I was. I turned to the woman for an explanation, but she looked at me with the same vacant expression.

Why was I being treated like a stranger by my own family? There must be some explanation. As I looked deeper at the woman—the woman I expected to be my wife—her face became clearer to me. I wasn't accustomed to identifying this person so I was shocked that she came into focus at all, let alone the fact that she was Natalie. I staggered back away from their table in disbelief that the woman who I loved did not know who I was. A well-dressed man politely passed by me, directing my body so I didn't crash into the other tables.

"Careful there," the man said to me.

My mind was racing for an explanation of what I had just seen so I couldn't even utter a response.

"Daddio!" exclaimed one of the boys at the sight of this man returning to the table.

The man held his hands out like he was a monster and proceeded to inch closer to the boys who were now practically squealing with delight. When he reached the table, he simultaneously tickled both boys with his extended hands, sparking an even more intense giggling fit which seemed to last forever. He leaned down and kissed Natalie gently on the lips and stroked her hair. She stared up at him in obvious admiration and love.

I realized then that this wonderful family, including Natalie, belonged to this man, not me. I was devastated. The haunting pit in my stomach reached a level far beyond what I could bear. I thought that living a lie and having a family that I couldn't provide for was rock bottom. But it turns out that the realization that I had no family at all was somehow worse. And that Natalie and my kids will experience all that life has to offer with someone else was worst of all. I felt desperately alone, and I felt like I had no one to blame for this but myself. I had the opportunity to create a loving family of my own but I was unwilling to give up one ounce of my selfish desires to make this happen. What a pathetic waste.

"Drew," I faintly heard a woman say.
"Drew," a bit louder this time.

"Oh, hey Sandra," I said, as I recognized my friend. "I . . . I must have dozed off for a minute."

I looked around quickly, trying to orient myself to my surroundings. I was in the college library and probably had been sleeping for a few hours.

"I'll say!" Sandra replied. "You started gasping and you sounded like you were being tortured."

"Ugh, something like that. I'm sorry you had to hear that. What a vivid dream."

"More like a nightmare, I imagine."

"That's about right. How have you been?" I tried to change the subject. My heart was heavy from the scene at the café and I wanted to think about something else as soon as possible.

"Fine. You sure you're OK? You don't seem like yourself."

"That's funny. I haven't felt like myself lately. You know, truthfully, I've been struggling with some things lately. Kind of a mid-life crisis, without the mid-life part."

"You don't know what you want to be when you grow up? Who does? Join the crowd."

Sandra was trying to make me feel better. She really was a sweet girl and we had some deep talks in the past—mostly about writing—so it didn't feel strange to open up a bit to her. Besides, protecting my innermost thoughts didn't seem to be my top priority these days.

"No. It's not what I want to do, but more like I don't know who I am or who I want to be."

"I see."

"In fact, framing it that way helps define the issue. I think I've spent too much time thinking about what to do, rather than who I am."

"Don't they say that you are what you do . . . or something like that?"

"I guess . . . and maybe that's my problem. I don't know if the person I have become is leaving me fulfilled, even though I like the things that I do . . . if that makes sense."

"I think it does. Sometimes, we have a vision for ourselves, our lives, and we do what we think we need to do to become that vision. But once we have done things for a certain amount of time, it turns out that what we've become doesn't match that original vision."

"Or that vision evolves over time," I added.

"Exactly! That's what makes it hard. It's like a constantly moving target."

"And if you don't stay in touch with it, you'll find yourself miles away from where you want to be."

"Very true," she agreed. "Same concept applies with writing. You start down one road that you think will get you where you want to go, only to find that it led somewhere else."

"How did you get so wise, Sandra?"

"I've had some good teachers to learn from, professor."

"You better not be referring to me. If I were as smart as you at your age, I wouldn't have screwed up as many things as I have."

"First of all, you're crazy. You've taught me a lot, believe it or not. And second, there's no screwing up and there's no regrets. It's all a journey and you always have the ability to change your future path. It's your script to do with it what you will."

"You're right, Sandra. You are right about that," I repeated as if trying to convince myself.

CHAPTER 23

"What has gotten in to you this week?" Big John asked me. "You go through the first slump of your life and then you come back better than ever. It must have something to do with that girl."

"Hey, what can I tell you? Some days they go in, some days they don't."

"It's got to be more than that," Tony chimed in. "I don't think you even hit the rim today, and from anywhere on the court. All net!"

I just shrugged. Normally, I'd be riding a major high after shooting that well, particularly four days in a row. These moments were what I lived for, literally. But for some reason I was not that excited. In fact, I felt depressed—and I never felt depressed. The better I played the worse I felt. Big John was just teasing, but he actually had guessed correctly. I could not help but think that I made a deal with the devil.

From the moment I stopped seeing Natalie, I hadn't missed a shot. Not in warm-ups. Not in games. Not from 10 feet and not from 30 feet. But my luck didn't stop there. For four straight days, it seemed like every pretty girl I saw smiled at me. Whether I was walking down a crowded street or trying to catch some game highlights in a crowded bar, it was like I had suddenly become a magnet. Again, this would normally make my day and I would be jumping at the chance to talk to these girls and hopefully hook up. But it just made me feel awkward. I didn't get that little rush I always sought. I couldn't even find the words to speak half the time. I wasn't charming or witty. In fact, I wasn't even interested. My whole approach to the opposite sex was predicated on this interaction and I simply couldn't be bothered. Maybe it would make sense if these women were not as attractive as Natalie, but it never got that far. I had not even bothered to try to compare.

It did not stop with basketball and women. All the other areas of my life were affected too. I got no thrill out of sneaking food from conferences, even though it seemed like I was catching all of the breaks. Hakim and Kijana never worked harder than they did on Tuesday, but I could not stop thinking about how I have been deceiving them all this time. Even the soup kitchen left me feeling empty. Nothing made me feel better than I did when I left there on Friday afternoons, but it was different the week that I stopped seeing Natalie. Everything seemed without purpose, even when I was helping people. Any personal satisfaction I may have had before was gone.

There was a bigger crowd in the locker room today because more people played on Saturday mornings than on the weekdays. People were in a different kind of hurry too. They weren't rushing to put their work clothes on and get to the office. They were rushing to get their weekends started. Most fathers were hurrying home for soccer practice or little league. Tony was in no hurry though, in fact, he seemed to try to keep my pace so he could talk to me more. After a few minutes of small talk about the New York Yankees, Tony could not take it anymore.

"Drew, you haven't been yourself this week. I have tried to give you some space because I know something went down with Natalie. But you're not getting any better. You're actually a huge downer to be around. That's not like you at all."

"Sorry, man. It's been a strange week, that's for sure."

"Are you going to tell me what happened? There's a lot going on in that head of yours but you're not exactly telling me much."

"Can we wait until we get out of here?" I asked, not feeling like opening up to a crowded room.

"Alright, let's go out to the lobby," replied Tony.

We spent another minute putting our belongings in our lockers and sending our laundry bags down the chute. We grabbed a seat on the chairs in the lobby after Tony bought us a couple of Gatorades. I didn't even bother to try to refuse the drink like I usually would. It wasn't the time to argue about it.

"So, I broke it off with her on Monday," I started.

"Now, why would you do that, you moron?"

"Well," I paused, considering how to put it plainly, "I saw my sister on Sunday. Ended up telling her about my unique lifestyle, coincidentally. But that's beside the point. She told me that she was pregnant and was never so happy in her life. I was really moved by it, and that's when I realized that as long as Natalie was with me, a virtual vagabond, she would never be able to experience life's greatest joys. So, I showed up at her house the next day and told her exactly that, and that we shouldn't see each other any longer."

Tony leaned back in his seat with a stunned look on his face as if he just took a jab to the chin that he didn't see coming. He was always so quick with the tongue that it took me by surprise that he seemed speechless.

"What's the matter?" I asked, concerned why he was not responding.

"This is worse than I thought."

"It's not that bad. I'm sure she'll get over it and I know she'll be better off."

"It's not her that I'm worried about."

"What? Me? I'll be fine too. I'll snap out of this little funk, and I'll start missing jump shots once again, don't you worry." I tried to be cheery so he would not think I was beyond repair.

"No, it's not the funk either. I'm sure you won't be in a bad mood forever. I just . . . what are you doing today?"

"I've got no plans. What's up?"

"Come with me. Come over for brunch this morning. I have something to show you."

"Ah, OK. You want to check with Nikki first?"

"We'll call her on the way. She'll be fine with it, trust me. She'll think it's a good idea too."

"Alright then," I agreed.

We got up and went over to the elevator to the parking garage where Tony's car was. We reverted back to our small talk as he drove out of town, talking about his car, his commute, my old cars and what it was like to never drive anymore. After about 20 minutes, we pulled onto Tony's street. There he pulled over to the side of the road and put the car in park.

"Drew, I've known you for a long time and you know I care about you. It really bothered me that you didn't tell me about your living situation because frankly, I felt left out— like you had to keep a secret from me because I would judge you or tell you that you should live your life differently. Well, sometimes friends will tell you what you want to hear, and sometimes friends will open your eyes to another perspective that might help. I'm not going to tell you what to do. I'm not going to tell you that you're wrong. I just want you to think about something that I don't think you've thought enough about before, OK?"

"Alright," I said, taking it all in, considering I was sure that it wasn't easy for Tony to say all of that.

"Enough talk. Just observe and hopefully you'll get it so I don't have to beat you over the head with it myself."

He drove down the street and pulled into his driveway. We got out of the car and walked to the front door. Just before entering, Tony turned to me, smiled and said, "Are you ready?"

"Daddy! Daddy!" I heard the screams as Tony opened the door.

"Where are my buddies!" yelled Tony in return.

Around the corner came two little people running just as hard as their little legs would take them. They were smiling from ear to ear, literally not able to contain their excitement at the site of Tony walking toward them with his arms out wide.

"Dadd-eeee!" continued the shouts, now getting louder. His one-year-old, Billy, was in the lead as they raced through the foyer. But his two-year-old, Christopher, caught him just as they reached Tony, who was kneeling down ready to catch them both in his arms. The boys plowed into him with enthusiasm I had never seen before. Tony had them in a bear hug and pretended to tackle them while making wild noises that for some reason had the boys in hysterics. It looked like a family reunited after being apart for three years. Nikki stood in the entrance to the foyer with a smile on her face.

Tony looked up at me with actual tears in his eyes, "This is what I get every day I come home."

I got it. In an instant, I got it. I was so focused on not depriving Natalie of the joys of motherhood that I never considered the fact that I was depriving myself of the joys of fatherhood. I had valued the other parts of my life as my high priorities and never considered whether there was something else that would make me happier. I was so obsessed with avoiding the difficult parts of life that I was blind to the magical moments that I was missing. I should have figured this out when I was talking to Devin, but I was so absorbed by my feelings for Natalie that I never moved past her to look at myself.

"Drew! Are you OK?" Nikki asked me as she grabbed my arms and looked up at me with concern. I had been staring at the scene with tears in my eyes. She must have thought I was crazy by this point. I hadn't shown her much else during our last few encounters.

"Yes, never better Nikki," I said snapping out of it. "Thank you for having me over on such short notice."

"Of course, you are welcome anytime, you know that."

"Say hi to Uncle Drew," Tony said to his boys. I squatted down to their level and extended my arm for a fist bump. Billy must be the only one-year-old in the world who knew how to fist bump.

"Boom!" I said with each bump. I had spent enough time with them that they were pretty comfortable around me. Every time I had seen them though, they were already with Tony. I never saw the extraordinarily touching reunion that this family had every time Tony walked through the door. It was truly inspiring.

We sat down at a feast that Nikki prepared for us. We laughed, we played and we ate everything in sight. It was great to take my mind off of things for a while. In fact, I felt better than I had in a week. I felt lighter, even though I must have consumed 5000 calories. It was like a switch was flipped. We didn't talk about it, but I knew what I needed to do next. I needed to make things right with Natalie. I thought I was following my heart by protecting her. But if I were listening more closely, I would have heard my heart tell me to pursue a life with Natalie as if it were the only thing that mattered. It's not about manufacturing some internal peace by pursuing our understanding of happiness. It's about love. Love breeds a depth of happiness that comes from no other source. I loved Natalie, and if I kept that as my guiding light, then life's greatest joys would surely follow, like the joy of children.

As Tony drove me back to the city, I thanked him for giving me such a gift and for being a role model to me. He wasn't perfect and he was the first to say that, but he understood the important things and he knew how to make them understandable to those around him, too. I would be forever grateful.

"I'll let you know how it goes," I said to Tony as I got out of the car.

"I can't wait," he replied before pulling away.

I had a sense of peace that I didn't have all week. Actually, it was a sense of peace I wasn't sure if I ever had. I knew what I wanted in life in a way that I had not previously known. I didn't just know what I wanted to do with my time. I knew what mattered most though—who I wanted to be. I think that peace was the only thing that kept me from fainting when I turned my eyes from Tony's car to the front steps of the gym where my parents and Devin stood waiting for me.

CHAPTER 24

Even though my heart sank because I knew this unannounced visit meant nothing but trouble for me, my mind immediately began to race on how I could defer this inevitable confrontation until after I spoke with Natalie. Within the time it took me to fake a look of happy surprise at seeing them, I had already played out the scenario in my head. My family was there for some type of intervention and I could care less about that as long as I could fix my self-inflicted debacle with Natalie before it was too late.

As I took a few steps toward my family, I was overcome with a feeling of dread that I had ruined things with Natalie and that she'd never be able to completely trust me again. How could I just abruptly end things like that, and expect her to put her faith in me to never do that again? I know I should have been disturbed by the way my mother looked at me –as if she didn't know who I really was—and that she hugged me longer than she normally did, like she thought if she held me long enough I would once again become familiar to her. But I wasn't disturbed. I was distracted.

After hugging my father and Devin too, I forced myself to turn my attention away from my thoughts about Natalie and to the matter at hand.

"What a surprise, my whole family waiting for me on the

steps of the gym," I said with a tone that suggested the oddity of the scene.

"Hi honey, it's so good to see you," my mother started. "We decided it had been too long and that we should just come to the city to see you."

"Oh, you shouldn't have," I said looking directly at Devin, clearly blaming her for this intrusion.

"Don't blame Devin," interjected my father who could see my annoyance with my sister. "We insisted on coming, and she just insisted on joining us."

"I wasn't *blaming* Devin for anything, of course I'm happy to see you guys," I said with sincerity.

"They were going with or without me, so I figured I'd just catch a ride to see you again," explained Devin, weakly.

"You had such a great time last week that you wanted to come right back, huh?" I said, laughing at all three of them. I shook my head and stared at them with my hands on my hips trying to figure out just what to do next.

"You know, I would have been happy to come home to see you guys. You know that's easier for everyone."

"Drew, we are worried about you and you haven't been home in ages."

"Worried about me? What would you be worried about?"

"Are you in trouble? Something is going on, I just know it."

I looked at Devin in disbelief. Had she actually told them everything I had shared with her in confidence?

"All I said to them is that they should try to connect with you at some point. They're the ones who started panicking that there was something serious going on. I tried to assure them but they think I'm covering for you."

"Real conspiracy theorists, huh?" I said to my parents, trying to keep it light.

"Don't joke about this, Drew. We are worried sick about

you. We have been for a long time. Are you dealing drugs?

"What!" I could not believe she asked me that question in all seriousness. "What in the world would make you ask me that?

"You just got dropped off by a large black man in a Lexus. That's a bit odd, don't you think?

"Not at all. When did you become so racist? Are you serious with that question?"

"I don't know Drew. I don't know what to think anymore. You don't tell us anything!"

"OK. Let's go somewhere to talk about this other than right here. And I'm not dealing drugs, so you can relax. I'm not in trouble of any kind, so be prepared to be disappointed. Your worry is much ado about nothing."

I wanted to alleviate their fears, but in the back of my head I knew they were not going to be thrilled if they found out about my lifestyle. I certainly was not in any danger like they expected, but they might be devastated in a different way if they knew my situation.

"OK, Drew," my father said calmly. "Let's find somewhere to sit and talk. We're only here because we care about you and want to be there for you . . . even if you don't want us to be."

"Thanks Dad. I know that. And I *am* happy to see you guys. I . . ." I hesitated to continue. I didn't know where to start. "Let's just go somewhere to eat and catch up, OK?"

My mother grabbed me by the arm and rested her head on my shoulder. I put my arm around her pulled her close to me and said to her, " . . . my little worry wart."

"I'm your mother Drew, that's what mothers do."

I felt incredibly selfish as we started to walk down Walnut to find a place to sit. I had always known that keeping them in the dark about my life wasn't completely fair to them but it was more evident than ever when I saw how concerned they were. I had partially convinced myself that they weren't that bothered because they never really pushed me on it before. But I could see by the actual pain in their eyes that they had wanted to confront me—more than just ask me benign questions like they normally did—for a long time but didn't have the courage to intervene like this. I guess something Devin said to them must have put them over the edge and here they were. Of course I never intended to cause such concern, rather I tried to spare them from concern. But here I was presented with an opportunity to come clean, precisely at the moment that I realized that my feelings—my love—for Natalie trumped any everything else in my life.

"Are you guys hungry for lunch?" I asked. It was just after noon and I figured they must have been on the road for a few hours.

"Yes, dear," replied my mother. "Is there some place you like to eat nearby?"

I cringed at the tentative tone in her voice. For the first time in my life, my mother was completely unsure how to speak to me, almost afraid to say the wrong thing like I was a ticking time bomb. I had never raised my voice to her in my life so I do not think she was afraid of some outburst. I think she was afraid that she would simply drive me further away from them. It was heartbreaking to hear and see.

"Let's try this bar and grill at the end of the block. I have heard they have good brunch food and it's big. Problem with a lot of these places down town is there can be a long wait sometimes on the weekends. Let's check it out."

The restaurant was only a few blocks from the gym. I never ate there but I had been to the bar a few times at night. As I suspected, there was no wait for us, even though there were a lot of people there. There was a nice back room that led to an outdoor patio area but it looked like it was reserved for a party. The hostess seated us in a booth in the main dining area not far from the entrance.

"You know what makes mothers happiest is to see their kids eat a full meal," my mother said to us as we slid into our seats.

"I'm not going to be able to eat at all, mom, I'm sorry," I replied.

"What? Your father and I will pay for it of course. There's no reason for you not to eat."

"It's not the money, Mom," I said ironically. "That big scary drug dealer you saw had me over for a lovely brunch at his house with his wife and kids."

"Oh, that's too bad," she said instinctively. "I just mean I wanted to feed you myself. That was very nice of him, is he a good friend of yours?"

I turned to Devin and said, "Is this the same woman from 10 minutes ago? Did racist mom vanish as quickly as she arrived?" Devin laughed and looked relieved that I was willing to joke with her instead of being upset with her for this intervention-in-progress.

"Drew! Stop saying that," my mother looked around to make sure no one overheard my chiding.

The waitress came over and took our drink orders. We told her we needed another minute or two before ordering our food.

"Sue, can you order me the strawberry pancakes?" my father asked my mother. "I'm going to run to the bathroom."

I knew my mother would want my father there when we got into a discussion about my life, so I tried to ease the awkwardness. "So what's new at home, mom? Anything exciting going on with you guys?"

"Not really. You know dad, he's constantly working around the house. He had a couple of projects this summer. And he's on that tractor all the time."

My parents were not farmers, but my father had a tractor

anyway. He claimed it was to help cut the grass on their five acres, but we all knew it was just a fun toy for him.

"What about you, any projects?" I asked, knowing my mother had a few hobbies and liked to keep busy.

"Well, right now I'm planning our trip to Ireland."

"Really, I didn't know you guys were going there?"

She raised her eyebrows at that response. It was too obvious to say why I did not know that. I had been out of touch too long.

"We're leaving in three weeks. Staying for two. We're going with John and Mary Griffin. They have been there so many times it will be nice to have some personal tour guides."

"I think that's great mom. You guys will have the best time." I turned to Devin and asked, "You guys aren't going too?"

"Not this trip," replied Devin rubbing her belly. She and Bradley had been on a few trips with our parents and I liked to tease her about it. I pretended that she got special treatment but we all knew I was welcome to go too. I just never expressed interest in joining.

Just after the waitress took our order, I saw my father exit the bathroom and stop to talk to a man who was about to enter. My father knew everyone in our small town so it was not unusual for him to stop and talk to people. But here, many miles from his domain, it was an odd sight. He looked genuinely excited to see this man, who was actually taller than my father's 6'2" frame. I watched him laugh and pat this man on the back and even give him a hug.

"Who was that, dear?" my mother asked excitedly.

"That was Casey Green. He was my biggest high school basketball rival. I hadn't seen him in years!"

"And you guys recognized each other?"

"Well, he hasn't changed a bit."

"And you still look like you're 18, too, dad," Devin chimed in sarcastically, knowing that was what my father wanted to hear.

"A little less hair and a few more wrinkles, thanks to you two," my father replied.

"Does he live down here?" I asked.

"Well, he grew up not far from Flemington, but I don't think he's been back since he left for college. His parents moved down here years ago and he lives in the suburbs somewhere, too. Funny running into him. He said he's here celebrating one of his kids' engagements."

"Oh, isn't that nice," said my mother.

"He's going to stop over in a few minutes to say hello. He said he followed your career, Drew, and he wants to meet the kid who made everyone forget about his father."

"You're kidding," I replied.

"This guy is a basketball junkie, you'll love him."

"Boys, we're not here to talk about basketball," reminded my mother. "We're here to talk about Drew and whether there's anything we can do to help him."

"Oh, God. I'd much rather talk about basketball."

"No. No more avoiding the issue, Drew. It's finally time to have a heart to heart."

"Fine," I said, resigned. "I'm done running and hiding from things. Let's just get it all on the table."

I shot a nervous look to Devin who gave me an encouraging nod. I continued.

"Look. Hear me out. Don't jump to any crazy conclusions. I'll just tell you the facts and we can talk about why I live this way, OK?"

"OK, son," said my father. "We just want to support you."

"Alright, here it goes. I don't have a house. I don't have a job. I don't have any money or really any things."

I ignored the audible gasps coming from my mother after each statement.

"But I'm completely happy and have chosen this life

225

because being happy is my number one priority. Not money. Not success. Not comfort. Just happiness."

I paused briefly and then continued, thankful that they let me get it all out in one shot.

"Now I've learned a few lessons in the last few weeks that have changed things for me. I've learned that relationships can bring you a type of happiness that other things in life can't. I met someone who opened my mind . . . . . . and my heart . . . to a joy that I did not know was in the cards for me."

At that moment, I noticed a small smile coming from my mother. I know she must have been devastated by the facts of my situation and I'm sure she had a thousand questions. But somehow, through those negative thoughts, she must have detected a glimmer of the love that filled my heart. She had always been a hopeless romantic so I shouldn't be surprised that she was so in tune with my spirit, even as she heard some harsh realities about my life.

"Drew, how are you surviving without a place to live, money or a job?" my pragmatic father asked.

"Well . . ."

I started to reply when I spotted a scene that I thought could not be real. Walking out from the party in the back room of the restaurant came Natalie. I stopped dead in my tracks and did a quadruple take to make sure it was her. But of course there was no mistaking Natalie. Even though I had known her a relatively short time, I would have recognized her walk, her posture, her body, her aura from a mile away. I could hear faintly both of my parents saying *Drew* as my attention shifted so abruptly away from our intense and personal conversation to something that must have seemed in left field to them.

The moment I got over the shock of seeing her there, randomly, at the time and place chosen for me to divulge my deepest secrets to of all people, my parents, I realized that seeing her was all I wanted to do. I had so much to tell her, so much to apologize for. I had realized my enormous mistake and I wanted to get her back in my life as quickly as I could and keep her there for as long as she would stay. I stood up and walked mindlessly toward her before I even realized I had moved. I was acting on pure instinct at this point and I gave no indication to my family what was going on. I had a one-track mind and I was determined to make things right with Natalie right then and there.

I was about 30 feet from her when I saw her smile at someone in front of her. I looked to my left and saw my father's friend walking out of the bathroom toward Natalie with his arms extended out. I froze where I stood, watching in disbelief as she practically jumped into his arms for a big hug. I was stunned, but did not fully comprehend what I was seeing until I saw William walking a few steps behind Natalie. He was smiling at my father's friend too and greeted him with a handshake and man hug, like they were close friends, like family.

That's when I pieced together that this man was here to celebrate an engagement: *Natalie's engagement!*

It must have been obvious that I was staring at the trio because they all turned toward me simultaneously. I did my best to shut my wide-open jaw and somehow found the strength to walk toward them with a smile. I knew I would have plenty of time to wallow in my misery when this self-imposed nightmare was over.

"Mr. Green, I wanted to introduce myself, I'm Drew Kelly, Jerry's son." I held out my hand and he shook it as if he had wanted to meet me all his life. His oversized hand swallowed mine and he stepped close to me to grab me by the arm affectionately with his other hand.

"Well it sure is great to meet you, Drew," he replied. "I was just telling your father how much I admired your basketball career. I kept tabs on you through the years, you know."

He hadn't let go of my hand yet and looked me so squarely in the eye that he was alarmingly captivating. My heart was breaking with every second that passed, but I could not help but be impressed with this gregarious man.

"That is very kind of you, sir. My father said you were quite the player yourself."

"Many years ago, Drew," he said with a laugh. "Too many years. Please, call me Casey."

He finally let my hand go. I hadn't looked at them yet, but I was sure that Natalie and William were watching intently and struggling to comprehend what was happening. I did not have time to consider their thoughts or feelings, let alone my own. I simply spoke from the heart.

"I have to tell you," I said, still not looking at Natalie, "your daughter is probably the best person I have ever met."

I shot a quick glance at Natalie, but knew I should focus on her father if I had any chance of handling the situation appropriately.

"I have had the privilege of getting to know her recently and you should know that she is a truly special woman. Congratulations to you and your family on this great news."

I turned to Natalie and for the first time, William, and said, "Congratulations guys. I wish you all the best. William, I would do anything in the world to be in your shoes right now."

Natalie and William were both speechless and I guess I could not blame them. They probably both figured that I could be unpredictable and I know this awkward encounter did not disappoint in that regard. I quickly shook Mr. Green's hand again and walked straight out the front door of the restaurant.

CHAPTER 25

I would like to say that I was so in the moment that I was not even aware of my surroundings, but that was not the case. I had never felt the heat from so many eyeballs on me as when I bolted for that door and took off on a near sprint down Walnut toward the park. I heard my name called by several different voices, but I purposely did not try to decipher who was saying what. I just pretended to not hear anything. My goal was to get as far away from this nightmare as fast as I possibly could. I was literally running away from my problems.

I knew it was wrong of me to walk out on my parents like that, but I had no choice. They came unannounced anyway, so it was not like I was responsible for wasting their trip. They actually wasted their own trip. That's the price you pay when you spring an intervention on someone who is in the throes of heartbreak. The beauty of not owning a cell phone or not having a place to live is that it is really easy to hide, if you want to. By walking out of that restaurant, I assumed that I bought myself an indefinite period of time to figure out what to do next. I needed time to digest what I had just learned, that my opportunity to be with Natalie had just passed me by. All I could think about as I entered the park was to get to my tree as quickly as possible. I learned at that moment that the tree was the closest thing I had to a home, not because of the minimal shelter it provided, but because of the peace and security I felt when I was under it.

As soon as I reached the tree, I sat down on the ground with my back resting against the trunk and put my head in my hands. It felt great to be in comfortable surroundings, but that was short-lived. The contentment I used to know when by myself no longer existed, not after the last few days. I was lonely. I was lost. This "home" lacked some critical features. It lacked family and it lacked friends. I felt a tear run down my cheek as I replayed the events of the day and the week in my head. I wasn't sad exactly. I didn't feel sorry for myself at all. I was simply moved by the depth of the opportunities that I failed to enjoy. Life with Natalie would have been wonderful. How could I have gotten this so wrong? I thought I was so clever but it ended up costing me beyond measure. I lost true love.

Even with my head buried and in the midst of wallowing, I sensed someone approaching. I looked up to see Devin walking tentatively toward me. I started smiling and shook my head at the absurdity of the whole thing. Devin did not say a word but sat next to me against the tree.

"Did you ever imagine we'd be sitting right here in this spot at this exact point in time?" I asked. "I mean there are so many things that happen in our lives, so many decisions that make up the path we take. And we're all so interconnected. We could never have predicted when we were kids that our path would lead us to right now. If even one little thing was different over the past 25 years, we might be somewhere else doing something else. That's crazy to me."

"That is crazy," she replied politely.

"I'm crazy, aren't I?"

"You are crazy."

"Thanks."

After a long pause, Devin finally asked, "So, I take it that was Natalie?"

"She's a dog, isn't she?"

"Bow wow. I'm sure she has a nice personality though."

"Kiss of death."

"So, what just happened back there?"

"Where are mom and dad?"

"Back at the restaurant, awaiting further instructions."

"From you?"

"No, from God."

"You ran after me?"

"Pretty much. If I didn't, I would never have known what in the world just happened. You looked like you got struck by lightning when you saw that girl, let's call her Natalie, walking across the restaurant. You were completely oblivious to the rest of us, like nothing else mattered."

"Yeah, she kind of does that to me."

"Judging by the hug, she's dad's friend's daughter, but you didn't know that."

"Pretty good. I don't think you needed to chase me to figure this all out."

"Well, I don't know who the other guy was, but I'm guessing you weren't too excited to see him."

"Correct. Actually, he's very nice. It wasn't seeing him that was the problem. It was the whole engagement party thing that put me over the edge."

"Ah, I see. That was the happy couple and you were just providing your well wishes?"

"Sort of."

"I'm dying to know what you said to them. Tell me already!"

"I told her father that she was incredible and I told her fiancée that I wished I were him."

"Nice. Hardly a well wish, but it was well said nonetheless. Might as well go down swinging."

"That wasn't swinging, that was me taking the high road actually."

"How big of you."

"Ugh, I really blew it, Devin."

"Don't say that."

"I had so much to say to her. So much I left on the table. She has no idea how much I actually love her, and that's a real shame."

"Why is it too late? An engagement isn't a wedding, you know?"

"I know. It's the significance of it all though. The fact that she went back to this guy so quickly shows me that she completely lost faith in me and I can't blame her."

"You don't know what happened though. Why don't you tell her how you feel and hear her out? What do you have to lose at this point?

"It's just so clear to me now that I was thinking my way through this situation instead of feeling my way through it. I realized it this morning and my biggest fear was that I was too late. Was I ever."

"Oh God, do they look lost," Devin said looking across the field.

"Who . . . oh great, now I get to show them home."

My parents were wandering aimlessly about 100 yards away, along a walking path in the park. My mother was looking at her phone, trying painfully to type a text message. My father was waving his arms in all directions clearly frustrated that he didn't know where to find us. Devin got up and yelled over to them, waving her arms like she was trying to land a plane. My parents spotted us and started walking in our direction, but my mother was still looking at her phone.

"Is she texting you?" I asked Devin.

"No and I don't think she texts anyone else. That is so strange."

My parents walked a few more yards and then stopped. My mother put her phone to her ear and started looking around as if trying to find someone. Then I saw her waving her hand back toward the entrance of the park. I followed the path of her wave and saw Natalie walking toward her with her phone to her ear. Moments later, they both put their phones down and Natalie joined my parents, together walking in our direction.

I looked at Devin with fright and confusion. She looked at me and burst out laughing. I failed to see the humor in this at all, only the humiliation. We were both standing at this point, looking off in the distance as if there was an imminent military invasion and it was too late to retreat.

"What—the—hell—is—going—on?" I asked slowly.

"I have no idea, but this is going to be good!" Devin could hardly contain her amusement. My parents and Natalie were walking slowly and talking. I was conflicted on whether I wanted them to go slower –to put off the conversation as long as possible—or to go faster so they could stop talking without me there to monitor the discussion.

"So I guess you guys have met?" I asked them lightly when they finally approached Devin and me at the tree.

"We sure have, honey," said my mother. She was smiling. That was a good sign.

"Hi Natalie," I said, for the first time that day actually addressing her directly.

"Hey Drew," she replied with a hint of encouragement in her voice.

"These are my parents, and this is my sister Devin."

"Nice to meet you Devin," said Natalie. She had obviously already said hello to my parents.

"Natalie, I owe you a few apologies."

"You don't owe me anything, Drew."

"I do. I apologize for that bizarre move back there. I know it was a special occasion for you and William and the last thing you needed was me to cause a scene."

"Drew, it's not what you think . . ."

"Let me finish," I interrupted. "I also owe you the biggest apology of my life for telling you we shouldn't see each other. I know it's too late now and it's really selfish of me to say this at this point, but I was dead wrong. I tried to make a decision about your future for you and that is not my place to do that, it's yours. Worse than that, I didn't make a decision based on what I truly wanted. I ignored what I was feeling and what would make me happy and instead relied upon priorities that I set for myself some time ago. Priorities that may have made sense for the person I was, but not for the person I have evolved into, thanks to you.

"I like the Drew who's around you more than the one who's not. I love spending my time with you. I love the thought of my future with you. I love the thought of having a family with you. I love the hope I have of growing old with you. That's what I felt in my heart the last time we spoke, but those weren't the words that came out of my mouth, and I'm sorry for that. I'm sorry if you can't trust me again but I will never let my head get in the way of my heart again. If I could just get out of my own way, I know I could love you like no one else could."

"Is it my turn?" she asked quietly, neither one of us acknowledging the fact that we had an audience for this conversation.

"Of course," I said, apologetically.

"OK, first, no need to apologize. Matters of the heart are confusing for all of us. No one gets things right all of the time, and this won't be the last time that things don't go perfectly for us."

Us? A glimmer of hope! My heart jumped at the thought.

"Second, I love you too. I was devastated when you left the other night, but I hadn't given up on you. I have been kicking myself for not fighting for you in the first place. I just let you go and I have been scared to death that I would regret that move. In fact, I've been plotting my next move to have you reconsider your ridiculous position."

"Consider it reconsidered."

"Well, I'll cross that off my list then."

"Was there a third thing?"

"Yes, my brother got engaged last week. The party back there would have been the perfect chance to introduce you, but you ran off rather quickly."

"And William . . .?" I asked, slowly piecing together what actually happened at the scene of the crime.

"William *and* his girlfriend were there to celebrate. Like it or not, he's a family friend and always will be at some level."

"I know that. I just . . . I guess . . . I just jumped to the wrong conclusion. Does your father think I'm nuts?"

"Well, he probably would have if he wasn't already such a fan of yours, and you probably have your father to thank for that," she said turning to my dad.

I looked at my parents sheepishly. "I'm sorry you had to see all this today."

"Are you kidding?" my mother said with tears in her eyes. "This was the most beautiful thing I've ever seen!"

"Mom, there's a reason I came to this spot. This is where I sleep most days. You're not freaked out by that anymore?"

"I am," sighed my mother. "But you are far happier than I could have ever hoped for. Everything else will work itself out for the best. Love is the one thing you can't just make happen, but it has happened for you."

She hugged me tightly—this time it was like I was her little boy again.

"Thanks mom."

"Drew," my father added, "thank you for your openness today. I am very proud of the man you have become. You certainly live to the beat of your own drum, but you are true to your principles and you are a good, kind person."

"Well isn't this one big love fest!" exclaimed Devin. "Let's all hug!"

I picked Devin up to swing her around and realized that she had a baby in there who would not appreciate our wrestling.

"Natalie, Devin is expecting!"

"Oh my goodness, congratulations!" Natalie and Devin embraced. I had no doubt that they would be fast friends.

"Thank you! We are so excited!"

"Well, let's celebrate," suggested Natalie. "Why don't you guys come back to the restaurant? You all can meet the rest of my family, the dads can catch up on old times, and we can announce the coming of a new baby."

"I love it," I said. "Can we officially end this intervention?"

"It's over," said my mother, still crying. "Saved by a love story."

I grabbed Natalie by the hand and pulled her close to me. I squeezed as if I would never see her again. If we didn't have company and a party to go to, I don't think I would have ever let her go. We held hands as we walked through the park, drifting behind my parents and Devin. I didn't know what my future would hold, other than that it would have Natalie in it, and that's all that mattered. I could figure out how to play some basketball, to read some and to pretend to write some. I could coach with head held high and nothing to hide. Life wouldn't go perfectly, but the magical moments would make all the struggles well worth it. And at the end of the day, I would always be true to myself.

The peace I felt walking with Natalie and my family was like nothing I had felt before. I had spent so much time and energy engineering a life that made me happy, but as it turned out, true and deep happiness cannot be created without its key ingredient, love.

The End

Read on for a sneak peak at *Go For Broke*,
the prequel to *A Shot at Happy!*

GO FOR BROKE

A Novel

Dear Firm,

I ~~need a break.~~

~~want my life back.~~

QUIT!

Sincerely,

CHRIS GUITON

Author of *A Shot at Happy*

"Live the life you've imagined."

– Henry David Thoreau

CHAPTER I

For a split second, I saw diamonds floating on top of the water, glistening magnificently in the moonlight. Thousands of them. I leaned over the railing on the top tier of the yacht, 30 feet above the Hudson River, hopelessly straining to see the fortune that could rescue me from my pathetic and increasingly meaningless existence.

But the diamonds were just bubbles. Countless bubbles, beautifully and miraculously reflecting light from the moon so many miles away. A phenomenal display of nature and science that should remind me how lucky I am to be part of such an amazing world. But they were bubbles just the same, and no one in their right mind would jump overboard for some sparkling bubbles.

"Scott, look at all these diamonds just sitting there for the taking," I said to my friend who was resting his back against the railing next to me, facing a packed dance floor.

"What are you talking about?" he replied, dismissively, not even bothering to turn around.

"Seriously, look at all those diamonds," I pressed. "Millions of dollars right under our noses.

Scott turned his head toward me, "You're losing it, Drew. If there were millions of dollars under my nose, I would have smelled it." He started to sniff the air.

"Well, I guess diamonds in water must be odorless then."

Scott turned completely around to look over the railing with me, but not because he believed a word I said. He just wanted to see what I was going on about. Scott and I were the kind of friends that could always entertain each other no matter what kind of misery we endured together.

"You know, it kind of does look like diamonds," he admitted with a slight smile.

Just then, the DJ shifted from Prince's *Party Like It's 1999* to Nikki Minaj's *Superbass*. Scott and I looked at each other with mirror expressions of confusion and amusement.

"Don't hear those two played back-to-back everyday," I said.

"I guess that's the challenge of catering to this crowd," he said, motioning over his shoulder to the series of painfully awkward body movements uniquely found at work function dance parties. Of the 40 people attempting to dance, nearly half were summer associates in their early to mid 20's. The rest were lawyers at the firm spanning in age from 25 to 70.

We had already completed a river tour of lower Manhattan and I guess technically parts of Jersey City and Hoboken. We were docked somewhere near the Chelsea Piers but weren't scheduled to be released from the boat for another hour. It was actually a very nice outing as far as work parties go.

"How can they dance like that at work?" I asked as I looked back at the shockingly carefree and noticeably uncoordinated contortions of my colleagues.

"Well, not everyone is as paranoid as you are about letting loose at work functions," Scott shot at me.

"I don't see you out there now do I?" I jabbed back.

"I'm paranoid like you—don't get me wrong—that's why we're friends. I'm just more tolerant of different approaches to work parties than you are," he said smugly.

Scott excelled at taking the contrarian position in any conversation. This made him fun to talk, but also hard to like. I mean, I loved the guy. I'd do anything for him. But I couldn't stand him most of the time. We bickered constantly.

"Is that right?" I responded skeptically.

"You are more open-minded about shitting where you eat, though, I have to give you that one," he said facetiously, digging into a known, open wound of mine.

"Ugh, don't remind me," I replied, scanning the crowd for Laurie. I spotted her on the other side of the dance floor near the bar. She was talking to Amanda and Becky, her supposed friends. Amanda and Becky were actually sweet. Just dull. And a little dorky. I liked dorky, but not combined with dull. I liked both of them more than Laurie, though, and Laurie was my girlfriend.

"Why don't you go ask your babe to dance?" Scott teased.

"I'd rather jump in the river," I snapped back, without exaggeration.

"I don't get it, why don't you just break up with her if you don't like her anymore . . . oh that's right, you work down the hall from her. I forgot."

Scott was having fun now, and there was nothing I could do to defend myself. I had no one to blame but myself for my predicament. He couldn't stop laughing at my pain.

"Sue me for dating the best looking girl at the firm," I responded, regretting it as soon as the words left my mouth. No one cared less that she was good looking than I did. In fact, given her propensity to be mean, selfish and controlling, I don't think I actually viewed her as good-looking anymore.

"Well aren't you just the prom king," Scott started to feast on me. "I guess your mama never told you about the whole *skin deep* thing? It's what's on the inside that counts? Any of this ringing a bell for you, killer?"

I couldn't help but laugh, even through the misery of laying in my proverbial bed.

"Look, I'm not saying this justifies anything, but I was really just a victim of circumstances." Although lame, I knew this to be true.

"Do tell!" Scott rubbed his hands together quickly. "This ought to be good."

I shook my head at a few summer associates who waved at me to join them on the dance floor. They had no idea how strongly I felt about not making a fool of myself in public. Especially at work.

"Well," I continued. " When you're put in an environment where you only interact with a few people, you don't have many partners to choose from."

"Slim pickings?" Scott loved cliché's. He laughed more loudly at his own choice of words than he ever did at someone else's.

"Yes. And it's not unusual to be drawn to the most attractive—even if just on the outside—person in that limited environment. You have to admit that from the moment we started working here, we rarely see anyone other than our co-workers."

"I'm tracking with you," Scott said reluctantly. Scott's wife was less than impressed with the long hours expected by the firm. Neither one of us had a life outside of our jobs. But at least I wasn't married.

"And Laurie can be . . . charming, at least when she really, really wants to be," I continued. "I just made a rash decision based on a short-sighted view of my immediate surroundings."

I knew she was trouble from the first moment I laid eyes on her. She had the look. The look of a woman who knew what she wanted and exactly how to get it.

"You hooked up with her because she is hot," Scott concluded. "Simple as that. No metaphysical explanation needed. Now you feel stuck, and I don't blame you." There was almost a hint of compassion in his voice.

"What are you two wallflower losers doing over here?" asked Bob as he and Allen approached us.

"Drew's thinking about jumping overboard for diamonds and I'm just telling him that's not a bad option, considering . . ." said Scott, his eyes darting in Laurie's direction.

"Loverboy can't get far enough away from his sweetheart, I see," noticed Allen.

Bob and Allen had been at the firm a few years longer than Scott and me, and had taken us under their wings—which really translated to making fun of us at every opportunity. Tremendous leadership.

"It's not like that," I lied. I never told anyone other than Scott how unhappy I was in my relationship, but it didn't take a detective to piece it together. She had created enough scenes around the office—and not just with me—that everyone knew her deal.

"You shouldn't complain, at least you're not married and miserable like the rest of us." Bob failed in trying to make me feel better.

"Hey, speak for yourself," Allen chimed in.

"I'm speaking for all mankind," Bob persisted.

"Let's face it, fellas, we're all miserable for the same reason," I posited. "And it's not because of our significant others. It's that we're all beholden to this damn firm."

Sweet & Reath notoriously demanded a lot from its lawyers. Beyond the expectation of more than 2000 billable hours per year, they wanted you to be in the office and accessible around the clock. The firm's policy stated that we had four weeks vacation, but everyone knew that you couldn't be out of touch for more than a few hours without earning the stigma of being a slacker.

"And the money," Scott added the obvious.

Sure we were paid well, but it came at a major personal expense—the expectation that everything in our lives played second fiddle.

"We spend every waking moment of our lives trying to please these guys and for what?" I asked. "So that they give us another case to work on? To get more important work? To become partner 10 years from now? To become one of them one day? They're all more miserable than we are. What are we doing here?"

I could feel my vein in my forehead protrude, my heart beat faster.

"Whoa Drew!" yelled Bob. "Let it all out buddy!"

I just couldn't take it anymore. How did I get myself in such a vicious cycle? All work, and almost no play—and what little play time I had was usually spent fighting with Laurie about not spending the entirety of my free time with her, even though I spent 18 hours a day with her at the office. I can't even talk on the phone with my sister without a fight that I don't pay Laurie enough attention. I don't think 20 minutes of my time every few weeks is too much to ask to keep in touch with family.

"This isn't Laurie's fault or your wives' fault I hate to tell you," I decided to continue my rare rant. "It's our life and this is how we have chosen to spend our time. All day, every day. How is someone else supposed to make us happy when we spend so much of our lives voluntarily being unhappy?"

"Dude, we all do it for the money," Allen tried to reason with me.

"But what good is the money if we don't have a life?" I fired back.

"Money is good for little things like food, a house, shoes, hair product for Scott," Bob said sarcastically.

"I know," I said, calming down. "I know it's the right thing to do economically. I just don't know when financial security became the be all end all for me."

I turned back toward the railing and leaned over to look at the water again. The diamonds were looking back at me again, begging me to save them. To save me. Just one rock would be enough to release me from this death sentence.

"Did you guys see these diamonds yet?" I asked Bob and Allen.

"Here we go again," Scott said only slightly under his breath.

"What are you smoking tonight?" replied Bob as he looked overboard, surprised at my uncharacteristically brazen attitude.

"I see what you're talking about," Allen came to my defense.

"How fast would you guys jump in that water if they were real?" I asked. I don't know why I chose this moment to philosophize, but I couldn't help but dream of another reality.

"I'd already be down there gasping for air and filling my pockets," said Bob.

"Yeah right, you need a tranquilizer to get on an airplane you're so scared of heights," challenged Scott.

"For a river full of diamonds, I'd get over my fear pretty quickly," Bob replied.

"You'd probably get fired," added Allen.

"I'd be a zillionaire," reasoned Bob. "What would I care about being fired?"

"I don't know," added Scott, playing devil's advocate as usual. It's probably the trait that made him such a good lawyer.

"Maybe there's not as many diamonds as there appears. What if it were just a few million dollars worth?"

"Are you kidding?" asked Bob incredulously. "I'd still jump."

"I'm with Scott," said Allen. "You might get a few million but you might lose your earning potential. Think about it. If you get fired for this, no one else is going to hire that guy that flaked out on the Summer Associate Boat Outing. You're legal career might be over."

"I beg to differ," argued Bob. "But even if it was career suicide, I could make a few million last me a lifetime. It's all about investment."

"True," Scott agreed. "Money makes money. But what if it was just one million dollars worth? Would you do it then? Where's the tipping point?"

"Ah, now it's getting trickier," Bob admitted. "You can't retire on a million dollars anymore. I'd have to think pretty hard about that one."

I couldn't hold it in any longer. "Do you guys hear yourselves? Most people out there would jump in for $1000, and you wouldn't do it for a million?"

I was nearly yelling. We all looked over our shoulders to see if anyone heard us. Thankfully the dance party was in full effect and Jay-Z drowned out our inane conversation.

"We have a lot more to lose than most people," defended Bob.

"That sounds so obnoxious," I remarked.

"But true," Scott agreed.

"If I didn't care about my job or my career then I'd do it for a million . . . or less," Bob reasoned. "Or if I wasn't here with work, maybe I'd do it for a grand, I don't know."

"Don't you think something is wrong that we care THAT much about work and career and money?" I asked the group.

"I'm not saying you guys are wrong, I'm just kind of disgusted with myself for being this way."

It wasn't that long ago that I was a poor law student living off my student loans. I ate cereal twice a day and peanut butter and jelly in between. All-you-can-eat $5 pasta night every Tuesday at the local Italian place was a splurge.

"Well, do something about it then tough guy," Scott pretended to goad me.

"What, like jump?" I replied, a bit more seriously then they expected.

"Yes!" they seemed to all say in unison.

"Ha," I replied, backing off a bit. "How much would you give me since all I see now are bubbles?"

"I'd give you a hundred!" Bob said enthusiastically, trying to encourage the others to add to it.

"I'll match it, if it would make a difference to you," Allen added.

"I'll double it, AND I'll help you pick up the pieces of your life if you ever pop your head back up above water," said Scott, playing along with this silly game.

"So what are you doubling, Mr. Coe?" asked Laurie, startling the whole group of us. She always called people by their last name. No one liked it.

"Jesus, where do you slither in from?" asked Bob. "Oh, hey ladies," he added, as he noticed Amanda and Becky standing quietly behind Laurie.

"Funny," Laurie said, fake smiling at Bob. "Seriously, what have you guys been so engrossed in conversation about?"

"Guy stuff," Scott offered, attempting to cover for me so I wouldn't have to get into the whole thing.

"Pathetic," replied Laurie in a special condescending tone she had all unto herself.

"So glad you stopped by," said Bob, blatantly suggesting that she leave us alone.

"Why so quiet, boo?" she asked me.

I cringed. I could actually hear five sets of eyes rolling at that term of supposed endearment. I must have begged her a hundred times not to call me that. Especially in public.

"No reason," I replied nonchalantly.

"Really?" she pressed me. "It looks like you guys are up to no good."

"We were just admiring how pretty the Hudson is tonight, that's all," Scott tried again to deflect.

"Yeah, right," said Laurie. "You guys are real sentimentalists. I'll believe that one." Along with being relentlessly sarcastic, she was maddeningly intelligent. This combination equated to unparalleled arrogance.

"Actually, we were debating how much money it would take for us to jump in that water right here and now." I decided Laurie should be able to handle the truth.

"*You* wouldn't do it for all the money in the world," she said sharply at me.

"Oh really, and why would that be?" I took the bait.

"Because you don't take chances like that," she said matter-of-factly.

"What?" I was taken aback by how cutting her statement was. Judging by the oohs and ahhs of the others, I wasn't reading too much into it.

"You would worry too much about the consequences to do something like that," she explained.

She was right.

I think that is what bothered me so much about this whole conversation. I was risk averse. I wanted my bosses to like me. I wanted to work hard so I got the extra bonus. I was willing to give up the things that truly made me happy just so

I could be successful. I wouldn't break up with my girlfriend because I was scared she'd retaliate and either make my life even more miserable, or just get me fired somehow.

She was right, but that's not who I wanted to be. It was finally time I controlled my own destiny.

"You're wrong!" I stood up taller.

"Oh I am, am I?" she replied with a wide, evil smile.

"I'm not that guy," I declared. "Not anymore."

"Tell her, killer!" Bob encouraged me like he was watching a street fight.

"You're telling me you'd give up your job for a dip in the river? You'd give up *this* for a bet with these assholes?" she asked, motioning toward her body with her hands.

"You're saying it's over if I jump?" I asked, leadingly, with both hope and horror. The fact that she'd leave me for jumping disgusted me, but didn't surprise me. Maybe this was my chance to escape it all, even without a fortune waiting for me in the water. A new beginning.

"That's exactly what I'm saying," Laurie confirmed with an extra dose of nasty.

"You're choice," I said as I started to take off my shoes. "And I don't even need a thousand dollars let alone a million. It's not about the money. It's about freedom from the money."

"Take it easy, big guy," said Scott when he realized what was happening.

"Hang on to these, will you buddy," I said tossing my iPhone and wallet to Scott.

In a flash, I flipped off my shoes, jerked out of my sports coat, catapulted on top of the railing and attempted to steady myself. I quickly glanced back at the party, then down to water one last time. Then I took a deep breath and dove straight into the bubbles below.

ABOUT THE AUTHOR

Chris Guiton is a devoted husband and a full-time father of three young children. In his spare time, he is an attorney at Johnson & Johnson and a novelist. Previously, Chris played professional basketball in Europe. Now he just plays in various old man leagues. Chris received an English degree from Haverford College and a J.D. from Temple Law School. Originally from rural Irish Hill, Pennsylvania (you won't even find it on a map), he currently resides with his family in the metropolis of Flemington, NJ.

CONNECTING WITH THE AUTHOR

Come check out my website at www.chrisguiton.com, join the Chris Guiton Author Page on Facebook at www.facebook. com/ChrisGuitonAuthorPage, and follow me on Twitter at @chris_guiton. If you prefer good old-fashioned email, you can contact me at cguiton32@gmail.com. I love to hear from readers so please feel free to reach out.

If you enjoyed this book, please help spread the word. You can leave a review on Amazon.com or on Goodreads.com, or you can share with family and friends through your social media networks or simply by word of mouth. Indie authors like me appreciate any help we can get!